By Max Wirestone

THE ASTONISHING MISTAKES OF DAHLIA MOSS

A Dahlia Moss Mystery

MAX WIRESTONE

REDHOOK

www.redhookbooks.com

Copyright © 2017 by Max Wirestone
Excerpt from *The Questionable Behavior of Dahlia Moss* copyright © 2017 by Max Wirestone
Excerpt from *The Shambling Guide to New York City* copyright © 2013 by Mary Lafferty

Cover design by Wendy Chan
Cover copyright © 2017 by Hachette Book Group, Inc.

Redhook Books/Orbit
Hachette Book Group
1290 Avenue of the Americas
New York, NY 10104
hachettebookgroup.com

First Edition: March 2017

Redhook is an imprint of Orbit, a division of Hachette Book Group.
The Redhook name and logo are trademarks of Hachette Book Group, Inc.

The publisher is not responsible for websites (or their content) that are not owned by the publisher.

The Hachette Speakers Bureau provides a wide range of authors for speaking events. To find out more, go to www.hachettespeakersbureau.com or call (866) 376-6591.

Library of Congress Cataloging-in-Publication Data

Names: Wirestone, Max, author.
Title: The astonishing mistakes of Dahlia Moss / Max Wirestone.
Description: First edition. | New York, NY : Redhook Books/Orbit, 2017. |
    Series: A Dahlia Moss mystery ; 2
Identifiers: LCCN 2016041492| ISBN 9780316386012 (softcover) | ISBN
    9780316386036 (ebook) | ISBN 9781478946588 (audio book cd) | ISBN
    9781478913436 (audio book downloadable)
Subjects: LCSH: Women private investigators—Fiction. |
    Murder—Investigation—Fiction. | Women detectives—Fiction. | BISAC:
    FICTION / Action & Adventure. | FICTION / Mystery & Detective / Women
    Sleuths. | GSAFD: Mystery fiction.
Classification: LCC PS3623.I74 A94 2017 | DDC 813/.6—dc23 LC record available at
    https://lccn.loc.gov/2016041492

ISBNs: 978-0-316-38601-2 (paperback), 978-0-316-38603-6 (ebook)

Printed in the United States of America

LSC-C

10 9 8 7 6 5 4 3 2 1

For Clay, expectedly, and Yoko Shimomura,
somewhat less so.

CHAPTER ONE

The Internet was making fun of me.

I couldn't blame the Internet, honestly. Things were going very badly. I had been on some disastrous arena runs, double 1-3 records, and the commentariat was letting me have it. That's what happens when you're losing while streaming to an audience on Twitch. Then again, it's also what happens when you're winning. The Internet, as a rule, just likes making fun of things.

This did not bother me so much. I mean, it bothered me in a global sense, as in: Internet, I See This Is Why We Can't Have Nice Things. But it didn't unnerve me.

What unnerved me was the tip jar, which suddenly had $500 dollars in it.

Grief I expect. Money I do not.

Let's be clear. I am not a major streamer. I'd only even started it a month ago when money from my last case meant I could afford a computer nice enough to stream without lagging. And while I'm sure there are big-shot streamers who wouldn't be all that surprised by a $500 donation, I'm no big shot. As my double 1-3 records would attest.

"Wow," I said. "That's super nice of you, Doctor XXX. Thanks for the cash."

The donor's name was Doctor XXX, incidentally. I'm not redacting to protect anybody. Nobody in this adventure gets protected.

"kool," typed Doctor XXX.

What the Fuck, said the rest of Twitch chat. What the actual fuck. I'm summarizing, because there were probably fifty guys in the channel typing away like spider monkeys, but this was the gist of it. Everyone could see the tip jar—there was actually a little animation of an oinking piggy bank that played—and the question of the moment was "Who the hell would tip $500 to me—a noob with a 1-3 record?"

Honestly, I was a little with Twitch chat on this one. Let's consider:

1. Some people on the Internet are Creepers.
2. People who give you large sums of money for no apparent reason probably have a reason.

Creepers be real, y'all. I don't want to hit this point too hard, but the two questions I'm asked most on Twitch are: "Do you have a boyfriend?" and "Where do you live?"

As it happens, the answers are "kind of," and "St. Louis," although when I answer this for Twitch, I round the "kind of" up to a "yes, definitely, he's very strong," and Missouri.

So I tried to play the $500 thing coolly, like this was the kind of thing that happened all the time. Oh, another five hundred bucks from a nameless stranger? Cool, I guess. Thanks for watching.

But Twitch chat did not play it coolly, because cool is not a part of the Internet's wheelhouse. How to explain Twitch chat, really? It's a bit like if the mouth breathers who wrote YouTube comments could type really fast and were also dangerously caffeinated. *Dangerously* caffeinated. Like Trish's maniac boyfriend on *Jessica Jones*, but *after* the mind-altering drugs.

Anyway, Twitch was all like: Doctor XXX wants some action. Romantic action, was the implication, because why else would anyone suck up to a girl with a 1-3 record, or so went their reasoning. Although, they conveyed this idea with considerably more lewdness than I just managed. It was moments like this that made me generally glad that Twitch didn't know my name.

My handle on Twitch is Sunkern, named for my second-favorite Pokémon. My favorite Pokémon is Jigglypuff, but I didn't want to run a channel with the word "Jiggly" in it, and even "Puff" suggests a marijuana-themed production that I do not have the funds or endurance to provide. So: Sunkern.

"Ha ha, you guys, let's start another arena run!"

Go hang yourself, said Twitch chat.

"Could I message you privately?" asked Doctor XXX.

And I thought: *Oh lord, here it is. Creeper City.*

"Let's not," I said, trying to sound cheerful and bright. "Just type whatever you want to say in front of everyone. Now, what class should we choose for the next run? Shaman, Warrior, Priest?"

Burnt! said Twitch chat—I'm paraphrasing—Dahlia Done Stole ALL your money. Only they didn't say Dahlia, because I am secretive. In fact, I've even "slipped" on the channel and accidentally used my "real name," which as far as they know is Louise.

"I'm opening the voting right now," I told the chat.

"I know this is going to sound forward," typed Doctor XXX, "but I was wondering if you could come to the Endicott Hotel in St. Louis tomorrow."

Um, no, I cannot. This is not *The Vanishing*, Doctor XXX. But I did not say that aloud, I just smiled at the votes, which were all for Priest—the worst possible class—because these guys were fucking with me. Every last one of them.

"Gosh, I don't know, Doctor XXX," I said, trying to sound positive and not at all concerned. "I have a plan for tomorrow."

This was true, in that my plan was not to be drugged and murdered in a hotel.

Meeting someone named Doctor XXX at a place I had never heard of was so obviously a bad idea that even Twitch was against it. DON'T DO IT!!! said Twitch chat, with all caps and exclamation points and Kappas, which are these screaming disembodied heads that are hard to explain because they don't make a lot of sense out of context. Actually, now that I think about it, they don't make a lot of sense in context. But no matter.

Even a Twitch chatter whose name was—and I'm not making this up—The Grim Raper—typed:

"Louise—I hope you're not seriously thinking of going to this hotel."

There was a lot of uproar. For a group of people who tended to complain about white knights—Twitch chat was being positively paternal.

Take his money and mute him, said Twitch chat. Take all the money.

But Doctor XXX just kept on typing.

"There's going to be a tournament there tomorrow. For *Dark Alleys*? Kind of a big deal. The winning team is going to take home $20,000."

"Yeah," I said. "I'd heard about that, but I don't really play a lot of fighters."

This was a sort of a lie, because I had gotten slightly obsessed with *Skullgirls* for a while, but this was a detail Doctor XXX did not need to know. Besides which—being good in one fighting game doesn't mean you're going to be any good in another. The sports equivalent is sort of like: oh, I heard you like soccer, so I'd figured you'd be great at ice hockey. Yes, the two sports are, very broadly speaking, similar, but the devil is really in the details, as you'll discover when you break your legs as you try to run across a sheet of ice.

"Some serious stuff is going to go down at that tournament," said Doctor XXX.

"Sounds like a fun day," I told him, right-clicking to bring up the mute option.

"And I think that there should be a detective on hand."

And that stopped me cold, because who was Doctor XXX to be aware of the Dahlia Moss, Geek Detective phenomenon? As far as Twitch chat knew, my name was Louise NoLastName, and the only mysteries I'd ever solved for them were Nancy Drew Hidden Puzzle games, which I actually struggled with a lot.

Doctor XXX knew who I was.

"Why do you think there should be a detective on hand?" I asked, with as much disinterest as I could feign.

"I don't want to say in chat," typed Doctor XXX. "But if you showed up, I could tell you in person. I'll be wearing a green hat if you do. I hope you do."

Girl, don't, said Twitch chat.

I don't know why I'm making Twitch sound like my gay best friend, because that is fundamentally not their vibe.

You better just take that money and forget this scrub. *swooshy hand* *finger snap*

See? I keep doing it.

But I listened to Twitch, actually. I know that seems out of character—actually taking someone's good advice. But with all those Kappas and exclamation points, how could I not? I clicked Mute on the drop-down menu and said: "All right; let's start another run."

I even went 7-3; and I made $500, so I was having a pretty good night. But that's just it, isn't it? Things are always great until the bodies start piling up.

CHAPTER TWO

My roommate, Charice, has this theory about curiosity killing the cat. People always throw that line out at you as though the cat has gotten into something he shouldn't have. Right? There was a mysterious noise that he shouldn't have investigated, or a scent that he shouldn't have tracked down. The implication is always that the cat looked for something evil, and the terrible thing he discovered bumped him off.

The moral is: Don't be curious.

Charice's theory, on the other hand, is that the cat never investigated the noise, never tracked the scent. He died from curiosity the way a young lover might die from pining. He yearned to find out what was around the corner, but could never check. He wasn't eaten; he wasted away.

Isn't that a great little idea? Okay, maybe not *great*, but it's a solid thing to tell yourself when you're contemplating doing something crazy.

And it's what I was telling myself while I sat at our dining room table and learned about the tournament Doctor XXX suggested I attend. Or it's what I was telling myself until I was interrupted by Charice's man candy of the month.

"Hellor there, Dahlia," said Daniel.

"Hello there," I said.

Although you may be wondering what's going on with me and Nathan—I'm here to report that the only major relationship upgrade of late has been on the Charice front. Point in case now: Daniel was standing in our kitchen, as he often did, partially naked.

I'm rounding down here, to be sure, as he was wearing short cutoff gym shorts and a tank top. But I had seen him in this kitchen wearing significantly less, and so I'm inclined to round toward clotheslessness. Daniel—whom you may remember as "Jesus Christ" or simply "a hot guy with abs" basically lived with me now, as he and Charice had formed some sort of sex alliance, the exact nature of which I did not understand. They were obviously dating, and Daniel slept over here constantly. Although, seriously—it was an alliance—the kind you would see on a reality television show. Their affair seemed to involve an awful lot of whispering and also bizarre physical challenges. Last week they went through Forest Park on a tandem bike.

"Hellor, Dahlia," said Daniel again. This time I noticed his weird pronunciation.

"Are you trying to do an accent?"

"I'm Australian," said Daniel. "An Aussie. I'm from Brisbane."

"It needs work," I told him.

"Yeahr," said Daniel. "That's why I'm practicing it. I don't go around practicing the accents I can already do."

This was not entirely true, because Daniel faked a British accent plenty, although he was usually being egged on by Charice. I could have reasonably asked him why he needed to learn an Aussie accent, but I was busy learning about *Dark Alleys*, and this tournament, which I was not going to attend, no sirree, because that would be crazy, and I am known for reason and clarity.

"What are you looking at?" asked Daniel.

I always found it very easy to talk to Daniel, largely because he usually wasn't listening to me. Even now, for example. Was he really asking questions, or was this just him practicing sound?

"I'm looking at a tournament that's happening tomorrow," I said. "Twenty-thousand-dollar prize. Split two ways."

"That sounds like a right good time," said Daniel. "An honest hoopla."

Yeah, Daniel was practicing sound.

"I was thinking about going," I told him. I never would have mentioned this to Charice, or even Nathan, because they would have freaked out, Charice with enthusiasm, Nathan with concern. But talking to Daniel—at least Daniel in practice-an-accent mode—was a lot like talking to ELIZA or some old chat bot. There was no through line. No development. He just reacted to the last thing you said.

"You should go," said Daniel. "It'll be a zinger of a time."

I don't think "a zinger of a time" is the sort of thing an Aussie would say, but Daniel made it sound strangely plausible. That was the troubling thing about Daniel. He was actually pretty good. I kept expecting him to disappear—not just because Charice's boyfriends always disappeared—but because he seemed like someone who was destined for New York or Los Angeles. Twentysomething actors as good as Daniel don't stick around the American Midwest.

"I want to go," I said. "But I'm thinking that it's probably a terrible idea. You should tell me that I shouldn't go."

"Why?" asked Daniel, who must have been interested, because he didn't throw any extra Aussie verbiage into the question.

"Well," I told him, a little surprised that he was listening, "a guy who watches my stream gave me five hundred bucks and wanted me go there. He made it seem mysterious, like something was going to happen."

"Something detective-y?" asked Daniel. "Charice told me all about this."

"That's what he made it seem like."

Daniel nodded. He was thinking. Probably he was doing that in an Aussie accent too.

"And you don't want to go because you think the guy could be crazy?"

"I think there's a reasonable chance."

Daniel sat down at the dining room table across from me. Charice's Max Beckmann self-portrait scowled down at us, as though he could see where this was going and did not like it one bit.

"Would you like some company?" asked Daniel.

"Nah," I told him. "I'm just going to read a bit and go to bed."

"Not now," said Daniel. "Tomorrow. I could accompany you. I could be your Aussie bodyguard."

This offer surprised me nearly as much as the $500, because Daniel had not taken a lot of interest in my comings and goings. Mostly it was just accents and tandem bikes and couples lacrosse.

"You realize the tournament's for a video game. It's not polo or mountain hiking or whatever Danielian nonsense you like to partake in."

"Yearh," said Daniel. "I figured. And for the record, mountain hiking isn't a thing. It's either mountain climbing or just hiking."

"Why would you want to go?" I asked, with just the sort of suspicion that had helped me solve my last case. "You don't spend time with me. And answer in your real voice, because I want to be able to tell if you're lying to me, and I find that accent distracting."

I really don't know what kind of answer I was looking for. I certainly didn't think that Daniel was romantically interested in me, because he was completely all-in for Charice. I'd seen the evidence. In his pants. But I also knew that he wasn't into geek culture, and so what else was left?

"Charice suggested that you and I ought to spend a little time together," said Daniel. And he did use his normal voice, which was actually pretty great, deep and authoritative, and yet still pretty friendly. You could see how he would get cast as Jesus.

But this answer made me anxious.

"Why would Charice want that?"

"She's a little worried that you don't like me. She wants to make sure that you and I get along."

There were a lot of things wrong with that sentence. For one, it had both the words "Charice" and "worry" in it, and those were things that should be paragraphs apart, if not entire pages. Possibly books. For another, the whole premise was dumb. I liked Daniel fine. I wished he would put on pants when he got up in the middle of the night, but this was a minor and ultimately solvable problem.

But mainly, it was scary. Something was happening to Charice and Daniel. I had a terrible feeling that it might be adulthood. Even more alarming was the idea that Charice and Daniel were going to couple up forever, and then they would *both* disappear to New York or Los Angeles, or wherever actors who could plausibly say dumb things in Australian accents went, and where would that leave me?

Anyway, this thought sounds very rational typed out like that, but in the moment I didn't type it out, even emotionally, and it hit me all at once, like the words were on top of one another and also they were maybe written in Wingdings.

"I don't want to go anywhere with you," I said quickly, and loudly, like a crazy person. And then I instantly followed it up with:

"No. Yes, I'm sorry, please come along."

Honestly, there was no time between those sentences. You'd have to measure the pause in quantum units, like the ones physicists used to discuss the beginning of the universe.

"Are you sure?"

I wasn't sure at all. I felt weird. Insecure, almost, although I couldn't have told you why. As exasperating as Charice was, I didn't want her changing. I had just gotten the hang of being a single twentysomething—just now!—and now friends were already leapfrogging into other stages of life.

I didn't say that, however, because that would be a monstrous and inhuman answer. I didn't even really think that answer. I just felt it.

What I said was "Sure."

"Banger!" said Daniel.

Because this book is titled *Astonishing Mistakes*, I will be honest with you and tell you that I did absolutely no other preparation for the tournament. I plugged the hotel into Google Maps, but that was about it.

I figured it would all work out. Probably Doctor XXX wouldn't even show up, and if he did, I'd have a fake Aussie bodyguard to protect me. What could possibly go wrong?

CHAPTER THREE

There are many things to admire about Daniel, aside from his abs, his actually-pretty-good acting skills, and his apparent ability to make Charice happy.

One of those things is his car, which totally functions. Yeah, that's a low bar to clear, but in terms of speed and functionality, my car rates somewhere between a pangolin and an elderly horse. So Daniel's ride—an old Ford Focus with a dangerous amount of miles—was comparatively amazeballs. Hell, he even had working heat. Heat! Truly, the vehicle of champions.

We thus got to the Endicott Hotel right on time, and were warm, even. Despite the Endicott's regal name, it looked less like some historic artifact of Old St. Louis and more like a Days Inn. That's not to say it was shabby—it was just nondescript in the way that hotels are carefully designed to be nondescript. A big, cavernous lobby with beige wallpaper and gold trim. Maroon-and-black-damask carpeting. It was nice, but you could have been anywhere.

Someone had put white plastic letters on a black sign that informed *Dark Alleys* players where to head for registration, although they needn't have bothered, because the direction and flow of gamers was pretty obvious.

In a few minutes, I would make the time to start getting nervous, but initially I was taking it all in. The people, I mean, not the place. I had never actually been to a fighting-game tournament before, and I was curious. I had watched some highlights videos here and there, but the thing about them is that you saw the gameplay but rarely the crowd.

Surveying the place, I could see why the crowd would not be a selling point.

There was nothing wrong with these guys, but they looked boring, businesslike, anxious. At PAX, or Comic Con or Zoth, these folks would have been exuberant and luxurious, decked out in costumes with makeup and hats. I got it; there was $20,000 on the line, and so it made sense to leave the wigs at home and bring your game face. But for an outsider, it was a little disappointing. Nothing much to look at. Although, at least I didn't have to worry about being attacked by a guy in a mask.

"So how is this person going to find you?" asked Daniel, back in Aussie mode. "Are you supposed to be wearing a carnation in your lapel or something?"

With ridiculous suggestions like these, you could easily see how Daniel might be a good fit for Charice.

"No," I told him. "He watches my stream, so he knows what I look like. I just can't identify him. He'll come up to me. Although, he did mention that he was going to be wearing a green hat."

We scanned the crowd together. There was no one with a green hat, although there was a lanky black kid with improbably green hair. I don't think he was cosplaying—he just had green hair.

"I'll go look around," said Daniel. "If I find a guy with a green hat, I'll tackle him."

"Don't do that."

"I'll break his legs."

"No."

"Maybe just one leg."

Daniel wanted me to negotiate violence with him, but I was mostly worried about being left alone.

"What am I supposed to do if he shows up while you're gone?"

"You're in a crowded public place," said Daniel. "What could he do?"

"He could pull a gun on me," I said, which only sounds nuts if you haven't had a gun pulled on you in a crowded place before, which I have.

"Well, if he has a gun, there's not much I can do to stop him," said Daniel, with altogether too good a humor. "So it wouldn't make any difference if I was around. Besides which," he said, tugging at the brown leather totally-not-Australian hat he was wearing, "I'm going to see if they have some kind of buffet here."

And, of course, no sooner did Daniel get out of sight than a guy with an olive toboggan cap entered the hotel. He was a huge guy, black, probably twice my weight, and very muscular. Or possibly fat. I don't know, he didn't take off his shirt. He looked like a linebacker, regardless. Or, at least, a linebacker who was slumming it, because he was a wearing a tatty black T-shirt that I guessed had to be lucky somehow, because otherwise it would have been thrown away or burned.

I came up to him quietly.

"Doctor XXX?" I asked.

He gave me just the sort of look a stranger would give if an unknown person came up to them and said "Doctor XXX?" Imagine right now, that as you are reading this, a person comes up to you and says "Doctor XXX?" Consider the look you would give them. That's precisely the look I got.

And because I like doubling down, I repeated it.

"Doctor XXX?"

"Is that supposed to be some kind of code?" asked the green-capped man.

"It's supposed be your username in Twitch chat."

"My username in Twitch chat is Mike3000."

I actually had heard of Mike3000, or at least run across his name in my extremely cursory searching about the tournament.

"Oh yeah," I said. "You're really good, right? You're, like, a favorite to win this."

Mike clearly liked being recognized but shrugged anyway. "Thanks," he said. "But we'll see. I've got a talent for coming in at second." He had a body that was somehow naturally good at modesty. Whenever I try to play off being really good at something, it feels false and off-putting. Mike was a prodigy at half smiles and shrugs.

"Is Doctor XXX supposed to be your partner for this event?" asked Mike.

This was not exactly it, but it was a very reasonable guess. *Dark Alleys* was a two-on-two game, which was unusual for fighters, and so lots of people would be looking for their teammates. There were probably other people there who had never met their partner in real life before. Which was good, because this meant that I didn't seem especially weird.

17

I lied to Mike, just because it was easier than the truth, and said yes.

"Is he a black guy?" Mike asked, probably curious why I had singled him out.

"Green hat," I told him.

"This hat is ocher," he told me, which is not a turn I was expecting the conversation to take. He also said it to me in a way that sounded vaguely offended. Thankfully, I didn't have to do anything, however, because he kept talking.

"He's probably waiting for you at the registration table. That's where my partner is. If I see him, I'll tell him you're out here. What's your name?"

I could have said Dahlia, but on Twitch chat I had been telling people my name was Louise, and if he told the guy Dahlia was waiting for him, maybe he would be confused. But I didn't really want to go around all day pretending to be named Louise, either, because the St. Louis geek community isn't _that_ small, and it was entirely possible that I'd run into someone I knew. I split the difference and told Mike that my name was Miss Moss-Granger.

"That's very formal of you," observed Mike3000.

If I had known Mike better, I might have suggested that he was the person splitting hairs between green and ocher, but with his slightly crabby forehead and Biff McLargeHuge body, I skipped that particular snark.

"In formal situations, I prefer to be called Dame Moss-Granger," I told him. Which I realize now is not much less snarky.

But Mike3000 liked the answer, because he flashed a toothy smile at me. "I'll tell him. Good luck in the tournament today, my lady."

"Yeah," I said. "Same to you."

Mike3000 lumbered off, and I was feeling a little more confident. I hadn't been drugged and murdered yet, and I had talked to a stranger and been here for nearly five minutes. This clearly meant I had an aura of invulnerability, and so I stopped worrying so much and headed into the main room.

Like the gamers themselves, the main room was disappointing.

I mean, it looked like a hotel ballroom. In contrast to other geek events I had attended, there were no giant inflatables or enormous banners. To be fair, it was a serviceable little ballroom—with a crystal chandelier and everything—but it wasn't particularly geeky. I was honestly a little let down. Were fighting-game players so competitive they couldn't spring for any tomfoolery? A chiptunes band? A black light? Something?

I was wading through the crowd of people, keeping my eyes peeled for anyone with a green cap—or for that matter, Daniel, who had completely vanished—and while I didn't see anyone I knew, I did spot a face I recognized.

"Sunkern," he called out.

And I figured that, even capless, this had to be the guy.

"Nice Guy Kyle," I responded in kind, chat name for chat name.

To be clear, I did not know Nice Guy Kyle at all. I had never met him before, and I honestly hadn't even seen his Twitch channel in several years. Ages ago, I used to watch him stream *StarCraft*, back when I was into *StarCraft*, and I couldn't believe that he knew my name.

I had two primary reactions to Kyle: one was being a little starstruck, because I spent a lot of time watching him stream way back when. The other was a dawning awareness of the passage of time. Kyle was one of those people who had once had if not boyish good looks, at least boyishly rugged looks. But he now appeared to have suddenly hit some aging avalanche. There was a TA in college I knew who did the same thing. She went abroad to teach in Germany for a year, leaving the United States as a young maiden of twenty-six or seven. And when she came back, she looked forty-four.

We all assumed that she had an amazing time in Germany.

I hadn't seen Kyle stream, in wow, okay, five years, but yikes, it looked like he had an amazing time in Germany. Also he had left about half of his hair there, although he appeared to have traded it in for an extra chin.

Despite all this, my main reaction was: starstruck.

"It's nice to meet you," I said. "I can't believe you know who I am! I'm a huge fan of your stream." I hoped that there would be no follow-up questions, given that I hadn't seen much of it in the past five years.

"Oh, thanks! My wife has started watching you. You make losing badly at *Hearthstone* look like so much fun."

This could be interpreted as a burn, but I chose to take it a compliment. Besides which, losing at *Hearthstone* was a lot of fun, at least the way I did it, which often involved gin. I had more fun losing at that game than most streamers did winning.

"What are you doing here?" I asked. "You don't—" and I was going to say "play fighters," but, again, I hadn't actually seen his stream in five years, so who knows? Maybe he did play fighters. "You don't usually stay in hotels."

That was my plan B answer. You don't stay in hotels. What can I say, I think fast on my feet.

But Nice Guy Kyle didn't seem to mind. "You gotta go where the money is," he told me. "And diversify. I can't just keep playing *StarCraft* forever. I've got mouths to feed."

I liked Nice Guy Kyle, then and there. I mean, I liked him before, but I was reminded exactly why I had gotten addicted to his channel in the first place. Yes, he looked a bit like Jabba the Hutt, and was wearing a sickly blue T-shirt that was easily two sizes too small, but he was a friendly Jabba. He was like an enormous plush toy—a Tickle Me Jabba—and even if he looked like he belonged on the training poster a nightclub would use to keep out undesirables, he was one of the good undesirables. He was one of us.

"So, what's it like at the upper tiers of Twitch royalty? Are you making crazy money?"

Kyle sighed and somehow looked even older. The question alone seemed to make him bald a little.

"Making money on Twitch is hard. Never gets any easier."

"Really?" I asked. "But the scene has gotten so much bigger."

"Yeah," said Kyle. "But so has the competition. There's always somebody younger coming around the corner, with faster reflexes and better ideas."

"You're losing your edge," I told him. This was not an insult so much as a reference—Kyle, as I remembered him, played a lot of LCD Soundsystem.

"I'm losing my edge," he said, smiling. "Hey," he said. "You should meet my wife."

At which point I was sort of clobbered by this pear-shaped woman who looked like she was auditioning for Miss Hannigan in a terrible production of *Annie*. Not physically clobbered, mind you, she just sort of thundered onto the scene. It was more of a psychic clobbering.

"Salutations," she said. I got the impression that this was out of habit, the way she always began conversations. Because the next line was spoken with a real glimmer of recognition. "Hey, it's that lady who always loses!"

She had a voice like a cartoon villain. Broad, is what I am saying. She frankly wasn't any less weird-looking than her husband, but I had had years to become inured to Kyle's weirdness, and this lady was coming at me all once. Peculiar face, tight blond ringlets that were decades out of style. And it was less that she was fat, and more she collected fat in odd places—she had tremendous thighs and no buttocks at all. She was perfectly matched to Kyle—so much so that creationists could have plausibly used her as a case for intelligent design.

"I don't always lose," I told her. "Last night I went seven and three."

This is, in case you don't play *Hearthstone Arena*, technically still losing, but it's at least losing with dignity, which I don't always manage.

"Good for you," she said. "You'll get there eventually!"

"This is Tricia," said Kyle, then pointing to a baby carrier that I had somehow failed to spot in my first assessment of her, "and that little harlequin next to her is Undine."

"Call me Dahlia," I said. How could I not? I was so among my people now—baby Undine was wearing a onesie with a Magikarp on it, which is really the perfect shirt for a creature that can't do anything.

"Oh. My. God," I said when I saw their baby, which is the normal human response to a tiny baby. And this kid was tiny.

So tiny that it struck me that Tricia's body shape was probably because she had recently given birth.

"How many days old is she?"

"Twelve?" Kyle wasn't entirely sure on this point, and Tricia didn't volunteer an answer. This was fine, because I was involuntarily cooing. I don't even like babies; just cooing.

"Oh. My. God." What can I say? You don't run into a lot of twelve-day-old people. It's not a big demographic.

"Do you want to hold her?" asked Tricia. "I can take her out of her carrier if you want to hold her."

In retrospect, it does seem a little weird that Tricia was going to risk waking up her baby so that she could hand her over to a stranger. But certain ladies could be real pushers about babies. They're like coke dealers, but for infants. You like this cocaine? No? How about you hold it for a second? How about this: smell the cocaine. Breathe it in deep.

Anyway, I did not want the cocaine. Or a baby, although I could understand the appeal of each. Separately, not together, although who knows?

"Maybe later," I told her. By this I meant "absolutely not," but it sounded softer. I coo at babies, as a normal person does, but that's where I draw the line.

"You seem like you'd be great with children," said Tricia, pusher.

"I'll let you ladies talk," said Kyle. "I've got to go register and find my partner."

"Oh God," said Tricia. "Don't get me started on his partner."

Kyle took off and I asked:

"What's wrong with his partner? Some kind of prima donna?"

"Nah," said Tricia. "I mean, I hope not. He's just a kid. He's, like, fourteen. It's just depressing to get paired up with someone that young."

"Why?" I asked.

"Kyle used to be paired with the very best players—he used to run in the big leagues."

"I guess this fourteen-year-old is not in the big leagues?"

"No," said Tricia. "He's not even in the little leagues. He bid for a chance to be Kyle's teammate in some kind of auction."

"Wow," I said jokingly. "Tacky."

"Yeah, well," said Tricia. "You gotta get that dolla. Am I right?"

Tricia, weird though she may have been, was right, and I told her so.

"Listen," she said. "I'm picking up that you're not super keen on spending quality baby time with Undine—"

This was true—I liked babies, but I liked them in the way that I liked heart transplants. It was great that they existed, and yet I positively did not require one now, which is what I told Trish.

"I feel you," she said, in a voice that suggested that she did not feel me whatsoever. "But could you just watch Undine for a couple of minutes? I've got a bathroom situation I need to resolve."

"You can't just bring her into the bathroom?"

"It's kind of a complicated situation," said Tricia. I had no idea what she meant, but there are certain lines of inquiry that are unwise to pursue.

"I don't know," I said.

"You won't even have to pick her up; just leave her in her carrier."

"What if she cries?" I asked.

"Okay, then, yeah, you have to pick her up. Please? Come on!"

And Tricia put her knees together in a way that suggested she had to pee very badly.

Which is how I became the caretaker of a strange woman's infant.

CHAPTER FOUR

For someone who did nothing—and I mean NOTHING—Undine was very good at keeping my mind off the business with my mystery client. She slept for the entire fifteen minutes Tricia was gone, but I kept expecting that she would explode somehow. She'd vomit or shoot poop out of her eyes or whatever dramatic, terrible thing babies did.

None of that happened. Undine slept. She even kept on sleeping when Tricia came back and took her away.

While I was in possession of Undine, I wasn't nervous at all. People don't mess with ladies with infants. Even in horror movies—they're pretty much off-limits, right? In part because it's unseemly to attack them, in part because people with infants don't have time for your Freddy Krueger bullshit. Haunt my dreams, Freddy Krueger? Ha, that's where I've got you. Since I had this baby, I no longer sleep!

But I digress. The moment Undine left, I started getting anxious again.

Where was this Doctor XXX, and why hadn't he found me? I'd been here a while now, and there weren't _that_ many people around. Maybe the idea of me with an infant had scared him. It had alarmed me a little, so why not?

Anyway, I took care of my own business in the bathroom, probably brought on by anxiousness. Then I continued to scan the crowd, this time not looking for hats, but more with the lens of contemplating who might kill me. Or at least, who might be Doctor XXX.

This was a reasonable enough plan, but not emotionally helpful, because most people, when you're in the right mood, have a face for murder. There was this shifty-looking kid, who had—I'm not kidding—absolutely no chin and one enormous eyebrow. There was this other guy with, like, thirty skull tattoos. Thirty! Who likes skulls that much? But the person who was really making me anxious was this weaselly-looking redhead. He had a head like a ferret, with a pointed nose and tiny little eyes and weird little fingers that he kept putting in his mouth. He also kept making eye contact with me, which I didn't approve of. Okay, probably he was doing it because I kept staring at him, but even so. Massively suspicious.

Weasel guy came over. He didn't have tats, or a particularly menacing body type, but there was something about him. He gave off henchman aura.

"Excuse me," he said. "This is awkward, but I feel I should inform you that you have toilet paper stuck to your leg."

I looked down at my leg, which indeed trailed an improbable amount of toilet paper.

"I hope that's not too toward," said the weasel.

I told him it wasn't toward, although it sort of was.

"I would want someone to tell me," said the weasel.

I agreed with the weasel, who seemed to imagine that this

was now somehow going to turn into a meet-cute. I am willing to admit that I was wrong about the guy, because he obviously had no immediate plans to murder me, but neither did I plan to embark upon a romantic comedy with him.

"Thank you for informing me," I told him. "Now, good day, sir!"

When he was gone, it dawned on me that I was possibly not a great judge of character. Still, it was good that he had come over there—not only for the toilet paper but because it made me realize that I ought to check in with Twitch chat. If something terrible did happen to me, it would undoubtedly be because Doctor XXX was here. I should let Twitch know what was up, because this would provide valuable clues to the police later when they were investigating my demise.

I had brought my laptop, and so I booted up and started my stream.

"Good morning, Twitch chatters," I told everyone. "Guess where I am right now?"

Oh no, said Twitch chat. Tell me you didn't go to that hotel.

"How did you guess? Yes, I'm at the Endicott Hotel. I decided I would take Doctor XXX up on his offer."

This is terrible, said Twitch chat. You will get killed. Although despite saying this, my viewers continued to swell. My getting killed was apparently an attraction. Streamers, it's all about bringing a unique service to the table. Take that, Nice Guy Kyle.

"I brought a bodyguard, so don't worry about that. But Doctor XXX hasn't shown up yet, which is why I'm checking in with all of you. Do any of you good fellows know what he looks like?"

Twitch chat diverged into a useless cacophony of theories, which is basically its natural state. Suggestions posited by Twitch chat:

- Doctor XXX never was going to show up and was just trolling me.
- Doctor XXX weighs 500 pounds and is sixty-seven years old and was too intimidated by my beauty to approach me.
- Doctor XXX weighs 145 pounds and is twenty-four years old and was too intimidated by my ugliness to approach me.
- Doctor XXX weighs 60 pounds and is seven years old, and his mother is too intimidated to approach me.
- Doctor XXX was waiting in a corner for me with some chloroform.
- Doctor XXX was waiting in a corner for me with a garrote.
- Doctor XXX was waiting in a corner for me with a blunderbuss.
- I have already been killed by Doctor XXX, like in *The Sixth Sense*, and do not yet realize that I am dead. Spoiler alert, I guess.

Additionally, they provided the physical descriptions of dozens of people. Among them:

- Charles Manson
- Hannibal Lecter
- The Cat in the Hat
- Aileen Wuournos
- RuPaul Charles
- Warwick Davis
- Dracula

So, they were essentially useless, although I realize now that if I am somehow killed by RuPaul or Warwick Davis, I have set myself up for an ironic death.

"Thanks very much, you guys," I told Twitch chat. "Your help is really invaluable."

Are you entering the tournament? they asked, quite reasonably. I was here to watch something "go down," and if that didn't happen, I might as well make a day of it. The odds of my winning was pretty low, but it would at least pass the time.

"Nah," I told them. Because, after all, it did cost money to enter. "I'm just kicking around. But if I do get murdered—which obviously I won't—"

Don't be too sure, said chat.

"One of you guys should contact the police. Like, avenge my death, won't you?"

"I've entered us into the tournament," said Daniel, who popped in out of nowhere. It was a trait that he shared with Charice. Was this a skill that dancers pick up, or was this something he had somehow acquired through their sex alliance?

Yippee, said Twitch chat.

"What, what?" I asked Daniel. "Did you find anyone in a green hat?"

"I didn't. There was one guy that looked really weaselly, though."

"I saw him," I told him. I should have been irritated at Daniel for entering us into the tournament, but mostly I was happy that someone else agreed with my weasel assessment. That guy was weird, even if I did vaguely appreciate him telling me about my TP situation—although I'm sure Twitch chat would have been more than happy to point it out. The sentiment did not last long, though, because I noticed that Doctor XXX himself had joined my Twitch chat channel. Or rather, the rest of the channel noticed, showering him with expletives, Kappas, and threats.

Don't kill Louise!!!!!!! said Twitch chat.

Doctor XXX did not respond to the abuse of the channel, which is always a good idea, actually, and instead privately messaged me:

"There's an unlocked storeroom on the second floor. Meet me there, ASAP."

CHAPTER FIVE

I did not immediately respond to this message. In fact, I smiled brightly, as though someone had tossed a little money into my tip jar. Because it dawned upon me that this guy—probably this creep—was watching my reaction. I didn't much care for the idea of being his puppet. Although, on the other hand, I had to admit I was curious about whatever might have been in this open storeroom.

"I'm glad we had this talk," I told chat. "Maybe I'll try to interview some players live on the stream later. That'd be interesting, right?"

No, said Twitch chat. It would be shit.

But that's the kind of thing they always say.

"We need to get to meeting room eleven," I told Daniel.

"We need to do a lot of things."

I'd have to brief Daniel on what was going on, but I'd want to do so after the channel was turned off.

"We play a game in five minutes," said Daniel.

"What, seriously?"

"Yeah, we're up first," said Daniel. "I'm lucky like that."

I closed my laptop and Daniel yanked me toward my first true humiliation of the day.

I had always imagined Daniel as a sort of Lesser Charice, and so I was always surprised when he did not react in a Charician manner.

"So," I told him, once the stream was entirely off, "this mystery doctor tells me that I should meet him in an abandoned storeroom upstairs."

This was not precisely the message, but I was embellishing it, because this was the sort of drama that Charice would enjoy. Daniel, however, just continued to walk along without any reaction whatsoever.

"We're going to be late for the tournament," said Daniel.

Had I given this piece of information to Charice, she would have combusted with excitement. I'm not entirely sure that I even mean that as a metaphor; she might have gone into *Firestarter* territory. Daniel didn't even slow down.

"Why are you pulling me? You don't even play this game."

Daniel shrugged, even as he continued pulling me.

"I threw in the cash to enter," he said. "I don't want to lose just because we show up late."

"But you don't even play! You're going to get crushed."

"It will make the day more fun," said Daniel. "We can root for the people who defeat us."

"I don't want to root for them. I want them to fail."

But I was being lulled into a conversation about gaming, or at least about competing, which was not the point.

"You understand we're going to have to check out this storeroom, right?" I asked. I couldn't even believe this was a point of discussion.

"Of course," said Daniel. "But if this guy really is some kind of creeper, it can't hurt to make him wait an extra fifteen minutes before he chloroforms you."

"Before he chloroforms *you*," I told him. "You're the designated victim. You're going in that storeroom first."

This notion pleased Daniel tremendously.

"If you had told me that ahead of time, I could have brought a wig and dressed up as you. Like a disguise."

And it was comments like these that made me think Lesser Charice. When plan A is "I'll dress in drag as Dahlia," you're comfortably in Charician waters.

"No one would mistake you for me," I told Daniel.

"I'm too tall?"

"That, and you'll have to walk schlumpier."

Daniel started mimicking my walk. I was sort of kidding about the schlumpier bit, mostly, but damned if he didn't start doing it. First, accurately—because I don't have Daniel's ridiculous posture—then in an exaggerated form, like I was some awful schlubby mime.

"Please stop that."

But he didn't stop it, at least until we reached our destination. Meeting room 11 continued our leitmotif of "underwhelming." For a $20,000 tournament, everything felt so pedestrian. That said, I understood how this worked. The first round had far too many matchups to do them all in one location, and so they were scattered in meeting rooms all over the place. There was a feature match area in the ballroom, and that match would be projected large, to a big audience. Naturally, the high-profile players would be sent there.

And then there was the place where they sent us, a featureless white room with a handful of folding chairs. We weren't even playing on a flat-screen TV.

34

This was where bad players were sent to die.

Our opponents were already there waiting for us. A kid with black hair and a red jacket stood there sneering.

"Dahlia Moss? Daniel Simone?"

We told the kid, yes, that was us.

"I hope you're ready to get crushed!"

Also, this kid was seven. Maybe I should have mentioned that first. And seven's not an exaggeration. I asked him his age.

A very tired woman in a plaid blouse was standing behind him.

"Jacob," said the woman, presumably his mother. "What have we said about being a good competitor?"

"It's called smack talk, Mom!"

Another kid, I supposed his partner, and even younger brother was also there, standing behind his mother. He was wearing an Oscar the Grouch shirt. Six? Possibly five. I asked him his age too, but the answer was hard to understand, because he told me one age and displayed fingers for a different number.

"This is a 'no smack talk' zone," said Fighting-Game Mom. "We're polite to strangers."

"Don't be mean!" yelled Oscar to his brother.

"Fine," said Jacob, with a lot of bitterness for a seven-year-old. "Good luck."

I was still wrapping my head around this all—this tournament of urchins—but Daniel took it quickly in stride.

"Good luck to you, Jacob," said Daniel. "Although I have to warn you—I'm pretty good."

Daniel Simone, as far as I am aware, had never picked up a controller before this moment.

"Oh yeah?" said Jacob. "Well, my dragon kick is unbeatable."

"We'll see," said Daniel. And he was doing this in such an appealing way. He wasn't being mocking, and he wasn't being condescending. He was getting into it with this kid in exactly the proper spirit. Fighting-Game Mom was smiling. "I'm really good at dodging," said Daniel, like the cool older brother you wanted to beat.

"Oh yeah?" said Jacob. "I'm too fast to be dodged."

"I hope not!" said Daniel.

"I eat children for breakfast," I told everyone. I wanted to participate in this junior version of smack-talk theater, but I just didn't have the knack for it. Jacob's mom frowned at me.

It wasn't long before the tournament organizers had everything set up. Most of the players there brought their own joysticks, and even here, in the purgatory of meeting room 11, the organizers seemed surprised that we did not have our own custom Mad Catz joysticks in tow.

Jacob had his own joystick. Even Oscar the Grouch had his own joystick, and he was five.

"You really don't have your own?" the organizer asked, quite surprised. Three times he asked us this.

"We totally have joysticks," I told him. "They're just being cleaned right now."

"I see," said the organizer. "I guess you're stuck with the controllers that come with the machine."

And we started.

I had never played *Dark Alleys* before, but it seemed to me that I was easily the most-skilled person playing. The game worked a lot like *Smash Brothers*, which was to say, there were four people trying to knock one another off a platform. If you're not a gamer, imagine an episode of *American Gladiators*—with folks trying to knock each other off a balance beam and into a pool below, although instead of Nerf-covered sticks for weapons, you had lightning bolts and a robot arm.

"Who should I pick?" asked Daniel, to me, in a whisper, apparently because he didn't want to show weakness to a six-year-old.

"The hell if I know," I told him. "This was your idea. I'm just here for dangerous and unwise mysteries."

My strategy for fighting games, and also for racing games, is always to choose someone big and slow. In my experience, speed and subtlety are overrated. This might also be my approach to problems in general, now that I think about it. I selected a large robotic sumo wrestler to be my avatar.

Daniel chose—I'm not completely sure—but I believe it was Amelia Earhart, and whispered to me:

"How does this game work?"

That's what he asked me. How does this game work? These are words that are rarely spoken by people competing in a tournament.

"You press buttons and try not to fall into the water," I told him.

"Any particular buttons better than others?"

"You'll have to press them to find out."

The match started, and my bodyguard immediately walked off the platform and fell to his doom. He wasn't punched, he wasn't dragon kicked, he wasn't hit with a jet of flame. He just walked off to his death.

"What does this joystick do?" asked Daniel.

Oscar the Grouch, apparently some kind of vampire, flew toward me and tried to bite my leg, and so I leaped away, and then swept him, knocking him on the ground, but not off the platform. His brother, a flaming ninja, started his dragon kicking at me, which was to say that he was kicking me, but the kicks somehow shot fire.

Fighting games are not known for their gritty realism.

Anyway, the kid was clearly very fond of using one move over and over again, and so it was just a question of watching him to figure out how this "dragon kick" worked.

Burst of fire, kick, shooting into the air, and then there was a moment or two where his character was vulnerable. You can see where this is going.

Once I realized what he was doing, I let him kick me, blocked the fire, blocked the foot, and punched him in the face.

Fighting games have a lot of special moves that involve complicated inputs on the joystick. Quarter rolls forward plus punches, half rolls backward, this sideways down diagonal motion that I could never do very consistently. It's sort of like playing the piano, I guess, if the piano were also being attacked by birds.

But the truth of the matter is that you can go a long way with just the basics, especially against beginners. People always think of fighters as being twitchy, and they are, but they are fundamentally about controlling space and about picking their moments.

So I picked my moments. I let Jacob jump toward me, blocked, and then I beat the living shit out of him. Dodging his brother was easy, because he would always yell out, "I'm going to get you!" right before he attacked. Again, five.

Jacob attacked and—blam!—I punched him in the face. He blocked his face, and then—blam!—I punched him in the stomach. He blocked his stomach, and then—blam!—I punched him the face again. Then he tried to dragon kick me again, and so I blocked for a second and then punched him in the face again.

This went on for a while. To be clear, I punched a kindergartener in the face seven or eight times in succession. By the time I knocked him into the pool, he was crying, and his brother had put down his controller and was hugging him.

I then knocked his brother into the pool.

"Victory!" I said, realizing only later that I should have looked more abashed. I wasn't trying to rub it in so much as I was surprised that I wasn't defeated by these two, especially with Daniel zerging into oblivion like that.

Anyway, Oscar the Grouch wasn't particularly upset by his defeat, cheering, "Now we get sodas!" but Jacob was really broken up, and I felt I should apologize. Happily, I had Daniel with me to handle this sort of people stuff.

"Don't feel bad, kid," said Daniel. "You did better than me."

And then he held out his hand for a handshake, and Jacob took it.

"Yeah," Jacob said. "You didn't do too well at all."

"I got confused by this joystick. I should have brought my own. The one you have is pretty cool."

"I got this at GameStop," said Jacob. "I saved my money for six weeks!"

Thank you, mouthed Game Mom to us, because Jacob appeared to be happy now that he had something else to brag about. The organizers cleared us out of the way to make room for the next victims, and Daniel continued to charm the kids. Also he charmed Game Mom, who I thought might give him her phone number.

I don't want to diminish the narrative that Daniel was pretty nice, because he is pretty damned nice, but he was acting, essentially. He was playing the role of the cool older brother, and playing it to the hilt. Maybe it's a strange response to someone being kind to children, but I suddenly realized that I couldn't really tell when Daniel was being genuine. Aside from cutting his teeth on new accents, Daniel could project whatever emotion he wanted. Like a sociopath. But a nice one, hopefully.

"Do you want to check out this storeroom?" I asked Daniel when we got away from the children.

"I'm not sure I do," said Daniel. "I feel a little nervous about it, actually."

He said that, but he didn't sound nervous at all. He sounded confident. He sounded like someone who was boldly heading into the future.

"We have to do it. That's why we came here." And despite my affirmative statement, I sounded like someone who was being dragged into the future, kicking and screaming.

The second floor of the Endicott Hotel was an extension of the first, with a balcony that overlooked the main floor. There were no hotel rooms on this floor, just amenities, like an "exercise room" and some sort of repurposed smoking lounge called the "office room," with rich dark wood furniture and an oriental rug.

I was feeling a little weird about coming up here, both because I wasn't sure who I was meeting, and also because I felt like I was trespassing. I had not paid for the privilege of using the "office room," and so who was I to go tromping around up here?

I had insisted that Daniel walk in front of me, as designated victim, but I was also anxious about the decision. From my limited experience playing *Dungeons & Dragons* with my brother,

Alden, whenever the DM made a point of asking for Party Order (i.e., who's in the front of the line), it was, about half the time, a trap, because you were getting sprung upon from behind. The truly safe place to be was in the middle, but I did not have enough victims for that. I would need to surround myself with bodyguards. Maybe they could carry me around in an egg, like I was Lady Gaga.

There were two primary halls to go down, and we chose, entirely at random, the one on the left, which led, sure enough to a room marked "Storeroom." Had we chosen the one on the right, this story might be very different. But this was not an astonishing mistake; this was pure chance.

I made it to the door of the storeroom—unassuming, uninteresting, and quite misleading.

"Try the handle," I told Daniel.

"You try the handle," he told me, again in a confident, firm, and very adventuresome voice. He sounded exactly like an adventurer; he just behaved like a sane person.

I opened the door, although I was prepared to leap back, in case someone had fashioned a dart trap to shoot out at me. (Note to self: I really haven't played a LOT of *Dungeons & Dragons*, but it has made an impression on me, at least when opening mysterious doors.)

There was no dart trap, but it was just as well, because there was Doctor XXX, sitting in the corner, bludgeoned to death.

CHAPTER SIX

I s he okay?" asked Daniel.

It's easy, and in fact, very tempting to make fun of this question, because Doctor XXX was clearly not okay, given that much of his skull was scattered across the floor. But there's no normal way to react to this kind of trauma, is there? Besides which, I leaned down and said:

"Doctor XXX? Psst. Hey, buddy?"

Which wasn't appreciably better. Doctor XXX, for his part in this, said nothing.

"These sorts of stories sound more fun when Charice tells them," said Daniel. This was true, although Charice had never stumbled across a corpse with me before. I had never stumbled across a corpse with me before. This was my first corpse, aside from my nana, and I didn't really so much stumble across her as visit her at the funeral home. Also, she hadn't been bludgeoned to death.

"I wish we had come up here before we beat up those children," I told Daniel. "Maybe we could have saved him."

It perhaps tells you more about me than I would like that my primary reaction to Doctor XXX's corpse was guilt.

"Maybe it's good we didn't," mused Daniel. "How long has he been dead?"

Daniel posed this question to me as though I had a reasonable way of answering it. True, I had managed to suss out a murderer once already, but it didn't involve measuring out how much blood had pooled on the floor and making calculations. It was an appealing idea, but to do it scientifically, I would need a control, Daniel presumably, whom I could bludgeon to death in a different room, and use the stopwatch app on my iPhone to gauge how much time elapsed before there was a comparable amount of blood.

I suggested this plan to Daniel, who did not spring for it.

"Maybe we should get the police," he said.

"I think that's a good idea."

"You stay here and guard the corpse, and I'll run downstairs and tell the desk."

It was undoubtedly Daniel's commanding voice that talked me into this plan. He sounded like someone who knew what he was doing. Someone vaguely Australian who knew what he was doing. But this was nonsense. He didn't know anything. I didn't know anything.

When you run across a dead body, no one has any idea what to do, so every reasonable idea and also unreasonable idea seem equally sensible.

Anyway, Daniel left. After he headed downstairs, I took a moment to look around. It wasn't so much that I was sleuthing as that I was afraid someone might jump out from behind something like the water heater.

The room wasn't anything special; there was a rack with cleaning supplies, the aforementioned water boiler, a floor sink where a mop could be drained, and, obviously, a bloody corpse. The corpse was definitely the highlight of the room.

I'm joking slightly, but it wasn't just the viscera. Whoever Dr. XXX had been, he was certainly natty, with copper-colored corduroy pants, an orange-and-blue-plaid shirt, and plaid socks that matched the shirt. He was a fellow who matched his socks to his shirts. I was happy if my socks matched each other, much less any other outside influence. It was hard to imagine what he looked like, with his complete skull, but I thought probably that he was Asian, although the blood and missing bits made the question a little open. Jet-black hair, though. Mostly Asian facial features, from what I could tell, but it made me queasy to look. Better to focus on socks.

I took a few minutes to ponder this sock-matching situation, which is probably just a way of coping with a terrible situation. You rest your mind on the less-terrible parts of the arrangement. Had he bought the socks and shirt together? Had them custom made? I wouldn't even know how to do such a thing if I tried.

But in terms of distraction, this was a thin soup, compared to a room with a dead body in it.

And the longer Daniel was gone, the edgier I started to get. Also, the less sense it made to stay in here. He had commanded me to "guard the corpse," but this was surely something ridiculous that had just been said in the heat of the moment. Guard it from whom? Was this some kind of sketchy spring break situation where someone was going to bust in here and take out Doctor XXX's kidney? How likely a concern should this actually be?

What seemed more likely, and in fact, suddenly became rather vivid was the notion that whoever killed the guy might swing back by. Maybe they got nervous about leaving finger-prints? I didn't see any fingerprints, but no matter. I also didn't see any obvious weapon. But those are sleuthing questions, and I wasn't sleuthing. I was just covering my bases. Maybe the mur-der weapon was in here somewhere, and the murderer wanted to drop by and pick it up. I did not want to stand in the way of this plan.

I decided that I don't like being left alone with very recently murdered people, for reasons that I think unnecessary to elu-cidate. It makes me anxious. And when I get anxious, I need human contact. This is probably why I decided to start stream-ing again. If someone came back in and murdered me, it would be on film.

"Hello, Twitch chat," I said. "How's everyone this morning?"

This was too casual an opening for a tiny room with a corpse in it, but I was trying to make myself feel calm.

To hell with you, said Twitch chat, their customary greeting.

"So, good news, bad news," I told chat. "The good news is that I met with Doctor XXX, and that he did not drug me at all. Not even in the slightest."

He stood you up, guessed Twitch chat.

"Not exactly," I said.

What's the bad news, Twitch chat began to eventually ask.

"The bad news is that he's been murdered."

!!! said Twitch chat.

"Bludgeoned to death, looks like. I'm in a tiny room with his corpse right now. Someone is fetching the police."

Pics or it didn't happen, said Twitch chat.

I had been holding the camera specifically so that it did not include Doctor XXX's corpse, because even I have some sense of propriety. Besides which, snuff was surely in violation of

Twitch's policy. Sexual harassment, certainly not. In fact, I believe that the official jingle for Twitch chat includes several pejorative terms for women and also some racial slurs. It's basically just harassment with some gaming in the background. But a single corpse, and they'd scream bloody murder, no pun intended.

"I think I'm going to keep that out of the frame," I told Twitch chat, who were surprisingly irritated by the development.

Show us the corpse! they kept typing.

"I don't think that's appropriate."

Corpse! Corpse! Corpse! they started chanting.

"No," I said. "Good God, no."

Maybe just describe it. What does it smell like?

I was finding their presence a lot less comforting than I had hoped I might, and I began to realize the wisdom of bringing an end to this conversation, and so I cut to the chase. I hadn't reached out to chat randomly, after all.

"Police are already on the way," I told them. "So you don't need to contact them. Just, you know, if I vanish, take a screenshot for clues."

What kind of clues, asked Twitch chat.

"I don't know, the last thing I was wearing. A time stamp that shows when I was alive..."

Do you think a murderer is going to come back and kill you? Get the hell out of there! typed Twitch chat, although there was also a side conversation about my incorrect grammar usage. (It should be the last "things" I was wearing, not "thing," lest I was wearing just a onesie. I did not engage on this point.)

"I'm guarding the corpse," I said in hopefully an authoritative voice, which sounded only a little Australian. Maybe New Zealand.

From whom? Who wants a corpse? asked Twitch.

"I don't know," I told them. I decided not to develop my Dahlia-might-get-murdered theme, and instead offered a cheerier proposition: "It's a hotel. If I don't keep watch, maybe some small children would wander in here and play with it. Or a dog or something. It might lap up all this blood and destroy valuable evidence."

All this blood. I really shouldn't have started talking about the blood at all, because it was a thing that was best to keep out of my mind. Best to focus on socks. Or chat. But there I had gone and started talking about blood.

And then it just sort of hit me.

The sensation manifested itself, initially, as a sense of numbness, an awful lot like what I imagine a stroke feels like. Then, I threw up. Over everything. Well, mostly the corpse. It happened very quickly, and my first thought was: *Don't throw up on your computer.* So I turned.

Okay, it mostly hit the wall, in my defense, but it was a small room and there was some ricocheting. A lot of ricocheting.

Then another wave hit me, this time not vomit, but guilt. Not only had I failed to prevent Doctor XXX's murder, I had thrown up on him and contaminated the crime scene. Seriously contaminated. I had a comically large breakfast this morning—with oatmeal and strawberries and orange juice and waffles. It was precisely the sort of breakfast that one sees on commercials for sugary cereal, a "Froot Loops is part of this nutritionally balanced breakfast" breakfast.

That the coroner would now study.

I am so sorry, Doctor XXX.

"You know what, guys," I told Twitch chat, whilst wiping vomit off my face. "I think I'm going to get back with you later."

Fuck you, said Twitch chat, which was its customary farewell.

I closed the computer and surveyed the chaos I created. It's hard to know what the etiquette is for throwing up on a crime scene. Should you clean it up? The corpse-y area, obviously not, but what about the non-corpse-y bits? Do I really just leave my vomit to pool throughout the room?

I also noticed on the floor by the door an extremely dampened sheet of paper—dampened with my vomit, that is—that appeared to be a program for the improv group that Daniel was a part of. It seemed to me that this was certainly Daniel's paper, and he somehow dropped it here in the scuffle and excitement. Given that I had thrown up on it, I thought the least I could do was to pick it up.

Later I would brood on this, and decide it was a mistake, but give me a break. I don't even consider this one an astonishing mistake—just a regular rookie error.

But I didn't get much time to consider it in the moment because I heard screaming from down the hall.

CHAPTER SEVEN

Maybe screaming is too poetic. Hollering? Let's go with hollering. Because screaming implies shock, or fear. And there wasn't a lot of that. This was more of an irritated yelling.

Regardless, when you're in a room with a corpse, and you hear yelling, you investigate.

So I left the room, leaving Doctor XXX's corpse totally unguarded. Although, I had vomited an awful lot in there, and if someone wanted to go in there and mess around, they would probably leave vomit-y footprints. They'd also smell. So in that sense, throwing up was a smart move! Next-level detecting.

As the crow flies, the voice was very close to me, and I felt I could hear it pretty well. A little muffled, because it was coming from the other side of the wall, but certainly audible.

Whoever he was, it sounded like he was yelling: "Albert Camus!"

I realize that sounds nonsensical, but in the moment, that's what it sounded like. Between the words and the hoarse, petulant tone, it sounded like someone had been extremely frustrated by French nihilism. "Fuck you, Camus! *The Stranger* is pretentious garbage." They didn't yell that, but it seemed possible that it may follow.

The layout of the second floor was effectively a U shape of hallways. To find the source of the sound, I made my way down the hall, to the main balcony of the foyer, where I couldn't hear yelling anymore, and back down the right hallway, where I could. This led to a storeroom and doorway similar to one I had seen in the other hall, only whoever was in this door was alive, because they were making a lot of noise.

"Hello? Can anyone hear me?" came the voice from behind the door. "Is somebody out there?"

I answered this question by opening the door.

There was a naked man handcuffed to a folding chair.

. . .

"Hello," I said.

. . .

"Hi," said the naked man. Okay, not *totally* naked. He was wearing tighty-whities—very tighty, from the looks of it—and also socks. But that was it.

"Listen," he said. "I know this is weird, but could you get me out of this chair?"

This seemed to me, all at once, to indeed be very weird and yet also exceedingly normal. Weird: finding a mostly naked guy handcuffed to a chair. Normal: wanting to get out of the chair.

I suppose I should have found the situation icky, but keep in mind that I had just thrown up on a corpse, and this was way more comfortable than that. Besides which, the guy—another Asian guy, actually—was trying very hard to be friendly and nonchalant. As if this was a normal thing that happened. He was a relatively slight fellow, about my height, but remarkably thin. The situation definitely wasn't sexually charged—if anything, he looked grateful that someone had found him.

"What happened?" I asked him, although I could formulate

some pretty randy guesses. The air here reeked of perfume, some of kind of tacky fougère.

"I don't want to talk about it," said the guy. "Can you get me my pants? They're over in the corner."

And they were. A pair of black jeans. I don't know how the guy planned to put them on, but they were there.

"I think you'll need to get un-handcuffed first, unless you have some sort of phasing powers," I told him. "Do you have a key somewhere?"

The guy's face told me that he didn't.

"Listen," he said. "This is not what you think. Like, I am not that guy."

"Really?" I asked. I was going to say, "I don't know what kind of guy you mean," but who was I kidding? I knew what he meant.

"Well," considered the guy. "Maybe it's a little bit what you think. I don't know what you're thinking."

"How long have you been here?"

"I don't want to talk about it. Just get me out of here."

He was about my age, maybe a bit younger, and so I asked:

"Are you here for the tournament?"

"I was," he said with frustration. "But I don't want to talk about it. Can you just get me out of this chair?"

I looked at the handcuffs and told him that no, I probably couldn't. I don't pick locks. I know there are detectives who specialize in that sort of thing—but honestly, who in this day and age picks locks? Nancy Drew would have plowed right through it, sure, but she also wouldn't stay in a room with a dude with bulging undershorts. So we're even.

"Everything will be fine," I told him. "The police are on their way here."

That was the wrong thing to say, because the fella looked like he was about to go feral. He was literally spasming against the chair. "The police? No! I don't want the police! I just want out of this goddamned chair."

And he actually looked like he was about to cry, honestly. It was hard to not feel empathy for the guy, at least in the moment, because it was a pretty sorry situation. I'm guessing the situation that led him to this point was pretty sketchy, but who knows?

"They're on their way already," I told him.

"I don't want the police to see me like this," said the guy. "And I haven't done anything wrong!"

"They're not coming for you," I told him. "They're coming here for a—"

And I started to say "murder," but that felt like a lot to pile on a man who had been depantsed and handcuffed to a chair, and so I said:

"Something unrelated."

"You have to get me out of here," said the fellow.

"Why?" I asked. What was the guy, wanted?

"This is humiliating," he said, and in such a defeated hapless tone that it was hard not to see where he was coming from.

"I'm sure the police have seen a naked guy in a chair before."

And our guy's whities were rapidly becoming significantly more tighty. Because I am a lady, I pretended not to notice, but it did not require Holmesian skills of observation to figure out what was happening.

"Should I leave?" I asked.

"There's not some dude out there that can help me?" he asked, his voice increasingly shrill and desperate.

"No," I told him. I should have gone out to find Daniel,

actually, but then there was the murder to contend with, and besides which, I wasn't sure that Daniel necessarily was in the mood to help a naked guy out, either. It was awfully early in the morning for naked guys.

The guy took a deep breath.

"My name's Swan," he told me.

"I'm Dahlia."

Transcribing that looks weird, but it felt natural that we should know each other's names in the circumstances.

"Dahlia," said Swan. "I'm just going to beg you right now."

"Don't do that," I told him. "It makes this seem weird."

"This IS weird. I am begging for you to get me out of here."

I shouldn't have, but I laughed. "What am I supposed to do?"

"Grab my pants, get my wallet. There's a hotel key for a room on the fifth floor."

This was an easy enough request, and I did it. I wasn't sure where he was going with it, but it was easy enough.

"Done. Now what?"

"Now I want to you pick me up and carry me to my hotel room."

"What?"

"Pick me up and carry me to my hotel room."

"I'm not going to do that."

"I am begging you," sobbed Swan.

I appreciated Swan's desperation—because this really was some sort of junior high nightmare situation—but that plan was nuts. Poor word choice. Crazy. Let's go with crazy. "I can't lift you!" I said.

"You look very strong," said Swan.

"It's three flights of stairs!"

Swan looked at me and said: "I. Am. Begging. You."

"How do I know this isn't some kind of trap?"

"Are you kidding me?" asked Swan. "I'm handcuffed to a chair. I don't have pants. What kind of trap could this be?"

"I don't know, maybe there are guys in the room waiting for me?"

"It's not a trap. Please, Dahlia. I am begging you. If my parents learn about this, they will kill me. You may as well just hit me over the head with a crowbar and leave me for dead."

An interesting choice, given what had happened in the other storeroom, but it was the bit with the parents that weakened me.

And this is how I was talked into transporting a naked man.

It helped that Swan was a very slight guy, because if he had been bulkier, I don't think I could have managed. I didn't so much lift him as drag him, chair and all. When we got to the stairwell, thankfully empty, I dragged him up step-by-step, making a booming echoing sound every freaking step. I kept expecting someone—police possibly?—to burst onto the scene, although no one did.

Amazingly, we made it all the way to Swan's room—502—without encountering another soul, which was great, because I had no idea how I intended to explain it to an onlooker.

Swan's room was nice—if absurdly small—and was pleasantly not filled with anyone waiting to jump me.

Honestly, he seemed to be shrinking each time I interacted with him. Not, you know, his tumescence—that was still holding steady—but the rest of him was getting smaller.

"Well," I said. "Here we are."

I draped his pants over him, which seemed not to be doing

the job, and so then I went to the bathroom and took out a towel, which I draped over his shame. I accomplished this in the most natural way—by tossing it at him, and something small and tiny fell out of his pants.

I picked it up, because I am not a slob, and observed that it was a tiny silver wheelbarrow. I really, really wanted to make some kind of "is this a wheelbarrow in your pocket" joke, but I appreciated that this was not the time or place. Still, it was quite a setup. How often do you meet someone with a wheelbarrow in their pocket is what I am saying.

I carefully put it on the counter, but I suppose it was all the same to Swan, who couldn't reach anything, anywhere.

"I don't imagine this is good for moving a lot of gravel," I said, which is not as good a line, but had the advantage of not being sexual or humiliating.

"Ha, ha, ha, no," said Swan, who looked and sounded incredibly embarrassed. Possibly there was nothing I could say that wouldn't be embarrassing.

"I've got to head back downstairs and deal with, um, an incident."

"Right," he said, shooting for neutrality. "I understand."

"I'm going to leave you now."

"I'll be right here," said Swan.

It struck me that Swan was not going to ask for any more help than he already had asked for but didn't like the idea that I was going to leave him in this room to starve to death.

"Is someone going to find you here later?" I asked. "Like a roommate or something?"

"No," said Swan, who appeared to be trying to summon dignity from some unseen and largely unreachable location. "I am traveling alone."

"Do you want me to send some dude up here later with pruning shears or something?"

This led Swan to squirm slightly, as though I were suggesting some bizarre sexual fantasy, and so I clarified: "for the handcuffs."

Swan tried to appear indifferent to this notion, although I could tell he was happy with the idea.

"If you could find the time for that," said Swan, as though he had lots of other things he planned to do. "It would be very appreciated."

"I'll get Daniel up here," I said.

"Great," he said.

It had been such an enormously awkward situation that I couldn't resist cracking a joke.

"Hey, Swan," I told him.

"Yes, Dahlia," he said, sighing.

"We've got to stop meeting like this."

No joke has ever been laughed at less.

CHAPTER EIGHT

After I left, I thought that I should have offered to turn on the television. I'll have to remember the idea for the next time I transport a naked guy chained to a chair. You know, for when that comes up again.

I came back downstairs, and in the intervening time, the police had shown up. This was actually comforting, because I had the idea that nothing bad whatsoever could happen to me if cops were around.

But of course, then something bad did happen to me.

The bad thing was a cop.

"Holy fucking Christ," said Detective Maddocks. "It's Dahlia Goddamned Moss."

Well, it's good to be remembered.

Detective Maddocks was a detective that I had encountered on my last adventure and who had never seemed to care for me very much. By which I mean that he threatened me and regarded me with abject disgust. His partner, on the other hand, the much more appealing Anson Shuler, liked me rather a lot. Arguably too much, although possibly just the right amount. I was still deciding.

"Detective Maddocks," I said. "How have you been? The family is well?"

I had no idea if Detective Maddocks had a family; I had never even noticed if a ring was on his hand. It seemed more likely that he had a brood, or perhaps a wolf pack. But I had no real idea. I was just being snarky, which he loved, because he totally got my sense of humor. Hashtag irony.

Maddocks stared at me. He had a fantastic craggy face; just the sort of thing you would want for a detective. It would be wrong to have a face like that on a publicist or an event planner.

"Are you the person that found the body? Tell me that you aren't."

"I did find the body. Also, I had sort of a reaction to it, and I may have, you know, thrown up a tiny amount in there."

"I've been in there," said Maddocks.

"Maybe it was more of a moderate amount."

"There are gallons of vomit on the floor."

"I was surprised!"

Maddocks sighed, but I thought possibly—just possibly—there was a glimmer of amusement behind his eyes. It pleased him, I think, that I had a normal reaction to a crime, as opposed to, you know, Hannah Swensening it up in there. He was probably nervous that I had dusted the place for fingerprints.

"Tell me, at least, that you're not here on some kind of ridiculous case. I'll remind you that you aren't a detective."

"I'm actually taking a class to become one," I told him, with way too much enthusiasm than was appropriate.

"Oh no," he said.

"I mean, online. University of Phoenix. I've only just started. But it's really easy to get certified to be a detective in Missouri."

"Just stop talking."

"You wouldn't believe how easy. It's sort of shocking. Some bureaucrats have really fallen asleep at the wheel."

"Tell me you're not here on a case. Until you're certified, you can't take cases, because that would be illegal."

"I'm very largely not here on a case," I told Maddocks.

"Why are you using weasel words?" asked Maddocks.

"I'm just being honest," I told him. "I don't lie to the police."

Maddocks made a face that indicated he had expected plenty of lies from me, which, honestly, was fair. I explained to him about the tip jar, and how "Doctor XXX" had suggested I show up here, after making a donation. I explained about his message asking me to come upstairs, and even about how "something major was going to go down here." The only thing I left out was the bit about Doctor XXX wanting a detective to be around, because that was just going to lead to a lecture.

"Where's Daniel at?" I asked him.

"Is that the guy you found the victim with?"

"Yeah, where is he?"

"Making a statement," said Maddocks. "I'll need you to do the same thing. And then we can see if your statements line up."

Maddocks had really spooked me the first time I had interacted with him, but there was something markedly less scary about him the second time around. Oh sure, he was vaguely threatening me, but I didn't have anything to worry about. I wasn't involved in the death of whoever this guy was. I had almost gotten involved, sure—but I got there too late. For once, I had nothing to hide.

"Yeah, okay," I told him. "Are you taking my statement? Is Shuler around?"

"Why are you asking about Shuler?" asked Maddocks. Did I say he wasn't scary? I should amend that. He was mostly not scary, because when he didn't like a question, you could feel it in your bones.

"Shuler's my bud," I said. "Besides which, someone's going to do it. Why not Shuler?"

"Shuler is not here today," said Maddocks. "My partner will take your statement."

"I thought Shuler was your partner."

"No," said Maddocks, which was perfectly Maddocksian in its lack of explanation. I knew full well that they were partners during my last case, but Maddocks didn't explain that, or what had happened in the intervening time.

"Maybe I'll just call Shuler," I said.

"Shuler is not part of this case."

I was mostly just trying to get Maddocks's goat at this point, which is playing a dangerous game, I realize.

"I understand that. I just meant to say hello. Hi, Shuler, It's me, Dahlia!"

And Maddocks looked at me in a way that was, what— ancient? terrifying? sort of paternalistic, but in a sweet Jerry Orbach-y way? All of these at once. He said:

"Dahlia. You should leave Shuler alone."

Which was really unnerving, actually. Not throw-up-on-corpse unnerving, but at least in the neighborhood. What really troubled me about it, and continues to trouble me even now, is that I'm not sure if Maddocks was trying to protect me from Shuler, somehow, or protect Shuler from me. I have a terrible feeling that it's the latter.

But I digress.

Maddocks's partner du jour was a stout woman in her early forties named Detective Weber. She was closer to Shuler in body type—her body might have been described as jolly in other circumstances—but somehow managed to be Maddocks's psychic twin. She was not one for small talk, Weber.

Giving my statement was pretty easy, actually, and I told Weber everything that I've told you. I even fessed up to the vomiting, which she was awfully understanding about. Maybe retching when you find a corpse isn't such an unusual thing, pop culture be damned.

The only thing that tripped me up was the business with Swan, which I sort of felt like wasn't my business to tell. Or at least, wasn't my business to tell right away. Because if I mentioned it the police now, they'd tromp upstairs, and he'd be just as humiliated as before. I'd have to tell them eventually—I got that. But later, after he had put on some clothes. I could tell Shuler. They could get their interview; but let them do it in a way that wasn't dehumanizing.

So when Weber asked what I did after Daniel went downstairs, I didn't lie, precisely. I just explained that I got queasy, which was true, and took a moment in the restroom. Which was true. It just so happened that the restroom in question was on the fifth floor, and the moment was so that I could grab a towel to cover Swan's tumescence.

Was this terrible? Is it a terrible mistake? I was inclined to think not, because after all, it wasn't like Swan was going anywhere. He was tied to a chair in a locked room.

What could possibly happen to him?

CHAPTER NINE

Daniel apparently took much longer than I did to make a statement, because despite starting earlier than me, he was still going. I didn't think much of this at the time, because I still was processing him as a sort of Lesser Charice. If Charice had to make a statement, it would have taken hours and hours and would probably have involved props, several dramatically smoked cigarettes, and possibly a musical number.

I called Charice, actually, even though she was at work, because this had been a crazy day, and Charice was still the person I called for crazy.

"This is Charice. What can I do for you?"

"Is there any way you can come out here?"

"Dahlia!" she said, alight with happiness. "Not at all. But tell me it's going well with Daniel."

"Of course it's going well with Daniel," I told her, which was sort of glossing over that he was giving a statement to the police, but this wasn't what would have concerned her anyway. "I love Daniel. Daniel's great."

I knew my roommate entirely too well, because even though I couldn't see her, I could picture the exact face she was making—this scrunched-up thing she did with her forehead when she was skeptical.

"That is just the sort of thing you say when you don't engage. And I don't want you just to deal with surface Daniel. I want you to deal with deep Daniel."

Even setting aside the altogether too-sexual way Charice said "deep Daniel," I was not sure I wanted to experience deep Daniel under any circumstances. What was wrong with surface Daniel? I said:

"There's been a murder here."

"Oh, that's wonderful!" Charice said, then instantly back-tracked. "I mean, yes, I'm very sad that a man is dead, but this is just the sort of bonding adventure that you two should go on! You'll be war buddies by the end of it."

"How did you know that it was a man?" I asked.

Charice was elated. "You're such a natural for detective work."

"I appreciate the compliment, but how did you know?"

"I suppose I'm just being sexist. Women can be corpses too. Feminism!"

"I would think it's misandry."

But Charice was not interested in this point.

"You're getting really good at deductions. How are you liking that online class?"

So yeah. I had just started this online course that was the first step toward getting licensed as a legitimate private investigator in the state of Missouri. It was fun but slightly surreal.

"I like it okay. It's a very strange collection of tea-making old women and bounty hunters."

"That sound like fun," said Charice. "We should invite them over!"

We should not do that. Emphatically, we should not do that, and besides which I was getting offtrack.

"Listen, is there seriously no way that you can come out here? I think maybe someone was trying to lure me into a storeroom and kill me."

"You know how to tempt me, Dahlia."

"Pretty please?"

"You have Daniel—he can be my emissary. Daniel will protect you."

"I don't need anyone to protect me," I told her, although in retrospect this would prove to be dramatically untrue. "I need a partner in crime. You're my right-hand man, Charice."

"Dahlia, you're adorable, but even I have work to do occasionally. How about this: I'll make an amazing penne when we get home. It has rampion in it."

"That penne won't save me if I'm dead."

"Well, then, there will be more for me. Spend time with Daniel. Get to know him. I like this one."

"I know Daniel fine."

"What's his favorite song?"

"'Colors of the Wind' from *Pocahontas*."

"That's not it at all," said Charice. "Did he tell you that?"

"I'm just making things up," I told her.

Charice sounded pleased and disconcerted all at once.

"You're getting much better at lying," she said. "This class is doing wonders for you."

I made my way back downstairs to discover that the tournament had been significantly disrupted by the arrival of the police. We had originally been scheduled next for an eleven fif-teen game, but now that had been postponed. Everything had been postponed, apparently, or so the signage told us.

The fact of this was sort of a comfort to me—this is what is supposed to happen when a person is murdered, but I was also slightly miffed. I had been shot last month at an event not com-pletely unlike this, and they carried on just fine.

There was a ginger-haired guy with glasses—not the weasel, a different guy—who seemed to be in charge of things, and I asked him what was up.

"There was an unfortunate incident upstairs," said the guy. "And so everything is just going to be thrown off schedule for three hours or so. But we will continue," he added, with a fake-sounding confidence.

"Do you know who was killed?" I asked him. "Was it one of the players, or just a guest at the hotel?"

"I never said anything about someone being killed," said the ginger.

"No, I realize you didn't. But do you know who it was? Have you heard anything?"

But the ginger guy was not putting up with me. He was a handsome guy, actually, with more shoulders than you saw on your average geek, but he had a fastidious manner that made him seem like a Roald Dahl character.

"You'll have to ask the police about that yourself. There's really a lot for me to manage here."

I had no intention of asking the police a damned thing, because I knew full well what they would tell me, which involved the various ways I might fuck myself. And this was just Detective Weber. But I was curious—was it a random hotel guest or someone here for the tournament? Because the way I saw it, there were two theories:

Theory One was that the dead guy was Doctor XXX. Something really was going to "go down" and whatever it was, it went down before he met with me. I didn't love this theory, not for any deductive reason, but because it involved me in his death somehow.

Theory Two was that Doctor XXX wanted me to see whatever had happened to Swan. Who knows whatever that was about? Some weird creeper sex thing? This theory hadn't dawned on me at all while I was dragging his naked body around, but now, with his badonkadonk safely out of sight, seemed not entirely improbable. Hell, maybe whoever had lured him in there was counting on me to bail him out.

This theory I liked much better, because it meant that I was not indirectly responsible for a man's death.

But reasoning-wise, it could go either way. When Daniel showed up, we'd get Swan into some clothes and grill him a little. Hell, we had three hours to spare until our next round. We'd have time to waterboard him, if it came to it.

But while I was waiting, I thought I could ask around a little.

And with perfect timing, Mike3000 came up to me. He seemed even larger than the last time I saw him, although maybe he was just puffed-up because he was high on victory.

"My lady," he said. "Were you ever able to find your partner?"

The answer to this question, as Douglas Adams would put it, was both true and not true at the same time. I did not wade into these existential waters with Mike3000, however, and decided to keep things simple and clean.

"I did. We crushed our first round."

"Crushed?"

"Well, narrowly clawed. Yourself?"

"I would have said *crushed* but you've already used it."

"Congratulations!" I told him. "Listen, I'm trying to find another player," I told him. "Asian guy, really dapper."

"That could be a third of the guys here." He laughed, then reconsidered. "Well, maybe not dapper."

"He was here earlier—he had socks that matched his shirt—"

I was going to describe the shirt, but Mike interrupted, because the socks were apparently enough.

"Karou Minami."

"Who?"

"Karou Minami. That thing of his with socks is weird. Downright weird."

"Yeah," I said, "that was his name. Karou. You know him well?"

"Not well," said Mike3000. "I suppose he's my competition. He's really excellent. I see him at most events I go to, but we're not really friends or anything."

"Cool," I said. And I was done with Mike3000, at least for now, because I had gotten a name, which was all I really wanted. Mike3000, however, was not entirely done with me. His face had gotten all schlumpy, with a frowning mouth and sagging eyebrows.

"Maybe I should haven't been so judgey about the socks," said Mike3000. "If you like socks, you like socks. What do I care?"

"It's not important," I told him.

"It's a victimless crime, snappy socks," said Mike.

"Yeah, I don't care." And truly I didn't. The socks were great. It was a useful detail that made it easy to figure out who this potential Doctor XXX was.

"No," said Mike3000. "I'm making Karou seem like he's weird. My therapist has been telling me that I 'other' people too

67

much, and it's what I'm doing now. It's just that I asked him about the socks one time, and he talked to me for forty-five minutes about them. I kept waving my keys at him—you know, the international signal for 'this conversation is over and I really must be going' but he kept talking."

I did not fully understand how I had gotten lured into a discussion about Mike3000's issues in therapy. Even as I type this up, I'm still not quite sure how that happened.

"It's good that you're being self-aware," I told him. Although I did not especially think that, actually. I was thinking about waving my keys at him, but I decided that would be too on the nose.

"He's a perfectly normal guy. Funny. He can dance pretty well too. He is a child of the universe, no less than the moon and stars. Just keep him off socks."

I was not worried about Karou discussing his socks with me. I was not worried about Karou discussing anything with me. If he managed to somehow return from the dead to bring up the topic of socks, I figured he'd earned the right to hold court. Besides which, there were certainly worse things to be haunted about.

Such as "you killed me."

That sort of thing.

"Thanks for the advice," I told Mike.

"Dahlia," said Daniel from behind me. "Where have you been?"

I knew it was Daniel because he was back in Australian accent mode. I suppose it could have been Guy Pearce that inexplicably wanted to know my whereabouts. As exhilarating as that thought might have been, let's be real: It was Daniel.

"Where have I been? Where have you been?" I said, wheeling around to see him. But he looked tired, and I had to remind myself again that this wasn't Charice but some other person, who just seemed to complement her in way that I didn't fully grok. I took it down a notch.

"Did the police statement wear you out?"

"It was exhausting," said Daniel. "I thought it would be interesting, at least. But the experience was terrible. That woman, Weber—she has eyes that look through you."

"Yeah," I said. "That's what they do. And you were with them for a while."

"I guess I'm not a known quality like you are," said Daniel. "Anyway, do you want to go out for lunch or something? Everything here is getting time-shifted by a couple of hours, and I really think it would be nice to get some air."

This was obviously a fantastic plan; and certainly if I hadn't a naked man to tend to upstairs, I would have jumped at the opportunity.

"I'm in," I told him. "Although, first we've got some business we need to take care of upstairs."

"What kind of business?" asked Daniel, apparently under the assumption that a murder, a fighting-game tournament, and a mystery client was enough activity for the morning.

"I don't want to tell you exactly," I said. "But it involves wire cutters and deceit."

CHAPTER TEN

I briefed Daniel on the whole Swan situation, who received the information with equal parts of poise and incredulity. Mostly this meant that he seemed very calm and unsurprised by the development, but repeated everything I told him back to me as a question.

"And he was in his Skivvies and handcuffed to a chair?"

"Yes."

"And you carried him up the stairs?"

"Yes."

"Still in just Skivvies?"

"As I said, yes."

"Still strapped to the chair?"

"That's right."

"And you did this while I was giving a statement to the police?"

And so on. But he didn't bug out his eyes or anything or, for that matter, run screaming. He gave the impression of being a reporter who wanted to get all the improbable details right. And he followed me all the way up to the fifth floor of the Endicott without so much as a raised eyebrow.

He didn't even raise an eyebrow when I used Swan's card key to open the door to find Swan flat on his back, still handcuffed to the chair.

"Who's there?" asked Swan. "All I can see is the ceiling."

"It's me again," I told him. "And I brought that male friend."

"Thank God," Swan said. He was happy to see me, but not happy to see me, if you get my drift. "I fell over."

"What happened?" I asked him.

"I was trying to get the handcuffs off," said Swan. "That's what happens in the movies. Not the falling over, I mean. The escaping. I ended up just falling over."

"This is Daniel," I told Swan, then whispered to Daniel, "Be bro-y with him. This calls for guy talk."

Daniel returned Swan to an upright position, a task he accomplished with an astonishingly small amount of effort.

"DUDE," said Daniel, trading in his Aussie accent for some kind of Californian Dell Guy. "What the hell happened to you, bro?"

"I don't want to talk about it," said Swan.

"You meeting some sweet piece of ass on the sly, and she cuff you to this folding chair?"

"Something like that." Swan sighed.

"Bro, we've all been there. Me, I've had some serious-ass chair-handcuffing problems. It's all cool. Right, Double D?"

It took me a moment to realize that I was "Double D." I really did want to smack Daniel at this point, but I had given him the instructions to be bro-y. I just didn't mean *this* bro-y. So I just said:

"Check yourself."

Which did nothing to stop him, or slow him down, and in

this way he was Charician again. Which was incredibly irritating and yet also sort of a comfort. I truly wished Charice were here, but maybe palling around with the two of them together wouldn't be the end of the world.

"Yeah," said Swan. "I'm not going to discuss any of this with people who aren't my friends. Frankly, I'm not sure I want to talk about it with friends."

Daniel apparently took this to mean that he should compliment Swan so that he could buddy up to him. However, most of the usual things you would compliment a stranger on were unavailable—clothing, accomplishments, an amusing joke.

"Cool briefs, dude," said Daniel, going for the only article of clothing available to him. "What are those, cotton?"

"I don't know," said Swan. "It is made from whatever underwear is made from. Can you guys get me out of these handcuffs?"

"We're going to try," I told him.

"Daniel, you said you've got a Swiss Army knife? You wanna see what you can do?"

And Daniel went around to Swan's, again, let's say badonkadonk, to see what kind of progress he could make. I was becoming iffy about Daniel bro-ing any info out of Swan, and so I took on the interview for myself.

"Listen, Swan," I told him. "I get that this is an embarrassing story you'd rather not remember, but I'm going to have to ask you some really direct questions about how you ended up in that chair."

"Why should I talk to you? You're not the police."

"No," I considered. "But I'm a private detective, and I'm also the woman that saved your sorry ass. And am still saving your ass, unless you'd like us to leave."

Swan sighed. "Yeah, okay," he said. "What do you want to know?"

I wasn't sure whether I should tell him about the murder next or wait until the end. Probably for the purposes of interviewing, it was better to wait until everything was over. But it felt sleazy to not mention it to him, and so I led with it.

"First, I need to tell you why the police were actually around."

Swan's eyes narrowed. He was very interested.

"There's no easy way to tell you this," I said. "But a man was murdered in a storeroom on the same floor as you. I found the body and called the police."

Swan looked appropriately shocked, almost even a little pale. This is how normal people react when exposed to a murder.

"Wow," he said quietly.

"You don't think there's any chance that whoever cuffed you to that chair"—and I went with gender-neutral language here, because what did I know?—"was also involved with the murder?"

"It was a girl," said Swan, noticing my tiptoeing around gender, and apparently being irritated by it. "You can just say 'girl.'"

"Hell yeah, it was," said Daniel, slapping Swan's ass. Too much, Daniel. Too much.

"So this girl. Do you think she was involved? Who was she?"

Swan was getting less and less agreeable the more I interacted with him. Admittedly, he had been having a rough morning, but there was something incredibly resentful and dyspeptic in his storytelling.

"First," said Swan. "I don't know who it was. I never saw her face."

"How," I started, trying to get the question out as neutrally as possible, "does that work?"

"So I checked into the hotel late last night," said Swan. "I really needed to network, because my partner flaked out, and I didn't have anyone to play with in the tournament. So I was planning on going out to this restaurant mixer thing to see if I couldn't find some other singleton to join up with me."

"Dude, that SUCKS."

"I know, right? Well, anyway, I'm getting ready, and I get this phone call at the hotel room. It's from a fan of mine—I stream a little, you know."

"A female fan," I guess.

"Yeah, and, like, super flirty. Actually, not even really flirty. More...dominant? She was more like 'We are going to have sex tonight. We are going to do the thing.'"

"Getting some action!" said Daniel.

"You've got to stop doing that," I told Daniel.

"I sort of like it, actually," confessed Swan. "Anyway, not to put too fine a point on it, but I don't get phone calls like that very often. Or, well, ever. I'm the guy at the bar who tries to buy you a drink, but the bartender can't hear me."

"What, dude? Chicks are totally after a piece of this."

"Honestly, no," said Swan. "And so, I don't know, she was kind of, I don't know, phone sex-y."

"What?! High five, dude!" said Daniel, despite the fact that Swan was still firmly handcuffed to the chair.

"There may have been phone sex."

"That's awesome, brah," said Daniel.

I was getting really irritated with Daniel at this point, but it actually seemed that his dude-bro affect was getting the job done, so I bit my tongue. I'm nothing if not objective oriented.

"It was awesome," said Swan, who looked dreamy for a moment. "It was pretty awesome."

Normally this is where I would say the word "vomit" aloud, possibly with hand gestures, but Detective Dahlia doesn't judge. Or she judges later, when she gets home. Also, I had done enough vomiting for the day already. I'd have been lucky to manage a dry heave.

"How did she get you downstairs?"

"She, uh, said that she wanted me to blindfold myself and leave my door unlocked. Then she came in here and brought me downstairs. Escorted me, I mean. She escorted me downstairs. To the storeroom. She said she wanted to try something crazy."

"Dude," said Daniel. "Freaky."

"I know," said Swan. "I wasn't really thinking at that point. I mean, not, clearly. But she walked me down there, handcuffed me to a folding chair in there—which at the time seemed AWESOME—made out with me a little bit, and then left."

"She just left?"

"She just left," said Swan. "She said she wanted to teach me a lesson."

"A lesson for what?" asked Daniel.

"I don't know," said Swan, who sounded troubled now. "She didn't say. It sounded sexy at the time. I kept thinking that this was some kind of game and that she was going to pop back in there, but she didn't come back. I kind of thought you were her for a little bit. I mean, right at the beginning."

"You were in there all night?" asked Daniel. "Dude."

"Did she sound like me?" I asked.

"Not really."

"You slept in there, bro?" asked Daniel.

"All night."

"You must have to pee," said Daniel.

"Like a horse," said Swan. "I didn't feel like I could ask Dahlia to help me with that."

"You thought right," I told him.

"If you can't get those cuffs off, you're gonna have to take matters into your own hands."

"I got you, bro," said Daniel, for whom helping another fella pee was apparently no big deal. Well, he was in *Equus*.

"How are you coming with those handcuffs?" I asked Daniel.

"Piece of cake, D," said Daniel, in a confident and bro-y voice. He then mouthed to me, in a less confident and concerned manner: *I can't fucking open these.*

"You can't open them, can you?" asked Swan.

"We're working on it," I told Swan.

"I don't want to put pressure on you guys. But my bladder is going to explode. I'm in like a Tycho Brahe situation."

"Siri," I said, turning to the Internet. "How do you open handcuffs?"

Siri suggested a YouTube video, which we all watched. The man in the video suggested using a shiv, a specially purchased tool, or a bobby pin, at which point Swan and Daniel both looked expectantly at me, as though I were some sort of girl detective from the forties.

"Dudes," I said, apparently infected by all this bro-talk, "I'm not a fourteen-year-old girl who loves horses."

They continued to look at me.

"I don't even have long hair."

"Well, we're fucked," said Swan. "I'm going to stay in this chair for the rest of my life."

"Actually," I told Swan. "Daniel and I were going to go out for lunch, and I was thinking we could invite a guy to join us. Someone who would have just the tools we need."

"Please don't leave again."

"I think we're going to have to."

Swan sighed. "Okay. But Daniel. Bro?"

"Yeah, buddy," said Daniel.

"It's time for you to free the beast."

CHAPTER ELEVEN

Daniel was growing on me, even excepting the "Double D" business—although if he ever tried calling me that again, the guy was in for a world of hurt.

"I'll say this for you, Dahlia," he said after exiting room 502, "you've certainly opened me up to a lot of new experiences. Beating kindergartners, making statements to the police, handling another man's junk."

"And it's not even noon."

"Where are we headed for lunch? I really need air now."

"You're the guy with the car," I told him. "You believe his story?"

"Shouldn't we believe his story?"

Oh, trusting Daniel. Admittedly, I didn't have any smoking gun I could point to, but I didn't buy it at all. Something felt seriously off.

"I don't know," I told him. "It was a little *Penthouse*-y, wasn't it? Turn down the dude-bro for a second, and tell me, would anyone ever behave that way?"

Daniel considered this. "Well, I wouldn't. Maybe the phone stuff, but I wouldn't leave my door unlocked and blindfold myself. That's, I don't know, very peculiar."

"You reverse the genders on that stuff, and it's straight-up implausible. No lady would do that for a hitherto unseen fella."

"Yeah," considered Daniel. "But the genders weren't reversed. And it wasn't me, or some guy that, well, you know, has a certain regular amount of sexual activity." I don't know why he was being modest; it wasn't like the walls at Charice's were especially thick. "It was a really lonely guy, and maybe he was just dumb. Guys are dumb sometimes, Dahlia."

Daniel told me this in a ridiculously confessional tone, as though this notion were going to come as a great shock to me. Whether guys could be dumb was not the point that I was hung up on. Actually, when you got down to it, I didn't know the point I was hung up on. The story had lots of implausible elements, but so does life, at least part of the time.

And yet—something about it was snagging on me. I was just about to put away the question when one of the wrong details came jumping out at me.

"He told me that he was alone in that room all night," I told Daniel. "But when I found him, the place smelled strongly of perfume."

"How long does perfume last?" asked Daniel.

"On the skin, a while I guess, depending on what it is, but the wake of it in the air? Not eight hours."

"You might be onto something," said Daniel. "Because come to think of it, he didn't seem to need to pee that badly."

I let Daniel call the shots on where we were headed for lunch, and he picked a sports bar that wasn't my speed or angle. Hockey sticks on walls, jerseys mounted behind glass, that sort of thing. But, the guy with the car makes the rules. And in retrospect, they grilled a mean mahimahi.

It was a little hubristic to expect Anson Shuler to show up

on such short notice for me, but he also struck me as the sort of guy who would always be there for you when the chips were down. I just had to make clear how down my chips were.

The conversation went like this.

"Hello?"

"Shuler? This is Dahlia. Moss."

There was a pause, possibly because I had never called Shuler before, despite him having given me his number, and he was probably running through his Rolodex of potential reasons.

"Dahlia," he said. "I didn't expect to hear from you. And you should call me Anson."

"Shuler suits you better," I told him.

And this was precisely the sort of vaguely flirty answer that I always seemed to veer toward when dealing with Anson Shuler. It wasn't the shore I was swimming for; quite the contrary. But it's where I always seemed to land.

"Well, if it suits me, I guess I can't argue," said Shuler. "What are you calling for?"

"I'm headed out for lunch, and I was hoping you could join me. Us."

"Who is us?" asked Shuler.

"I'm spending quality time with Charice's new boyfriend."

"The actor? Or is this a newer boyfriend?"

"The actor. Daniel's a keeper apparently," I said, which got a glance from Daniel, who was driving during this conversation.

"Yeah, okay," said Shuler, who I was pretty sure was doing the three-second let-me-pretend-to-consider-this shadow play. "I suppose I could join you guys. When are you having lunch?"

"We're on our way now."

"I enjoy your complete lack of planning. Where are you headed?"

I gave Shuler the name of the joint. I also took this moment to explain that this was not entirely a social call.

"There's also some police-y stuff I want to talk to you about."

"Yeah," said Shuler. "I figured there was something like that in the mix."

"Did you hear about the murder at the Endicott Hotel? It just happened."

"I did not," said Shuler.

"Really?" I was surprised.

"I'm not Batman, Dahlia. I don't stand on rooftops and monitor the city on my day off."

"Oh," I said. "I'm sorry if I'm dragging you into stuff when you'd rather take it easy."

"Eh, forget about it," said Shuler. "But you're buying the meal."

It took a while for Shuler to join us, but you couldn't blame the guy given the lateness of the situation. I admirably waited for his arrival before having anything other than mozzarella fries, but it seemed to take forever, especially because this was the opportunity that Daniel took to ask me personal questions.

"So tell me about this Shuler guy," he said, after a pregnant pause between fry consumption.

"You met him," I told Daniel. "Once."

"Yeah, but there were ten other people there, and I was sort of making out with Charice."

"He's a police detective and he'll know how to break handcuffs. That's all you need to know."

"He's sort of sweet on you, isn't he?"

What fresh hell was this? Daniel was asking me about my romantic life? No. Emphatic no. No, with reverb and powerful echo effects. I do not like talking about my feelings, Daniel, as I prefer them to be unknowable and ill considered.

"Daniel, I don't know what Charice told you about me, but I don't really do girl talk."

"Why is it girl talk? Guys can't talk about feelings?"

I hate actors.

"Okay, then, I don't really do people talk."

"Come on, Dahlia. Is he sweet on you or not?"

"I think so," I told him. Although there was no need for weaselly words here. It was pretty clear that Shuler was interested in me. He was coming to a sports bar on no notice. After my having not spoken to him in two weeks.

"So," said Daniel slowly. "Are you sweet on him?"

"What's with all this 'sweet on' business? Are you my grandmother now?"

This seemed to amuse Daniel, who then asked, "How about this? Do you see yourself spooning with him?"

Jesus, I hate actors. Anyway, this question resulted in my choking on a mozzarella fry, which resulted in the waiter coming over. At which point Daniel asked the question a second time, this time raising the ante to "fucking."

"I could use some water," I told the waiter when I was done choking.

"I'm sure you could," said the waiter, whom I now regarded as irresponsibly sassy.

Anyway, before I was able to answer or get water, Anson Shuler himself showed up, waving to us like he was hailing a cab.

Here's the thing about Anson Shuler. He doesn't look like a cop. Even a little. If I had to assign him a profession based solely on appearance, I'd go with Muppeteer. He has close-cropped hair and a cute round face, and he smiles very, very easily. He gives the impression of being someone who might suddenly sing a song, possibly about subtraction or maybe the importance of good citizenship. He also has this perfectly smooth caramel skin—and I know you're not supposed to describe biracial people with "food" words—but there is something decidedly dessertlike about the guy. He has—just very slightly—a little muffin top, which I feel, very strongly, that someone should pinch.

Not me necessarily. Just somebody.

"What are you guys talking about?" asked Shuler.

I shot a glare at Daniel, who gave me a faux-angelic look that I swear he knicked straight off Charice.

"Dahlia was telling me that I sound like her grandmother," said Daniel, eyelids actually fucking fluttering at me.

"You must have a pretty salty grandmother," observed Shuler.

Which was actually true, but not the waters I wanted to wade in right now. Shuler, incidentally, looked like he had started out dressing for a date and changed his mind at the last minute. He was wearing a shiny maroon dress shirt that looked like it should have been doused in cologne and black dress pants that he appeared to have actually poured his body into. And it was topped off by the dirtiest, filthiest trench coat I had ever seen. It was like the trench coat that Columbo had worn, only filthier. This trench coat looked prepared to solve crimes on its own. He was wearing, to summarize, pants that asked: "What are you doing later?" and a jacket that said: "Me? I'll be eating Cheetos at home alone." No wonder I didn't know how I felt about him.

"Grandmother Moss was a saint," I told Shuler.

"So," said Daniel, spilling the beans all at once, "we found a naked man."

"What kind of restaurant is this?" asked Shuler, glancing around.

"Not here," said Daniel. "At the Endicott Hotel."

"Where there was a murder," added Shuler. He was admirably unflappable about the matter.

"Right. And we need your help to de-cuff him."

One of the things that is most notable about Anson Shuler was his eyebrows, which were expressive to the point of possibly being independently sentient. He said nothing for a long moment, but his brows told an entire epic, a journey of hope and sadness and loss.

Finally he spoke.

"He's alive, this naked man?"

"Very much," I told Shuler.

"So," he said. "Who handcuffed him? You guys, or the police?"

"Neither. He claims it was some kind of sex thing," said Daniel. "So naturally Dahlia thought of you."

"You know," I said, talking mostly to get the narrative away from Daniel, "I was planning to wine and dine you a little before we led up to the chained-up naked man," I told Shuler. At which point the waiter returned, naturally. Given the snatches of conversation he'd heard so far, I couldn't really blame him for hovering over us.

"Can I get you something to drink? Some alcohol, I assume?" said the waiter.

No one got any alcohol, although I strongly wanted some

pinot grigio at the moment. It was arguably a little early in the day for booze, but I'd already seen a corpse and a naked dude, and surely that provided an exception. But no one else drank, and so I skipped too. Shuler and Daniel both ordered exactly the same soup and sandwich, apparently untroubled to get the same thing. I put in for the mahimahi, which I felt would make me look worldly and sophisticated at least relative to the rest of the menu.

Over lunch, we told Shuler the story of the morning. About the stream, and Doctor XXX, and the police, and about poor shirtless, shoeless Swan.

"I wonder why she left his pants," mused Shuler, which was a point that I hadn't considered.

"I don't know," I said. "Maybe she wanted to humiliate him, but not too much?" Although the suggestion sounded wrong as soon as I said it.

"So," said Shuler. "Do you want me to chastise you about having not told this all to the police already, or should we just skip over that part and take it as a given."

"We're telling you," I told Shuler. "And it's only an hour later. Honestly, come meet this guy. He's the saddest person you ever met. You wouldn't have left him in that room to get discovered by Detective Weber."

Shuler looked prepared to argue on this point, until I mentioned Weber's name, at which point his eyebrows conceded my point.

"You don't believe his story, though?" said Shuler. "I can tell that just from your retelling."

"Why does no one believe his story?" asked Daniel.

"Yeah, I don't buy it. But I don't think he's involved with the murder."

"What do you think happened?" asked Shuler. I wasn't sure if he was just making conversation or if he had somehow worked it out and was testing me.

I hadn't really given the matter a lot of thought up to that point, because I hadn't had time. But when you're retelling someone else's story, it either feels true in your mouth, or false. And Swan's story felt false.

"I think," I said slowly, "that he's downplaying his involvement in the sordidness of it. I don't think some random girl called him out of the blue. I think it was probably his idea."

"A call girl?" asked Shuler, who looked like he might book Swan.

"Maybe," I said. "But probably not. Why would a call girl leave the guy cuffed to a chair? It's not good business." And I had handled Swan's wallet. "Plus, he had cash in his wallet. Not a lot but, like, twenty bucks. Why leave the twenty bucks?"

"I love a mystery," said Shuler.

Daniel, at this point, got a phone call. It was a phone call that he apparently wanted to keep private, because he quickly made an excuse and left our table. I took this to mean that the caller was not Charice, because he was perfectly comfortable having inappropriate conversations with Charice right in front of me.

I didn't know who it was, which was maybe what led me to the conversation I had with Shuler.

"So," I said. "You don't think Daniel would kill anybody, right? I mean, if you had to put the odds down for that?"

Shuler gave me eyebrow.

I procured the flyer for Daniel's improv group from my purse, and tried to give it to Shuler, who wouldn't take it.

"Is there vomit on that? Jesus, Dahlia!"

"I found it on the ground in the room where we found Karou.

I think maybe Daniel dropped it in the excitement. Or, alternatively, maybe he was in there earlier for some reason."

"Just put that away," said Shuler. "I was wondering what that smell was."

"It's a clue," I told him.

"You should give it to the police," said Shuler. "Other police, not me. But I don't think it's a clue."

"Do we really know Daniel? Can we really trust him?"

Shuler was not having this.

"Let me ask you a question," he said, softly and carefully. "Would you be suspicious of Daniel if he weren't getting very involved with your best friend?"

"Who said they're getting very involved? They're just involved. Just regular involvement."

"I think you should give this to the police and not really worry about it anymore. I think the odds of Daniel being involved in the murder are pretty close to nil."

A tinge of pity had crept into Shuler's voice, and I was suddenly very uncomfortable.

"Do you think I'm being crazy? I'm not being crazy, am I?"

"I think you ran across a body, and you are understandably on edge. I don't like the word 'crazy' anyway."

Daniel popped back into our table literally at the speed of teleportation. Like, there should a *BAMF* noise that accompanied his arrival.

"I love the word 'crazy,'" said Daniel. "It's useful both in freestyle rapping and in Scrabble."

This comment understandably provoked silence, which was not helpful, because I was trying to quietly tuck Daniel's vomit-covered program back into my purse.

"So, you wanna go see this naked guy?" asked Daniel.

"Let's call him Swan. It's objectifying to just keep calling him the naked guy," I said. "Besides which, someday he will be clothed again, and what will we call him then?"

"I helped him pee," said Daniel.

"You didn't have to tell me that," said Shuler.

"I wanted you to know," said Daniel.

We drove back to the Endicott in separate cars, but we waited for Shuler in the parking lot so that we could all go up together.

"Are you ready for this?" I asked Shuler.

"As ready as I am for anything."

When we arrived at room 502, however, it turned out that there was nothing to be ready for. Swan was gone.

"I like the room, at least," observed Shuler.

I didn't like this development one bit.

"He's been murdered," I blurted out. "Someone broke in here, kidnapped him, and he's probably been murdered."

"Dahlia," said Shuler, "I'm a homicide detective, but even I don't think that the answer is always murder."

This was probably a fair point. I looked around the room, and noticed that the chair was still in the room, neatly tucked under a desk. There wasn't an extra chair in the room, so this was where it had started from in the first place? But regardless, no handcuffs and no Swan. Swan had gotten free—or at least free of the chair.

"There's a note," said Daniel.

He picked up a piece of hotel stationery and read:

"Sorry to skip out on you, but I was able to get out after all. Daniel, thanks for all your help. Pls. leave my key card at the front desk.—Swan"

"Thank you, Daniel? What about me? I'm the person who rescued that fucker!"

Daniel looked very pleased with himself. "It's a bro thing, Dahlia. You wouldn't understand."

Shuler, on the other hand, looked contemplative. "I'm weirdly disappointed that my services weren't called for, actually. I was geared up for an adventure."

As was I. There's a moment, sometimes, when events spin away from you that I just love. Often it's the moment right before the meteorite hits the earth, but there's something serene and perfect sometimes right at the dawn of the chaos. I assumed that's what Shuler meant. If so, I agreed with him.

"There's still sort of a mystery, though," I said. "Where did he find clothes?"

"This is his hotel room," said Daniel. "As long as he packed for more than one day, he'd have extra stuff to wear."

"Yeah, but he wouldn't bring more than one pair of shoes."

Shuler and Daniel both seemed to consider this idea.

"Okay, so we're looking for a barefoot guy," said Shuler.

"What happened to the handcuffs? Why wouldn't he leave those behind?"

"You are very good at asking questions," said Daniel. "I don't know why. Maybe he wanted a souvenir?"

"He doesn't want a souvenir," I told Daniel. "What do you think, Shuler?"

Shuler sat down on the bed, and said, "I think those are both interesting questions, but you should just go downstairs and ask him. He's probably at the tournament."

"Is that what you would do?"

"It is," said Shuler. "That, and keep the key card."

"Right," I said. "Well, let's do it. You coming with us, Anson?"

"We need to get down there anyway," said Daniel. "Our next match will be coming right up."

"You're competing in the tournament?"

"Sort of," I told him.

"Nah," said Shuler. "I should probably get out of here. Also, I'll give you about a half hour before I tell that story to the police, so you'll want to make sure Swan fesses up before then."

"On it."

"And, Dahlia," said Shuler, just a hair more softly. "You don't have to wait for a naked guy to get handcuffed to a chair to call me for lunch." That is what Shuler's mouth said. His eyebrows said that and added: "I could be the naked guy in the chair." This is the sort of statement that might offend me in a verbal form but through the veil of eyebrows seemed vaguely acceptable.

"Fair enough," I said. "Thanks for coming out for lunch."

"Say hi to Nathan for me," said Shuler.

"Well, that was weird," said Daniel as we were heading down the stairs and back toward the lobby.

"Yeah," I said. "Swan said he didn't have a roommate, so who came in and let him out?"

"No," said Daniel. "Well, actually, that was a little weird too. But I meant the sexual tension between you and Shuler."

"Listen, Daniel, you're great, but you've got to stop doing that."

"Doing what?"

"Observing my life."

CHAPTER TWELVE

For some reason, I had expected that it would be easy to find Swan downstairs. He was barefoot, and how hard could it be to find a barefoot man? However, no one confessed to having seen a barefoot man downstairs, which meant that either he had brought a second pair of shoes or hadn't been downstairs after all.

"Are you regretting leaving Swan alone?" asked Daniel.

This was an unnecessary question. Yes, Daniel, I was. But I appreciate it when awkward questions are not posed to me but simply left unspoken to hang in the air, like, I don't know, a Japanese hungry ghost. That is how I do things. I did not acknowledge Daniel with a response, but simply set to asking yet another gamer if he had seen a barefoot Asian man, getting the same blank response as before.

It dawned on me, at that moment, that I did not have a lot of vocabulary to describe Swan. It would have been helpful if he had some remarkable signifying characteristic—like a scar or a goiter. Not only did he not have a signifying characteristic, he was pretty ordinary. Black hair, medium length, straight.

I wish I had taken a picture of him. More notes for the next time I drag a naked guy up a stairwell.

"We have a half hour to find Swan before the cops go ape shit."

"Do you think they're going to come after you?"

Again, with the horrible questions. If Daniel had been a Harry Potter character, he would have just been running around shouting "Voldemort, Voldemort, Voldemort." But no matter.

"If he's gone missing, they'll certainly give me a ring."

"You know what would take your mind off that," said Daniel. "And by 'that' I mean your potential imprisonment. Our next match is starting soon! I think we should go do that."

I really didn't understand Daniel's interest in continuing on in the tournament. Did he just not like to lose? I was about to object to him, but he must have anticipated that I didn't get his reasoning.

"I don't give up on things," said Daniel. "I might get beaten down, but I don't give up."

This was, probably—along with his implausible knack for accents—another reason that he was going to make it as an actor. I knew the odds, and I wasn't expecting that Daniel was going to become a superstar or anything. But when your mission statement is "I get beaten down, but I don't give up," you're probably going to eventually succeed somehow. And come to think of it, this sounded an awful lot like a "Continue?" in *Street Fighter* anyway: Ryu, or possibly Cody.

"I appreciate your point of view," I told Daniel. "But you're not the person who lost a murder suspect."

"Eh. He's not a murder suspect," said Daniel.

"He might be," I told him. "I mean, I don't think he's a murderer, for sure. But a suspect? The police have wild ideas sometimes."

I was just making things up at this point, hoping to impress Daniel. But he was like one of those snapping turtles that wouldn't let go of a thing until there was a thunderstrike.

"Come on," said Daniel. "We can lose really quickly, and maybe Swan's over there anyway. You know he came for the tournament, so it's a reasonable guess."

This did not seem like a place you would go without shoes, but unlike Daniel, I give up on things very easily. If I had a spirit animal, it would not be a snapping turtle. A sloth perhaps, or maybe a sturdy goldfish. And so I went along.

We did not lose, as it happened. But won. And we did it very quickly.

"Dahlia Moss? Daniel Simone?" asked the redhead who was trying to run this thing. He looked even more put out than the last time I saw him.

"That's us," we told him.

"I'm sorry to tell you that your opponents have gone home."

"No need to be sorry," I said, since I didn't particularly want to play again. "What does that mean for us?"

"It means you advance," said the redhead.

I wasn't sure why this was bad news, and started to ask him why this was the case, but I noted the deep scowl lines in his forehead and suddenly remembered my own advice about posing uncomfortable questions. Instead I asked, "Why'd they go home?"

"They heard about the murder upstairs." The redhead sighed. "Everyone's heard about it."

Oh, so we all knew it was a murder now, did we? I wondered how that bit of information had made it around, seeing as it was only an incident earlier.

"I see," I said. "Are many players missing now?"

I got angry forehead for this, but I wanted to know. "It's like *Outbreak*. Half the people here are missing. Just because a man was murdered! It didn't even happen on this floor!"

I had noticed that the crowd was looking a little thinner, but I had just assumed this was somehow the natural progression of things as players got eliminated from the tournament. I hadn't thought that people would willingly drop.

"Hooray," said Daniel. "We win again!"

I did appreciate how untroubled Daniel was by this turn of events. He didn't guard me very effectively, but he did have an excellent temperament for uncovering corpses and naked men. But I was still aiming to find Swan, and despite the craziness, I hadn't put the mystery of Doctor XXX completely out of my head.

"You don't have a guy named Swan signed up for the tournament, by any chance, do you?"

"What's his last name?"

Great question, redhead dude! Come to think of it, what's his first name? Probably not Swan. That was probably a nickname. Further notes for the next time I drag a scantily clothed man up a stairwell. In addition to getting his picture and making sure he stays put, I should also learn his given name. Hell, I had even held his wallet. I don't know if this was an epic fail, but it was certainly at least rare or uncommon.

"I'm not sure," I told him. "Swan doesn't ring any bells for you?"

"No," said the redhead, who, for whatever reason, appeared to just want me to go away.

"How about Doctor XXX?"

"Are you just making up words?"

I would have said something scathing and witty here, except

for the fact that I didn't have anything witty. That's the problem with being witty; it requires a lot of quick thinking.

Besides which, Tricia, wandering around with Undine in tow, came up to me.

"Hey, Dahlia, were you looking for a barefoot Asian guy?"

"Yeah," I said, surprised. "Where'd you hear that?"

"It's a weird thing to go around asking about," said Tricia. "It's making the rounds."

This was spoken by an oddly shaped woman whose hair was so eerily wiglike that it absolutely had to be real. Her hair was askew. Not dashingly asymmetrical, just off. I don't mean to pick on Tricia, whom I had taken a liking to, but merely want to point out that when she regards you as weird, you've kind of accomplished something.

"We are," I told her, bringing Daniel into this if for no other reason than to keep him from gloating about our success in the tournament. "We are both looking for a barefoot Asian man. Named Swan."

"You keep yourself very busy," observed Tricia, eyeing Daniel with an expression I couldn't quite place. Concern? Lust?

"This is my bodyguard, Daniel," I told her, because when you're already branded as being weird, why not go all in?

"G'day, mate," said Daniel.

If any of this seemed strange to Tricia, she did not comment on it, although baby Undine looked remarkably doubtful.

"The guy you're looking for is out in the hotel lobby. He's sitting on the sofa. You can't miss him."

CHAPTER THIRTEEN

I did not anticipate the possibility of there being a second bare-foot Asian man. Even given the relatively high density of Asian guys at the tournament, it seemed altogether too unlikely that the barefoot Asian in the lobby would not be Swan.

And yet, here it was.

It would make a better story if I had gone up to him in confusion and told the stranger: "Swan, you must call the police!" as he stared at me in bafflement. But for once, I was actually not so dumb. I went up to him in the lobby, joining him, in fact, on the sofa, and said: "What the hell?"

That was my conversation opener. "What the hell?"

The fellow raised an eyebrow at me. "Hello?" he offered.

He looked a lot like Swan, at least in the way of Swan being somewhat generic-looking. Like Swan, he had medium-length black straight hair. Similar facial structure, about the same age. His eyebrows were very different, though, and their skin tone wasn't exactly the same—this guy was the slightest bit ruddier. And when he smiled, I noticed he had a little bit of a snaggle-tooth. Not a bad-looking fella, but not Swan.

"Seriously," I told him. "What the fuck?"

Our guy was looking irritated, which was fair. But I was

working it out, as I lay back on the hotel sofa, this cream-colored Queen-Anne thing that was miles nicer than the furniture in Swan's room. Real drop-off between the lobby and the hotel rooms here.

"You must have found Swan," I said. "You guys friends?"

"Not exactly," said the fellow, astonished that I made this deduction. "Do you know him?"

"I'm Dahlia Moss. He didn't mention me to you?"

Daniel, who'd been just sort of hovering around for this conversation—body guarding, I suppose—was happy to have the chance to jump in.

"Or Daniel? Did he mention Daniel?"

"I'm Chul-Moo," said the guy, I guess feeling that my introduction required his own. "And he didn't. But I don't know him well."

"What happened to your shoes?" I asked him.

Chul-Moo looked down at his bare feet as though he were surprised that they were missing. Then he looked at me uncertainly. I expected that he would say something, but he didn't.

I was gradually working it out, however. Chul-Moo came in, somehow, and found Swan in distress. He had somehow gotten the handcuffs off, and Swan persuaded him at some point to lend him his own shoes. This was the only possible explanation, right? Probably Chul-Moo was being cagey around me because Swan had given him some other version of the story and was maybe worried that I was the woman who had taken his shoes in the first place.

Those were the assumptions I was working under. None of them stopped me from pursuing my goal.

"You need to call Swan right now and tell him that he needs to talk to the police."

"What?" said Chul-Moo, who was still on shoes.

"Do you have his phone number?"

"Yes," said Chul-Moo uncertainly.

"Call him, and tell him Dahlia Moss says he needs to call the police. They already know, so it's going to come out anyway. It'll be way better than the alternative."

Chul-Moo continued to look at me in bafflement. "Just call him," I said. Still bafflement.

"On your phone," offered Daniel. I would have put this down as a ridiculously unnecessary detail, but they were apparently the magic words needed to provoke Chul-Moo into action. Very slow action.

He picked up his cell, looking ever uncertain, and pressed an icon on the screen. He held it up to his face, watching me and waiting, and after a moment spoke:

"Hello, Swan," he said. "There's ... a woman here."

I could not hear what Swan was saying.

"Yes," Chul-Moo said after a pause, "exactly."

If this sounds strange and ominous to you, then congratulations, you and I are of like minds. If this doesn't sound suspicious to you, I'm sorry, you are wrong. I took the phone from Chul-Moo's hands, who clearly hadn't expected this as a possibility at all, and held it up to my face.

"Yes, Swan," I told him. "It's Dahlia."

"Wait, what? Who is this?"

"You can't possibly have forgotten me already. How are you doing?"

"I'm ... fine. How did you find Chul-Moo?" asked Swan.

"Well, he's not wearing shoes, which tends to make a fella stand out in a crowd," I told him. "But who cares about that. You need to call the police, pronto."

"The hell I do," said Swan. "I'm not involved in any of that."

"You're involved now, because I told the police, and they're going to come looking for you."

"But I didn't do anything! I thought you were keeping me out of things."

"Yeah, well. You vanished on me," I told him. Although, to be honest, this actually wasn't related. I had ratted him out before he had vanished.

"I didn't vanish," said Swan. "You left me tied to a chair, and I got out. What, I was supposed to just stay in the chair?"

"I found a man that could cut handcuffs for you!" I told him. Is it wrong that I should expect a guy to be grateful for this service? This goon thanked Daniel and not me.

"I appreciate that, Dahlia," said Swan. "I really do. But as it happens, I didn't need him. Chul-Moo came along, and now I'm golden. What I need, actually, are shoes, because mine were apparently stolen by that woman. I can't fly home without shoes. The TSA just won't allow it."

"I'm assuming this is all a preamble to say that you're going to call the police?"

"No," said Swan. "Maybe. I mean, what would I say? It's a very strange conversation to start."

"Tell them you have information that's related to the murder at the Endicott Hotel."

"I don't have information related to the murder at the Endicott Hotel. I didn't even know that happened until you told me."

"Tell them you have information that might be related to the murder."

"Well," said Swan. "Maybe."

Swan, I could tell, was reconsidering the story that he had told me, which was so dopey that it couldn't possibly be true in its entirety. Which bits of it were lies I wasn't entirely sure, but I was willing to bet my teeth there was some solid fibbing in there somewhere. I preyed upon this very detail, in fact.

"They're going to call you very soon, probably. So you'll want to figure out what you're going to tell them. If you have to make it up on the fly, they're going to be on to you, and you're going to end up stuck with the unadulterated truth."

"I *told* you the truth," said Swan, but his heart wasn't in it. And he left out the word "unadulterated," besides. "But fine," he said. "I'll call them."

I had not observed that Mike3000 was watching me have this conversation until it was over. He certainly wasn't hiding; he was built like a truck and had neither the body nor temperament for sneaking about. I just wasn't looking at him.

Daniel was looking at him, and was even standing between the two of us, which I suppose might count for body guarding in some circles. Circles in which people are easily assassinated, probably.

"Mike3000," I greeted him, regretting the 3000 only after I said it, because it managed to both seem formal and really dumb at the same time.

"Miss Moss-Granger," said Mike. He sounded a little pricklier than the last time I'd spoken to him, and this wasn't just because he wasn't calling me Dame. "I have a question for you."

"I am filled with answers," which, friends, was clearly bullshit.

"Why were you looking for Karou Minami earlier?"

As this tale is filled with unforced errors, I think it wise to bring extra emphasis to the rare situation when I get things right. Case in point: I could have lied here, but I didn't. I kept my cards close to my chest and answered with a question.

"Why do you ask?"

"Well," said Mike. "You seemed to think that Karou was alive when I spoke to you earlier, but from what I've heard, you two were the people who discovered his body."

Chul-Moo, who was watching this conversation, made a face as though he were a reality-show contestant about to witness a catfight. As though I were about to throw a drink at Mike, who in turn would tear off my wig. (Please note: I was not wearing a wig. This is a wig of proverb.) I believe Chul-Moo even mouthed the words *oh shit*.

But I had no intentions of getting in a catfight with Mike, or anyone. But especially Mike, who would have been—if we are to continue the cat metaphor—a much larger cat than me. Like a jaguar or a puma. So I deflected.

"I was trying to figure out who it was that had been killed, actually."

"Why not just say that?" said Mike. "I mean, it's very weird to pretend that a murdered man is alive. It's more than weird—it's suspicious."

I was annoyed. For once, I was completely on the up-and-up, and Mike3000 seemed to be implying that I was some sort of backstreet skulker. "Well, I wasn't walking around with him like it was *Weekend at Bernie's*, Mike. And I figured it was the business of the police to mention murders."

"I don't find that explanation very believable," said Mike.

"I think you're 'othering' me, Mike. This is exactly the sort of thing your therapist was talking about."

"Leave Gwendolyn out of this!" said Mike.

It struck me that Mike3000 was very upset. Like, I think he might have been crying earlier, which made me wonder if he didn't know Karou better than he had initially let on.

"You seem a little broken up," I told him.

"That's a normal person's reaction to finding out your friend was killed," said Mike.

I was caught between the precipice of wanting to investigate and not wanting to seem like a dick. Were they friends or not? Why had Mike said that they weren't earlier?

I decided to ask, but I went for it in the gentlest tone that I could manage. Which just came out as: "So were you guys friends, or what?"

"Karou was my bro," said Mike. "I'd known him for years."

"You said he was weird and he was obsessed with socks."

"He was weird and obsessed with socks. These things are both true."

"You also said that you didn't know him well," I told him.

It was, traditionally, at this point that my boyfriend, Nathan, would add that I had an "interrogative manner." I honestly looked for him to say the line, but he wasn't around. Daniel didn't say it either, and Chul-Moo just yawned at me, apparently disappointed that we hadn't descended into wig-ripping chaos.

But it was now Mike3000 that was on the defensive, and he looked surprised that I had called him out. In fighting games, this is called a reversal.

"I thought you were maybe meeting him." said Mike. "Like, sort of a groupie."

"What difference would that make?" I asked.

"Well, then you would ask personal questions about him. Like: Is he a nice guy? That sort of thing."

"He wasn't a nice guy?"

"He was a nice guy, but maybe in the way that Tony Stark is a nice guy."

"He was nice but megalomaniacal and an alcoholic?"

"He's nice, but under a crusty shell of not being nice. And he's sort of a cad. Honestly, I assumed that he had ditched you. Karou's always hooking up with girls at these sorts of things—and he's been known to, you know, if a girl doesn't look enough like her picture, sometimes bail."

"You're saying that you think I'm not attractive enough to meet up with Karou?"

I was really just toying with Mike at this point, because what did I care? I had a boyfriend and a half at this point, and Karou was missing large parts of his skull. Chul-Moo was interested in this turn, however, and leaned forward. Honestly, some reality show ought to use him for reaction shots.

"I misread your relationship to him," said Mike. "And for that I apologize. But if you have questions about Karou, you should ask Chul-Moo, there. He's his partner."

CHAPTER FOURTEEN

Yes," said Chul-Moo. "I'm out of the tournament now. That's why I let Swan take my shoes."

Mike3000, weird and sweaty, seemed obviously torn up over the death of his friend. But Chul-Moo on the other hand was rather cold and distant about the affair. Not serial-killer cold, but arch, as if this had been a curious but interesting development in his day. I know there's no correct reaction to death—people are sometimes suddenly inclined to fits of laughter, after all. But damned if Chul-Moo didn't seem a little distant about it all. Part of it was that he was just watching me and Mike, like we were actors in his drama.

"What the fuck are you looking at?" I asked him.

"I'm sorry," said Chul-Moo. "I should go. I have a pressing appointment."

He said this in such a dignified and authoritative voice that it was easy to forget that he wasn't wearing shoes.

"You don't have an appointment," I said. "And I've got some questions for you too."

Chul-Moo pouted at me—a gesture he managed well, despite committing very little of his face to the activity. "Who are you," mused Chul-Moo, "to be asking us all questions in the first place? I'm very sorry you ran across Karou's body, but I don't see how that gives you the right to be entering into everyone else's business."

"That sounds like something a dodgy person would say," I told him. "A person with something to hide." This was the sort of technique I'd developed playing *Werewolf*, and it rarely worked there either. But Chul-Moo, for whatever reason, seemed to accept this.

"Fine," he said. "I can answer your questions. But later," he said, glancing at Mike3000. "And privately. My room is across the hall from Swan's. Which I guess you know where."

We bid adieu to Chul-Moo, and Mike as well, because Daniel had to drag me along to another *Dark Alleys* match. No time for murder when there's an extremely important fighting tournament to tend to. Priorities is what I am saying.

The tournament was going very quickly now, it seemed, with so many players missing. A bludgeoning will really wreak havoc on your scheduling, I guess.

Speaking of quick tournaments, we won, again, handily, as our opponents failed to show up. There's a line in *WarGames* that goes: "Sometimes the only winning move is not to play," and I thought of it now, as it was also apparently our strategy for advancing in the tournament.

The redhead running the desk was increasingly apoplectic at the state of affairs because the crowd just kept getting thinner. Arguably there was too much of a police presence for people to have fun, but by this I mean any police presence at all. I had noticed that there were a number of gents who smelled pleasantly of marijuana, and the aftermath of a murder investigation was probably not their scene.

"I can't believe that so many good players have left," said the redhead, "and yet you two are still here."

"It's a good thing we beat those kindergartners," said Daniel, which made the redhead's face contort. Usually snooty people like this are the sort of folk I tend to beat up on, but I actually felt sort of bad for the guy.

"Why not just reschedule this whole thing?" I asked.

"We can't," said the guy—I never learned his name. I'm sorry—"do you know how expensive it is to rent a steamboat?"

Feel free to read over that sentence a few times before we go on to see if it makes any more sense to you. It certainly didn't make sense to me. I tried thinking of something that rhymed with "steamboat" that would have been more logical. "Dream coat"? "Scream throat"? "Themed float"? I had nothing.

The redhead could see that I was confused and explained.

"The finals of the tournament are on the *Major Redding.*"

Daniel and I both looked at him blankly, and for once I was glad Daniel was there, because looking uninformed always goes down better with an accomplice. This is why Fox News usually has more than one caster.

"Right," we said.

"Why are the finals on a steamboat?" asked Daniel, and I was again glad to have him around to voice the question. You know, maybe it wouldn't have been so bad if someone went around saying "Voldemort" all the time either. It's kind of a pretty name, if you can divorce it from its connotations.

"Take a flyer," said the redhead in a tone that made it interchangeable with "go to hell."

I picked up a flyer, but I didn't look at it. I wasn't overly concerned about the finals, because we still had two more matches, and it seemed statistically unlikely that absolutely everyone we faced would disappear ahead of time. Besides which, I got a phone call.

"Dahlia Moss?"

I had expected that the phone call might have been from Charice, or possibly Nathan, who was due for a call. But it was neither of these possibilities. It was Chul-Moo, of all people.

"Can you come up here?" he asked.

"Chul-Moo. Up where?"

"To my room. Across from Swan's. We went over that."

"How did you even get my number?"

But I already knew the answer. Swan had shared it with him. Thick as thieves, those two were.

"You're ready to talk about Karou?" I said. Although, now that he was volunteering, I wasn't exactly sure what questions I wanted to ask him.

"I suppose," said Chul-Moo. "But mostly I'm anxious about Swan. He's not back yet. He should be back by now."

"You'll see your shoes again someday."

"Please," said Chul-Moo. "Just come up."

I had commented earlier that there was a marked scent of marijuana wafting about the tournament, and I found the source of it now.

"Hey," said Chul-Moo, who seemed different from when I spoke to him earlier. For one, he was clearly high. "Come on in," he said. "Can I get you anything?"

Anything in this case would appear to be a hit off his bong, or at least this was what I assumed. It was a tiny hotel room that mirrored Swan's completely and it wasn't as if he had a minibar at his disposal.

"I'm fine," I said, stepping in again. These rooms were starting to become comfortable to me, even with marijuana smoke, or hell, perhaps because of it. "Why did you want to see me?"

"Swan told me that you were a private detective," said Chul-Moo.

This was only mostly true, as I was simply taking classes in that direction, but I decided to just say yes I was.

"I think I might need a private detective," said Chul-Moo.

"Why?" I asked.

"Because I'm a little worried that the attack on Karou was meant for me."

Chul-Moo said this in an even tone, as if this were just the sort of thing people often and casually said, but he looked a little wild-eyed. I gave a look to Daniel, who looked dutifully opaque, as a good bodyguard should.

I do not, as a rule, usually partake of pot, mostly because it makes me very paranoid, and I've got plenty of paranoia without drugs in the first place. It was perhaps through that lens that I regarded Chul-Moo now, because he did not seem overly broken up in the lobby when he *wasn't* high.

"Why would you think that?" I asked him.

"He was my teammate," said Chul-Moo. "We were entering the tournament together."

"Okay," I said. "But that wouldn't explain why the attack was meant for you."

"Well," said Chul-Moo, "Karou and I were the favorites to win, and so I think someone decided to weed the field."

I was pretty sure this was all paranoia, because there were

some logical problems with Chul-Moo's theory. First, even if we assume everything he said was true, why kill someone before the tournament even starts? At least wait a couple of rounds—your opponent might get eliminated, and then you'd be saved the trouble of committing a murder. Right? If you're going to kill a guy, you ought to be efficient about it. But I played along with the idea.

"How much is the prize money for this thing, again?"

"Twenty thousand—ten grand per person," said Chul-Moo.

Ten thousand dollars was not, in my mind, a lot of money to kill for. You couldn't buy a used Kia for this kind of money, and was it worth killing for a used Kia? A Honda possibly, but a Kia? Probably not.

"Also," said Chul-Moo, "the winners get to pick a character to add to the game. That's maybe the bigger deal."

"You mean you design your own character?"

"No," said Chul-Moo. "There's a list of fighters the developers are thinking of adding as DLC. You just pick one of those."

Cool, actually, but still not worth bludgeoning someone in the head. And I had another problem with Chul-Moo's theory, although it admittedly was sounding more plausible the more secondhand smoke I inhaled.

"Assuming you're right," I said, "aren't you in the clear now? I mean, your partner has been killed, so you're out of the tournament, regardless. Who'd want to kill you now?"

"I'm not out," said Chul-Moo. "I spoke to the folks running the tournament, and, given the extremely unusual circumstances, they're letting me enter late. That was the pressing appointment, incidentally, that you claimed did not exist."

"But you have no teammate. It's a partner-based game."

"I'm teaming up with Swan. He got disqualified because of

the chair thing. It's a lucky break for me, actually, because he's really good. We actually used to be teammates, once upon a time. We could actually win this thing, especially with everyone leaving."

Maybe it was the induced paranoia from the haze of marijuana smoke, but I was getting awfully suspicious of Swan. I mean, I didn't exactly think that he murdered Karou and then stripped and handcuffed himself to a chair on the off chance he could be re-paired with his old teamie, but I certainly noticed that things were breaking his way.

"Did you speak to the police already?"

"Yes," said Chul-Moo, but not before taking another hit. "At great length."

"Did you tell them about this theory of yours?"

"Nah," said Chul-Moo. "I didn't think of it then."

You thought of it now, I observed. After smoking up. Noted.

"Well," I said, "what do you want me to do?"

"Talk to Mike3000," said Chul-Moo. "And tell him not to kill me."

Daniel, who'd been very quiet and actorly, at this point actually gasped, which made me feel better about my own reaction, which was a stifled laugh. Mike was a teddy bear.

"I'm not telling him that," I told Chul-Moo.

"Actually it's probably his partner, Imogen. She's the one you have to watch out for. Mike might be her accessory, but she's the one pulling the strings."

I hadn't met Imogen yet, and, who knows, maybe I would and think: "Yes, there goes a cold-blooded murderer," but my reaction at the time was that absolutely no one named Imogen was going to bludgeon you in the head.

"I think," I told Chul-Moo, trying to sound cool and reasonable and hip, and not at all like Nancy Reagan, "that maybe the smoking is making you a little paranoid. If you're still in the tournament, maybe you should just be relaxing and focusing."

"This is how I prepare," said Chul-Moo. "It improves my reflexes."

"Even so," I told him.

"Please? At least go meet Imogen, and talk to her. I'm sure that if you spend any time with her at all you'll take me seriously. It would really make me feel better."

"Sure," I said. "That's what I'm all about. Unpaid work that makes people feel better."

CHAPTER FIFTEEN

Are your days usually as full as all this?" asked Daniel on the way back down the stairs. It was a fair question.

"Alas, they are not," I told Daniel. "Although I've had worse."

"So, that guy was loony tunes, right?"

"Probably," I said. And this was true. Well, perhaps paranoid more than crazy. I didn't feel an overwhelming need to get involved here; I didn't have a client paying me, after all. But apparently my sarcastic remark about helpful unpaid work being my scene wasn't all that sarcastic; I already knew I was going downstairs to talk to Mike again. I just wanted to see what his reaction would be.

I shouldn't have been worried about any of that. I mean, setting aside the moral implications of trying to solve a murder when there are actual police for that. What I should have been worried about was the Doctor XXX thing. This is hindsight talking, but I had let the gruesome business of Karou Minami's death overtake the less-gruesome, but certainly irksome, business of an anonymous stranger jerking me around on the Internet. That's what I should have been investigating. But I kept getting distracted.

And I continued to be distracted, because when we made it

downstairs, there were Tricia and Undine, on that same sofa as before, only now Undine was naked on it. Tricia was changing her—having thrown down a cloth first—but there was a naked baby. And Undine wasn't even the first naked body I'd seen that day.

"Dahlia," said Tricia, who was adept at diaper changing and multitasking. "You find your barefoot man?" she asked.

"I found a barefoot man," I said. "And even though he wasn't the barefoot man I was seeking, it all worked out."

I sort of love that Tricia did not feel the need to ask follow-up questions about why I was seeking out such a person. Maybe having Undine around kept her grounded? Or maybe she thought I was just a really desperate foot fetishist. Instead she asked me:

"Are you still in the tournament?"

"We are," I said brightly, although Daniel spoiled my glow by explaining that all our opponents had been dropouts.

"Get out!" said Tricia, happily folding up Undine's diaper and putting it in an enormous Ziploc bag. She was prepared, Tricia. "Kyle's had to fight every damned round. We haven't skipped one!"

As if on cue, Kyle showed up, scooping up the now-changed Undine one-handed. "Score another victory for Kyle," said Kyle, apparently comfortable with the third person.

Another kid trailed behind him, a mop-headed boy who looked like he was twelve, thirteen. He was sort of a perfect model of awkward adolescence—unflattering Buster Brown haircut and the skin that was the "before" half of a Proactiv ad. I half expected him to speak with the creaky voice of a teenager on *The Simpsons*, but no dice.

"Good job, Kyle," said the kid. His voice was actually

improbably deep. Not quite Barry White deep, but not that far off either. Poor guy—it was going to be decades before his body caught up to that voice.

"This a groupie of yours?" I asked Kyle, who took the question graciously, although I caught Tricia wincing.

"No," said Kyle. "This is my partner, Remy. Say hello, Remy."

"Hello Remy," said Remy.

I looked at Tricia, who shot me a look that said: "Don't say anything."

How the mighty had fallen. Kyle used to be the cool kid, the master of the scene. Now he was pairing up with a random deep-voiced fourteen-year-old.

"Oh, right," I said to Remy. "You won some sort of online contest?"

"It was really more of an auction," said Remy. "It was super-cool of my dad to spring for this."

"And money well spent," said Kyle. "Because look at how well we're doing!"

"Kyle's teaching me all about the game," said Remy. "We could actually win this thing. I mean, as long as my mom doesn't find out about this murder. I'm hoping she doesn't check the news, because if she does, she's totally picking me up and taking me home."

"I see," I said. "Yeah, that would be bad."

"Right?" said Remy. "So I'm not going to mention it to her until after. Nobody tell her when she picks me up today."

I did not know Remy, and I was not sure why he thought I was going to bring up a randomly murdered stranger to his mother, although come to think of it, I had brought up the topic to a lot of strange people so far. But I told him that I would skirt this issue with her, in the unlikely circumstances of our meeting.

"I appreciate that," said Remy. Seriously, he had the body of a piccolo and the voice of a euphonium. It was disquieting to hear him at all.

"We better be on our way," I said, although we actually had nowhere to go, as our next match wasn't for another forty minutes. Then, thinking of an activity—and changing the subject—I asked: "You guys hear of a player named Imogen?"

"Yeah," answered Tricia. "Kinda creepy, isn't she? I think she's in the bar."

"This hotel has a bar? This changes everything."

CHAPTER SIXTEEN

So are you investigating a murder now?" asked Daniel. "Or just dicking around? Because I can't really tell."

"What do you want the answer to be?" I asked him.

"I feel the answer should be dicking around, but I want to say murder."

I wanted to say murder too, honestly. But the police had interviewed everyone; I'm sure Weber and Maddocks had everything under control. Besides which, there was no actual reason to assume that Karou getting bumped off was related to the tournament in the first place. Unless he was Doctor XXX. Which, well, okay, then that would be a good reason.

Two options. One: Doctor XXX was Karou, who wanted to tell me something. Something that he thought a detective would be useful for—and he didn't get the chance. But why me? And what sort of secret was worth getting killed over?

Option two: Doctor XXX had intended for me to find Swan. Maybe Doctor XXX wasn't necessarily a guy at all. Maybe our good doctor was this implausible gal who had persuaded him into the chair. But why would she want me to find him? If you're worrying about Swan starving to death in a closet, why not just call the hotel desk?

In neither situation was it clear how I was getting roped into the situation.

Actually there was a third option, which was always worth remembering. Maybe Doctor XXX was just making things up, yanking me around because he could. For all I knew, he was a forty-three-year-old IT guy in Spokane, who wasn't even at the tournament, and was just another random troll. When we're talking about the Internet, random troll is never an option that should be completely discounted.

"I'll meet you in the bar in just a second," I told Daniel. "I've got something private I want to deal with."

"You won't need any body guarding?" asked Daniel.

"I think I can manage a minute or two."

Daniel went off without objection, which was another way that he was fundamentally not like Charice, who would have grilled me. This element of difference in his personality was a good thing, because by "something private" I actually meant "something unwisely broadcast on the Internet."

I dug out my laptop, popped it open, and started up my stream.

Are you dead yet? asked Twitch chat.

"No, not yet," I said. "So, guys, this tournament is totally fucked, right?"

Totally, said Twitch chat. Completely and totally fucked.

Twitch chat, incidentally, likes it when you curse, which is maybe not a good thing for me to be exposed to, because I like cursing enough as it is.

"Is anyone else streaming it?" I asked.

I learned that a guy named Reynard was supposed to deal the finals tomorrow, but the qualifiers today were deemed a little too penny-ante for coverage. If this were television, we'd be on ESPN 30.

"Does anybody follow the teams?" I asked Twitch chat. "There was a last-minute shifting around of players, as far as I could tell."

Most of Twitch chat didn't know a damned thing, which was to be expected. But if you ask enough people, someone is bound to have the details, and sure enough, one commenter knew plenty.

"Karou dropped Kyle about a week before the tournament," the user said. "Replaced him with Chul-Moo. There's a thread about it at EventHubs."

EventHubs was a website, but I didn't need to read the overblown details. The big picture was good enough. So: Karou dumps his teammate Kyle, who is forced to grovel for the affections of a rich fourteen-year-old. Swan loses his teammate and can't play at all. Then, post murder—Swan is back with his old pal. And Kyle is still screwed. Was this enough of a motivation to kill someone? Financially speaking, certainly not, but maybe there was a personal element I had yet to uncover?

So Twitch chat hadn't been a complete loss. See, I'm not insane for speaking to these clowns. But neither was it a smashing success, because I was hoping that I'd find a pressing and revealing message from Doctor XXX, which would say something like: "Meet me out in the gazebo; it is a matter of the utmost urgency," which would really answer questions, but no dice.

"Do any of you guys know anything about Doctor XXX? What he looks like? If it's even a he?"

Twitch knew nothing, at least on this front, but they had a lot of ridiculous speculation, which I will spare you, except that many of their theories inexplicably involved cat suits.

In retrospect, it's strange that I should have trusted these guys at all. Because let's face it, they're a bunch of morons. But I also sort of felt—and still do—that they're my morons. It's sort of like spending Thanksgiving with your racist grandmother. Yes, she has a lot of problems. But it's family, right?

Just testing the waters, I asked: "You guys know a player named Imogen?"

CREEPY, said Twitch chat, all at once, like it was a meme.

"Thanks, guys," I told them. "You're like my Synergy. Except, you know, not awesome."

I was profoundly disappointed by the time I met Imogen Morland. For someone whose appearance was presaged by "creepy creepy creepy" and "talk to her for a second and you'll know I'm not crazy," she looked like a real estate agent. She was dressed a little too nicely for the occasion, with a rose-colored blazer that honestly looked a little eighties secretary. But this was bizarrely offset by blond spiky hair, and the resulting creation was a little confounding. On top of all this, she looked profoundly bored.

I spotted her because she was next to Mike3000 at the bar. I was willing to bet that the clear glasses in front of them contained water and not alcohol, both because they were competitive and because of the annoyed look on the bartender's face.

"Hey, Mike," I said, sitting down next to the two of them.

"My lady," said Mike. He still wasn't exactly amiable toward me, but he was warming back up. He was also a polite guy, because I didn't even have to ask for the introduction.

"This is my teammate, Imogen," offered Mike. "For this tournament, anyway."

Imogen, who continued to look more impassive than creepy, gave me a curt nod.

"Cool," I said. "I'm Dahlia Moss. Online pugilist and private detective."

Imogen cocked her blond head at me, but it was Mike who looked surprised.

"You didn't tell me you were a detective," said Mike. He sounded suspicious, and I was sliding back down the ladder of his good graces.

"I didn't think it was important," I told him. "I don't know what either of you guys do."

"I teach music theory," said Imogen, who looked pleased to have broached the topic. There was a hungry look in her eyes, which I would describe as "let me tell you about twelve-tone composition," but I may have been extrapolating this unjustly from my friend Steven Yang, who was a music librarian and is emphatically someone who you do not want to let get started on classical music as a conversation topic. I was quickly moving to head Imogen off but maybe Mike knew the same thing, because he cut in for me.

"Are you saying that your being a detective is important now?"

I still didn't know what Mike did for a living. He had the physicality of a plumber or a roofer, but who knows? Maybe he was just a really slouchy florist.

"Sort of. I appreciate how quickly you're coming to the point," I told Mike, although I can't begin to tell you why because I didn't appreciate it at all. I was, if I really was going to follow Chul-Moo's half-baked instructions, casually accusing him and his partner of murder. This was the sort of that thing that small talk is called for.

Case in point:

"Hello there, friend. How are you?"

"Excellent, yourself?"

"The same. Nice weather we're having, isn't it?"

"Yes, although I hear it's supposed to rain next week!"

"Oh? Say, you didn't bludgeon a man to death by chance, did you?"

And scene. See how nicely this imagined conversation went? That's the sort of thing I was hoping for. But it did not appear to be the sort of conversation that Mike or impassive Imogen wanted to have, because she stared at me blankly and Mike clearly wanted me to bugger off.

"Then get to it," said Mike.

Imogen drank from her water with a neon-green twisty straw, which I point out only to reiterate how utterly non-creepy she was. Hannibal Lecter may have made scary slurping sounds, but there were certainly no fun straws.

"So this is a sort of don't-shoot-the-messenger scenario," I ventured. This seemed like a good start because it immediately separated me from Chul-Moo's message.

Mike seemed neutral about it, but Imogen suddenly looked ready to punch me. Not creepily, though. Just a straight-up whacking. I'm guessing she didn't like Chul-Moo, because she just tensed up at the mention of his name.

"Yes," I continued. "So I ran into Chul-Moo earlier."

"He produced this message that we're not supposed to shoot you for?" asked Mike3000.

"Yes, exactly," I said. "So, he suggested that either you or Imogen murdered Karou."

Imogen and Mike took this idea very, very neutrally. Surprisingly so. Imogen slurped a little, but she did not do it in a gasping or particularly offended manner.

It got so little response that I actually repeated it, because I thought maybe they didn't understand.

There was more silence, and then Imogen said:

"Me or Mike? It's an either/or situation, is it? We couldn't have killed him together?"

I did not really have much of a read on Imogen, because she was a strange amalgamation of things that on their own did not make a lot of sense. But I had the impression that she was amused, and not taking this accusation very seriously.

"He didn't really specify. I would guess that there's an implied and/or in there, but this is his theory not mine."

"If you're going to kill a man," said Imogen, still slurping on her straw. "I would think that it would be nice to have a backup. Besides which, this is a partner's tournament. Killing a man solo seems against the spirit of the thing."

Yes, she was definitely not taking me seriously. I didn't blame her. But Mike on the other hand was moving from neutral to gradually troubled.

"Why would we kill Karou?" asked Mike, in a tone that I would describe as concerned academic.

"He thinks that you wanted to get him out of the tournament. So you killed off his teammate."

Mike shifted in his seat. Rare is the lunch in which you are casually accused of murder.

"Wouldn't there be easier ways of disqualifying him than murder? We could have slashed his tires. Or a kidnapping? What's wrong with a kidnapping?"

So far Mike's and Imogen's responses had been: (1) it's troublesome to kill alone, and (2) why not kidnapping? I did not think that they had murdered Karou, but they seemed like excellent criminals.

"This isn't my theory, you know," I said.

"So you've said. I have a follow-up question," said Imogen. "Was Chul-Moo high when he suggested this possibility to you?"

Imogen, it seemed, had interacted with Chul-Moo before.

"Like a kite," I told her.

"You might run this theory by him again, later," posed Imogen, still calm, still neutral. "And tell him that I was not amused at hearing about it."

That's what she said, but she looked profoundly amused. She was smiling now, actually. The suggestion that she might have bludgeoned a man to death seemed to brighten her.

Not looking amused, however, was Mike. He wasn't angry, exactly, but I could tell that he was thinking about, if not shooting the messenger, at least kicking her shins.

"Why would Chul-Moo even want you to tell us this?"

"He's afraid you're going to kill him."

Mike's face creased in incomprehension. "But he's not even in the tournament anymore. Why would we murder him? Just to be symmetrical?"

"No, he's back in the tournament."

Mike was still confused and unhappy about the previous matter—vis-à-vis being accused of murder—and did not seem to immediately process the bit about Chul-Moo playing. But Imogen was immediately annoyed.

"You're fucking kidding me," said Imogen. "He's missed, like, three rounds. You can't skip three rounds!"

"He's playing tomorrow. That's what he told me."

"That's even more rounds!"

"I guess if your teammate gets killed, you advance to day two," I said. "It's like getting all As in college if your roommate commits suicide."

"People have no respect for rules anymore," said Imogen, sounding saltier than you're probably imagining. Although, she returned to her usual placid self before adding: "And that roommate-suicide thing is just an urban legend."

"Tell that that to my sister's roommate's cousin."

This was a joke, but no one laughed. (I don't even have a sister!) This could be because my joke wasn't that funny, but I prefer to think that Imogen and Mike were deep in thought. Imogen was looking very displeased about Chul-Moo still being competition, whereas Mike seemed to struggle with the idea that Chul-Moo would assume that he'd bludgeon his friend in the head. I could start to see where the whole "creepy" idea was coming from with Imogen, though. She was an emotive person, and as she scowled at the idea, you could almost feel black storm clouds around her. These clouds were admittedly more Lucy van Pelt than Son of Sam, but even so.

It was also at this moment that I noticed Imogen's bracelet. I'm not much of a jewelry gal, but Imogen had on an old-school silver charm bracelet that looked awfully familiar. There was a dog on it. And a top hat. And a car.

They were Monopoly tokens, of course. Just like the wheelbarrow that had been in Swan's pocket. I tried checking to see if she was missing a wheelbarrow, but her arm was on the bar, and half the bracelet was obscured.

"Who's his teammate, then?" asked Imogen.

"Swan," I said. "I, uh, don't know his last name."

"Oh, fucking A," said Imogen. "Of course it's Swan, like a bad penny. Well, we'll just have to beat them the old-fashioned way."

Imogen was chumming it up with Mike as though she expected commiseration over the Swan development. But

Mike, looking increasingly devastated, continued to be on an entirely different plane.

"How could Chul-Moo think that I could kill a person?" asked Mike. "I'm, like, the nicest person here."

I noted that he didn't say: How could he think that Imogen might kill a person? But regardless, Mike was looking rather sad all of a sudden, and I felt that it was best to get him off the whole suspected-murder topic.

"You never did tell me what you did for a living, Mike."

"I'm a taxidermist."

Well, there was your answer.

CHAPTER SEVENTEEN

Astonishingly, we made small talk after the murder accusation. Although, this was mostly Imogen, who could talk about the upcoming weather with a lot of knowledge and enthusiasm. Mike just stared at me, glazed over, and I started feeling a little guilty about the whole exchange. He looked so troubled that I began to wonder if Chul-Moo didn't really suspect these two at all. Maybe he was just trying to knock Mike off his game.

I didn't much care for this idea, because it meant that I was a pawn in someone else's machinations. And not even great machinations. If I was going to be a pawn in someone else's game, I would at least want it to be a big game. Like a *Game of Thrones* situation, with shifting seats of power, murderous widows, and psychic wolves. Not for a *Smash Brothers* knockoff with a $20,000 prize.

After I left, and only after, I remembered the fougère perfume that been stinking up the storeroom I had found Swan in. I should have smelled Imogen. Admittedly, this is a little personal, but once you've accused someone of murder, why not just go all in? If I ran into her later, I would give her a sniff.

Daniel was still missing. He had messaged me that he had to go "meet a guy," which seemed ridiculous.

"Here?" I had asked him. "In the hotel?"

"Sorry," Daniel had texted. "It's a thing."

At the time, I had just taken this all to mean that Daniel had wanted to steer clear of the aftermath of a scene in which I casually accuse a man of murder. This was the sort of thing that was probably not his style. So I did not interrogate him on the point.

However, when I returned to the lobby of the Endicott, I observed that Daniel was indeed meeting with a guy.

I know that Shuler had cautioned me about being unreasonably suspicious of Daniel. And he had very carefully suggested that my suspicion was maybe grounded in some personal reasons that I won't dwell on. These were fair points, and I cop to them.

But believe me when I describe the guy Daniel was meeting with as "looking like a criminal." He was middle-aged, maybe in his late forties, and looked like a grubbier Steve Buscemi. Brown hair, tangled and unwashed. Wrinkled clothing. Weird teeth. And he kept scratching himself. All over. Like he had a skin disease.

I had planned on walking over and introducing myself, but the scratching made me nervous, both because it was suspicious and because I didn't want anything that's communicable. But I was very curious who this person was, and I couldn't possibly imagine what he would be doing with Daniel. I mean, I suppose I could imagine, because he looked like the sort of person who you would meet for a drug deal. Not in real life, because drug dealers, in my experience, dress pretty well. But on CBS.

I remained on the other side of the lobby and just watched from a distance. I was not, I want to clarify, spying on Charice's fella. I was just making casual observations unseen and from a distance.

They were having a conversation, but it was very quiet and not particularly animated, so it was very difficult to guess what was being discussed. After a moment, they both began to look around as if they were concerned about being observed, and so I ducked back around the corner.

Once again, not because I was spying, but because I was observing. I'm gunning to be a detective, right? We are an observing people. And if I wanted to hide behind a corner or a shrub and observe, what was to stop me?

Anyway, they didn't see me. Although, there was a guy in the hallway who seemed to regard me with great amusement.

"Are you hiding behind this corner?" he asked me.

"No," I told him, making a sort of *pssht* noise with my lips that was properly the domain of fourteen-year-old girls. *Pssht*, what? I don't have a crush on Billy Tomlinson. What? You're crazy.

It was no more effective here than it was for me in eighth grade. (And here we take a moment for Billy Tomlinson, wherever you are.)

"Really?" said the guy. "Because you leaped back here like a panther."

This guy, incidentally, was wearing purple overalls. I assume he was planning on shooting a nineties-style hip-hop video later, because there is really no other explanation for his clothing. I was not taking guff from this clown.

"I suddenly changed rooms is all," I told the guy, who was way too keenly interested in me.

"Who are you hiding from?" he asked, peeking into the lobby himself.

"I'm not hiding from anyone," I said, peering out as well. "Oh shit," I said. "They're gone!"

Purple Overall Guy thought this was hilarious, but fuck him. I caught a glimpse of what I hoped was Daniel going down a hallway that led away from the gaming area, and so I jolted after him. I was keeping my eyes on two places at once—one eye on Daniel's departing figure, the other on Purple Overall Guy, who I hoped was not going to follow after me for fun and games. He was laughing his head off, and clearly considering tailing me himself, but thankfully he decided to stay put. Purple Overalls? I mean, honestly. I was able to gain enough ground on Daniel to see him and our CBS Criminal disappear, together, into the men's room.

Am I wrong in thinking that this was a bit weird and suspicious? Men don't go to the bathroom together. Women, yes, men, no. I don't think this difference is so much due to gender difference as much as the state of men's restrooms, which typically look as though they have recently housed feral rhesus monkeys.

Even so, I didn't really have a lot of alternatives. I didn't feel that I could bust in there, because it would be difficult to explain. Besides which, there could be other guys in there. Pooping guys, who might not take kindly to my presence. Even worse, there could be pooping guys who did take kindly to my presence. Also, rhesus monkeys.

So I waited outside.

What was going on in there? I had three possibilities, just off the top of my head.

1. Sex.

This did not seem like a very likely possibility, because Daniel was, to my knowledge, entirely straight and pretty damned into Charice, regardless. And even if Daniel did swing both ways, a subject that I had not, and never will, broach with him, it seemed to me that he could do a lot better than a bathroom tryst with haggard Steve Buscemi. If I were writing Daniel-based fan fiction, which is actually not an unappealing idea, I'd pair him with a Poe or Finn. Or perhaps Poe and Finn. Why limit myself? Maybe I'd even throw in the robot. But quality fellas, and age appropriate. Not Steve Buscemi. Steve Buscemi does not does fit into this picture.

2. Drug deal.

I mean, Daniel's weed had to come from somewhere. After all, just because one looks like a drug dealer on CBS doesn't mean that this guy couldn't actually be a drug dealer. And it would explain why Daniel hadn't taken that phone call earlier in front of Shuler. You wouldn't talk to your drug dealer in front of a cop. That's just lazy.

3. Pooping.

Or peeing, I suppose, but they had been in there for a while. Maybe the guy just came up to Daniel and said, "Hey, buddy, do you know where the gents room is?" and Daniel was like, "Sure, dude, and whoa, that reminds me—I need to release my bowels too, now that I think about it." This exchange, as I type it, does not exactly have the ring of truth, but it has to be a possibility.

Those were my three theories. I didn't say they were good theories. But I didn't get a chance to come up with anything better, because Mr. Buscemi appeared in the doorway of the restroom. I had to repress an impulse to hide, but there was no reason to. This guy had never seen me before, and even if Daniel were to pop out as well, it wasn't as if I had done anything wrong. I gave him a curt little nod when he noticed me looking at him, which he returned before walking away.

So two options, Dahlia. I could wait for Daniel and ask him what that was all about. Which would seem a little pushy, particularly if it were nothing. I could also wait for Daniel and not ask him about it, which would be much more reasonable, if less emotionally satisfying. I liked these two options about as well as my three theories on what was going on in the bathroom.

So I came up with a third option, which was that I followed Steve Buscemi.

CHAPTER EIGHTEEN

I followed the guy from a distance, and I thought I was doing a pretty good job. No one had really taught me how to tail anyone, but I felt I was doing pretty good for a rookie. Those years of playing *Metal Gear Solid* really paid off for me.

Also, not to pick on anyone's infirmities, but now that I was following Mr. Buscemi without any distractions, I observed that he was walking with a limp. A limp! This guy was one facial scar away from being a goon in a Cinemax movie.

He left the hotel and headed toward the parking lot. I have no idea which car he was getting in, but I did observe that there was an El Camino in the lot, and for the sake of poetry, let us assume that was his car. It certainly wouldn't have been right for this guy to pile into a Chevy Volt.

"Hey, you," I shouted.

This was wasn't a great opening, but I didn't know the guy's name.

"Yeah?" said the guy. For a second—just a second, I thought that perhaps our guy had an Australian accent—which might have explained why Daniel would want to hang around him—but the more he spoke the more I realized this wasn't the case.

What can I say? When you've been listening to an iffy Australian accent all day, everything starts to sound like one.

Anyway, my next question was sort of hard to get out, which was something considering that I had casually accused a man of murder about twenty minutes earlier.

"Were you meeting with a guy in the men's restroom?"

And the guy gave me exactly the same fourteen-year-old's *pssht* that I had employed only a few minutes before.

"No," he said. Billy Tomlinson? You're crazy. "What the hell is wrong with you?"

This was, and in fact continues to be, a salient question. But it wasn't the issue at hand.

"Because it looked like you guys were going in there in secret or something."

"What are you, his fiancée? You're a real piece of work."

"I'm not his fiancée. He doesn't even have a fiancée."

"That's not what I hear. Anyway, if you're not the fiancée, it's none of your business. Stop bothering me."

And I did stop bothering him, because he was right. And, I was a bit tripped up about the fiancée business. It sort of made a lump in my throat. Daniel didn't have a fiancée, did he? Unless he had some secret family I didn't know about. But who has time for that? I don't even have time for my regular family, much less an extra secret one.

Unless he meant Charice, which was where the lump was coming from.

This possibility was very unnerving. More unnerving than Doctor XXX skulking around the Endicott and sending me cryptic messages online. Even more unnerving than poor Karou, who had definitely been killed by someone, and was a point that I really should not lose sight of. But that was mystery stuff, and while that can definitely impact my real life (case in point: the bullet wound in my left arm), this wasn't a side project that was drifting into my regular day-to-day. This was the main event.

Had Charice gotten engaged and not told me about it?

I was a little shaken by the time I made it back into the Endicott. I had always been unsettled about Charice's relationship with Daniel, but the idea that it was developing behind my back really disquieted me.

Okay, I grant that sentence seems a little Single White Female, and that's not it at all. I had absolutely no intention of killing Charice and wearing her skin as a dress. (Besides which, she wouldn't fit me. I'd have to kill someone else and sew them together.) But—I don't know—I'm the sensible one, and Charice is the wacky sidekick. There are rules for this sort of thing. The wacky sidekick can't get married. We're talking about a woman that released a poisonous Gila monster in our apartment. She can't go walking down the aisle! Not unsupervised. She's like the textbook example of the runaway bride.

Anyway, I was freaking out a little. This was naturally a good time to get on Twitch, because when you're feeling unmoored, there's nothing like an angry mob of borderline abusive gamers to talk some sense into you. And I didn't want real life, at least for a moment. I wanted mystery. I wanted to see whether Doctor XXX had sent me a message. He hadn't, and so I sent him a message:

Hey Doc:

Let me know if you get this. Meeting you in that storeroom didn't turn out so well. But I'm guessing you figured that out.

This was a strange message to write, given that I had no idea with whom I was messaging, whether they meant me good or ill (or were just jerking me around), or, honestly, if they were even alive at all. You feel a bit strange sending a snarky note to a dead person.

Strange, but productive. Although, I still felt sad and weird about Charice. She was engaged. Or was about to be engaged. This was a piece of news that I knew I would acclimate to, but I just needed some time. Maybe it was a blessing that I had figured it out ahead of being told, because now I would have time to practice being happy. I imagined Charice telling me, and I tried smiling. I didn't have a mirror handy, but I felt pretty sure that my smile looked like something that Heath Ledger would have created with a knife.

I still had time.

Focus on Doctor XXX. He maybe wanted to kill you, and that felt like more comfortable waters than engaged Charice, typed Dahlia, in the weirdest fucking sentence ever. And I had never even been to a wedding before. What do you wear? No, wait, Doctor XXX. He was shady, right? And I essentially knew nothing about him. He may or may not be wearing a green hat; he may or may not be alive. He may or may not have ever existed. He may or may not be engaged, like Charice.

No, stay on track, Dahlia. Intel. Find now.

All I really had for the good doctor was Twitch. So, let's expand on that. I'd streamed some, but I'd never really gotten deeply under the hood with Twitch. I wasn't exactly sure how it worked with commenters—I knew I could search for streamers, and "follow" them so that Twitch would let me know whenever they came online, but I wasn't sure if the same was true for the commentariat. I would love if Twitch sent me a message letting me know if Doctor XXX showed up online. In any channel. I'd even watch a little *FIFA '16* if it meant a conversation with this clown.

So I prowled about on my laptop and discovered that sadly, no, this was not how it worked. No alerts, unless he streamed, which seemed unlikely. I followed him, just in case. But it wasn't a total wash; there was a hubpage for our doctor, and I could see who else he was following. Which was, interestingly, only two people: myself and someone named LadyBlazer.

It made sense that he was following me, since he was able to mysteriously appear whenever I came online. He was getting a notification every time I streamed. But who was LadyBlazer?

I started streaming again.

"Hey, Twitch chat," I said. "I'm still in the tournament!"

Go fuck yourself, said Twitch chat. Has no one killed you yet?

"Not yet, but there's still time. Listen, I'm still trying to find information on Doctor XXX."

He's just not that into you, said Twitch chat.

"Well, he's a little into me, because he led me into a room with a corpse in it. He's potentially sending me into death traps. You have to be a little into someone to arrange a death trap." This was undoubtedly an unwise thing to say to Twitch chat, or perhaps to anyone, but they took it with their usual nonchalance.

Girl, said Twitch chat. We don't know where he is. Ain't nobody got time for that. This is the Internet, we got porn to look at. Hashtag #alttab.

Seriously, I don't know why I keep giving the Twitch chat people a gay BFF vibe. They are seriously not like that at all.

"I don't want to cut into your porn time, but I am just the teensiest bit concerned that maybe someone is trying to kill me."

Back on that again, said Twitch chat.

I was suddenly more empathetic to Chul-Moo and his drug-induced paranoia. It's not fun sounding paranoid. Although, I didn't really think that Doctor XXX was trying to kill me, honestly, because I'm probably not that hard to kill. I just think that he was up to something nebulous that I couldn't figure out. I would have said that, but I actually think it makes me sound more paranoid than the murder. Funny how that works.

"No one has seen him? At all?"

No, said Twitch chat. How many times do we have to tell you no?

"How about this: Does anyone know who LadyBlazer is?"

She's at the tournament, said Twitch chat. She's playing with Mike. CREEPY CREEPY CREEPY.

Daniel *BAMF*'d back in front of me. Okay, he probably wasn't involved in the murder, but he would have made a great assassin. Ninja skills, this man has. Hollywood, if you need a fake Aussie ninja, here's your man. If you need a real Aussie ninja, perhaps Geoffrey Rush? I realize that he's probably too old to play a ninja, but now that I've typed it, I really want to see a movie where it happens. But I digress.

I was obviously not in the mood to see Daniel at this point. Engaged Daniel. Fiancé Daniel. Yeesh. I tried my smile at him, which apparently Heath Ledger had hacked up further in the intervening time. Maybe it was getting to Two-Face at this point. But I logged off and dealt with him anyway.

"What happened to your face?" asked Daniel.

"I'm smiling," I said. "Because I'm so happy."

"That's not a smile," he said, hitting a perfect Paul Hogan. He then beamed with the glorious grin of someone who was walking into the matrimonial future. It was a smile with the force of a Thousand Splendid Suns. I haven't actually read that book, so I apologize if that reference is inappropriate. But that's what it felt like.

"That's a smile," he said, not willing to let the joke go by. And it was a smile.

"What are you so happy about?" I asked.

"Secret things," said Daniel.

Secret fiancée things. Ugh. Forget Doctor XXX. This was the mystery I wanted solved.

"Hey, I love secret things," I said. "You can tell me."

"I could tell you," said Daniel. "But then it wouldn't be a secret."

Literally, happiness was shooting off Daniel in waves. Like, you couldn't look directly at him. The happy was too strong. It was going to knock you over.

"Is it related to Charice?" I asked.

"Can't say," said Daniel. The waves of happy were crashing into me, like tides of joy against grim rocks. Yikes was Daniel happy.

"I could figure it out," I told him, which was probably true.

"I suppose you could, but I would think that you'd be more interested in the murder and the guy who tried to lure you to a murder."

"You might think that."

"Well," considered Daniel, "it was a little strange."

"Strange like meeting a weird-looking guy in a men's restroom strange?" I asked. "Or strange in a different way?"

"You have been using your detective powers," said Daniel, with the exact sort of gladness that Charice would have responded to the situation with. "Anyway, you shouldn't bother with that. You'll find out soon enough anyway." And then he winked at me. Not even a real wink, but a Lucille Bluth stage wink.

"Why did bathroom guy think that you have a fiancée?"

Daniel seemed unruffled by the idea that I might have been spying on him, but consider: he was in love with Charice, who was basically impropriety on legs. Apparently he decided the best way to deflect my question was with another one about my case.

"Do you think that the guy wanted you to find Karou's corpse? Or was Karou hoping to meet you alive?"

This was, of course, an excellent question. I still wasn't even sure Karou was what we were supposed to find. Maybe I was supposed to find naked Swan. Or, hell, maybe I was just supposed to wander into a closet for laughs. This seemed unlikely, but I'd been shot at before by a woman in a tree costume, so "unlikely" felt like it belonged on the table. Hell, sometimes there was so much "unlikely" on the table that it spilled onto the floor and got mixed up with "the merely improbable." I really should keep cleaner tables.

"I don't have a clue," I told him. And this was true.

"Well, pull yourself together," said Daniel, "because we've got one more round to go."

CHAPTER NINETEEN

Our last match of the day was—and forgive me if you could see this coming—also canceled. Statistically, this was really unlikely—we were the only pairing who didn't play a single match following the murder. Everyone else—even with the quasi collapse of the tournament—played at least two or three rounds more than us.

I knew this because the redhead who was manning the tournament table appeared ready to explode.

"I cannot believe your opponents are not here," he said.

"We're just lucky, I guess," said Daniel, still oozing happiness out of his pores. "Everyone's lucky sometimes."

"They were here earlier," said the redhead, who was not oozing happiness so much as shooting daggers.

"I'm happy to wait for them," I told him.

Daniel, apparently insane from the thin air he's getting up there in his Clouds of Love, was perfectly delighted to advance to day two. I was frankly ready to bail. Day two of this thing would have an audience. There would be crowds. Our games would be projected on a giant screen. I could barely play this game at all, and if it weren't for the excellent tutorial in *Skullgirls*, I would have had my ass handed to me by a kindergartner.

"If they're not here," said Daniel, "it's not our problem."

Mike3000 and Imogen—aka LadyBlazer—crept up behind us. "Don't tell me that you're advancing again without playing a match," said Mike.

"How'd you hear that?" I asked.

"Everyone's talking about it," said Imogen. "People are calling you the Cinderella Couple."

"They're saying what?" I asked.

"The Cinderella Couple. You know, like you're enchanted. How are you doing it?" asked Imogen. "You bribing them or something?"

This idea that I have enough money to bribe people to take a dive in a tournament is so innately laughable that I actually pig-snorted at Imogen. Although I maybe should have been concerned, in retrospect, that this was the prevailing wisdom.

"I'm not bribing anybody."

"And they will have opponents," said the redhead. "They were here earlier. And I'm sure they'll show up any second."

"Hey, Imogen," I said. "You know a guy on Twitch called Doctor XXX?"

"Nope," said Imogen, without even thinking about the question. Which I thought was odd, because if you posed a question like that to me, I'd at least take a moment to think about it. But Imogen didn't even pause.

"He follows you on Twitch," I explained.

"Yeah? So do about twenty thousand other people."

"That's a lot of people," I said.

Imogen shrugged.

"He's never messaged you and asked you to go meet him in a storeroom?"

Imogen answered this question with a look. She said nothing

at all, but her glance answered the question more effectively than paragraphs of denial ever could.

"No weird messages at all? Nothing?"

More looking. Daniel was also unconcerned about the indirect accusation of bribery because he unhelpfully mused aloud:

"I hope our opponents weren't murdered."

"Yes," I said. "That would be a sticky wicket."

Anyway, most of this conversation I was just looking at Imogen trying to work out a reasonable way that I could smell her and see if she, by any chance, smelled like the fougère that stunk up Swan's room. I was never going to come up with a great opening, so I just embraced a lousy one.

"What's that smell?" I said, invading Imogen's personal space in a terrible and almost Charician way. "You smell wonderful! What is that?"

Imogen was not prepared for this—either the invasion, or the compliment.

"Uh, what? The hotel shampoo, I guess? I forgot to bring anything."

Imogen smelled like nothing. By which I mean, actually, nothing. Not perfume, not shampoo, not sweat. Maybe she was a cyborg. Even so, I pushed.

"It's this wonderful fougère—what is that scent? It's familiar to me, but I can't place it. I'm such a perfume nerd." This was bullshit, but you can't blame a gal for trying.

Imogen looked a bit stunned. "Oh!" she said. "Could it be the Lion's Cupboard?"

"That might be it," I said. "Is that what you're wearing?"

"It was my boyfriend's cologne—my ex—but I would wear it now and then back when we dated because—well, never mind why because. I wonder if some of it got in these clothes?"

But she looked very uncertain.

"It's a great scent," I told her, hoping that this compliment would redirect her from wondering how the scent could have stayed with her all this time. It must have, because she got out her phone and started fiddling with it. Hopefully she wasn't googling "cologne half-life."

Meanwhile, Mike, who had zero interest in this perfume discussion, politely interjected:

"Who were you supposed to play?"

"Jason 'Trenchet' Saltz and Jonathan 'SoggyToast' North," answered the redhead.

"Yeah," said Mike. "They were here."

"Bribed, probably," said Imogen, apparently off the topic of the Lion's Cupboard. I didn't really appreciate the jab, although I could see she was just playing with me now. Imogen wasn't creepy really, not at all, but she did have the catlike quality of being someone who played with her food before she ate it. And as far as she was concerned in this tournament, Daniel and me were food.

Then Imogen pulled me aside. I had kind of imagined she was going to give me more perfume intel, but she had something else on her mind, and she spoke in a hushed tone.

"Hey, I just checked my Twitch account to see if that Doctor XXX of yours ever tried sending me a private message—and uh, yeah, he has."

"Did he ask to meet you in a hotel storeroom?" I asked her, maybe a little too quickly.

"No," she said. "That's crazy. No, these are just death threats."

I had never heard anyone toss off the phrase "just death threats" with such natural nonchalance. Death threats seem like the sort of thing that ought to concern you.

"He sent you death threats? How did you not know about this earlier?"

"Well," said Imogen, "I have a filter that blocks most of that stuff, and I don't read messages on Twitch, because why? If anyone worthwhile wants to talk to me, they'll use email." She stopped to consider. "And they're not death threats exactly. It's more 'you should have been a blow job and not a baby.' That sort of thing."

"Jesus Christ," I said. I looked at Imogen, who remained completely composed through this conversation, maybe even a little bored. "How are you so calm about this?"

"It just comes with the territory. If you want to make it in this scene, you have to be thick-skinned. And you never read the comments."

It was weird making small talk after that, but we managed it. Imogen actually did have more to say about perfume and cologne, and I instantly regretted my little white lie about being a perfume nerd, because she certainly had the knowledge to call me out, going on about top notes of bergamot and gourmands and other words that I didn't even know.

By the time the redhead came up to us, I was immensely grateful.

"Well," he said. "I guess I have no choice but to let you move on to day two."

"This really is my lucky day," said Daniel.

Daniel and I headed back to our apartment, Daniel driving through a surprising amount of traffic for that hour in St. Louis, which usually tends to clear out pretty well at night. I suppose

I couldn't say at that point that I was completely uncomfortable around Daniel, because I could ride with him in silence without the need to make dumb small talk. Which is the mark of friendship for me. I guess I did like the guy, even if I had at least somewhat contemplated him being a killer.

But the silence was good.

There was plenty to think about, and not being at the Endicott Hotel gave me breathing time to actually think about and consider it. I watched the city pass—there's also something deeply disorienting about riding in a car when you're used to walking and public transit—and tried to categorize my thinking on the day.

We arrived at my apartment to yet another mystery, which was that Charice was not there. As mysteries go, this wasn't the Piltdown Man, but it was curious. If it had been someone else, we probably wouldn't have thought twice about it, but when Charice is up to something, it's generally wise to be on the lookout.

"Wasn't Charice supposed to be here?" I asked Daniel, who was familiar enough with her to be wary.

"Yes," he said. "She promised me penne."

Maybe we were friends, Daniel and I, because we shared a look. It was the look right before someone opens a door in a horror movie. Charice was into tomfoolery, and we were the self-aware ingenues that were destined to face down her Jason in the woods.

Daniel, self-starting fellow that he is, took to making his own pasta. And I logged on to Twitch again, because I am a glutton for punishment.

CHAPTER TWENTY

Charice entered the room, and we were shocked. Which was saying something because we expected to be shocked.

Charice was dressed as Balrog. In case you aren't familiar with who that it is, allow me to briefly sketch it out for you by listing several things that Balrog is (and that Charice isn't).

Male
Black
Huge
A professional boxer
Evil

I could go on, but if those things don't concern you, there's no point in dwelling on the niggling bits. Certainly Charice didn't.

She did notice that we were looking at her, mouths agog, however, and she asked:

"How's my look? Too much?"

Daniel did not immediately answer, and I decided to follow suit. Besides which, it wasn't the right question. The issue wasn't whether the look was too much, so much as it was wrong. It's like stabbing someone in the head with an awl, and then asking if the hole was too big. The size of the hole is not the point. It is the placement.

Daniel made an observation.

"Balrog is black," he said.

"Yes," said Charice. "I decided not to wear any face paint because it would be culturally inappropriate. Why, do you think I could get away with it?"

"No!" Daniel and I said together, as involuntary a reaction as heartbeats.

"It does make my hair look weird, though." Charice was wearing a bald cap—a dark-skinned bald cap—with Balrog's triangular hair stitched into it. "Weird" wasn't even close to being the right word.

"Why are you dressed as Balrog, Charice?"

Charice laughed. "To celebrate your victory, obviously. I'm going to wear this tomorrow to the tournament. If I'm going to be there, I may as well make an entrance."

"Where did you even find that?" asked Daniel.

"I'm borrowing it from a friend," said Charice. "I wouldn't have gone with Balrog if I'd more time to put this together. I'd be Cammy or Rose or something."

Now that I had gotten over my initial shock, it actually was pretty apparent that Charice's costume was a hand-me-down. Her blue tank top and pants hung off her obscenely. But dear God, her head.

"You know you can't wear that bald cap," said Daniel whose thinking was running alongside mine.

"Oh," said Charice. "I'll rouge this thing up so much, you'll never know."

Then we had pasta. Charice was unwilling to take off her boxing gloves—"I'm feeling the fantasy," she said—and so this forced Daniel fully into chef mode. A role he seemed to relish, actually, although his cooking was always more enthusiastic than skilled.

"So," said Charice, once we had food. "Tell me about this murder, and your tournament, in that order."

I told Charice everything, who could, despite all appearances, be a pretty good listener. She was especially piqued around the part about the naked guy, which I expected, but also about the appearance of Shuler. I won't say that Charice didn't like Shuler, because Charice likes everyone, but she was wary of him. This was perhaps because of her frequently illegal behavior, but also because she was more firmly in the camp of Nathan.

But I digress.

"You need to figure out who this Doctor XXX is," she observed when I was done with the story.

"Do I, though?" I asked. Now that I'd had a moment to not be in the maze, as it were, it seemed to me that it would be much easier to not figure this out at all. Not everything that happens around you is a mystery to be solved. Besides which, I didn't actually have a client here.

I explained this to Charice.

"Then I'll hire you," said Charice. "What do you charge?"

"You can't afford me," I told her, although this was plainly untrue. Charice made obscene amounts of money and, despite her apparent extravagances, didn't actually spend all that much. Take our apartment—it wasn't that nice. Charice could afford a house in a suburb. But making cuts on housing things meant that she could go big on places where it really mattered, like colorful hats or randomly assigned detective work.

"One month's rent, free," said Charice.

"If I solve the murder? That's nuts, Charice."

"Not even that," said Charice. "Just figure out who this guy is who lured you into the storeroom."

"Why?" I asked.

"I'm curious," said Charice. "Besides, it will make you proud, and you'll walk around for the next month all puffed up, and that makes you easier to live with."

For the moment, let us skip over the implication that I am difficult to live with. An implication made, once again, by a woman who had released a Gila monster in our apartment.

"Why would that make me happy?" I asked, very honestly.

"Because you are a person who yearns for vengeance."

I was prepared to argue this point, but it was, like many things Charice said, uncomfortably true. It would be nice to stick it to "Doctor XXX," even if he was, I don't know, a twelve-year-old girl in Guatemala.

"Fine," I said. "But how would I make that happen?"

"Beats me," said Charice. "You're the detective. Have you tried googling the guy?"

I had, actually. I had figured it wouldn't work. I needed someone with a username like VertiginousPigeon or Topiary-Spider. Doctor XXX was too common. Also, when I did a search for "Doctor XXX," the first hit was for—and I quote—"a crazy nurse with a dick." This did not inspire me to do a lot more searching, although if your tastes run toward crazy nurses with dicks, consider yourself in the know.

"I suppose I could do that," I said, not bothering to expound upon the nurse with dicks angle. Because there were things I could do. If the guy had used the handle for anything else, I could search for pairs: "Doctor XXX" + "Dark Alleys" or "Street Fighter." Or hell, I could just try names. "Doctor XXX" + "Mike3000." These were all long shots, but it couldn't hurt to try. Honestly, I suspect that in this day and age most murders could be solved by the correct Google search. It could be a web series. *CSI: Bing.*

I had an idea to try that now, which seemed a natural thing to do, because Charice and Daniel were beginning the long process of retreating to their bedroom, which was presaged by Daniel feeding her pasta. Looking at the two of them, I was simultaneously sort of disgusted and struck with the thought that if Charice was going to get engaged, it was good that she was going to do it with a man that cooked and fed her pasta.

But the doorbell rang, and I had a visitor. Nathan Willing.

Nathan was wearing a green-and-white-checked blazer and a V-neck, which on its own would have looked plausible on a nice Floridian golfer lady. But on him, it looked great. Nathan looked, as he always did, scruffy and winning, and with a grin big enough to be seen from space.

"Dahlia," he said. "I've come bearing gifts."

He held out a small ornamental cactus. This happened because Nathan, a botanist, is fonder of buying flowers for women than most fellas. I told him I did not want flowers, because I am not good at keeping things looking good or alive. His response to this was, apparently, to simply switch to xerophytic plants. And he held one out now, a small round cactus with tiny purple flowers and needles that looked a bit like snow.

"May I come in?" he asked.

I gestured to come in, and Charice stopped being fed pasta and waved at him.

"Don't I have one of these already?" I asked. I was amassing quite a little cactus garden, because Nathan had taken to giving me one of these every time he saw me.

"Not one like this," he said. "I'm keeping a database. How was your day?"

And more pasta.

Here's the thing about Nathan Willing. I feel about him a little the way that I feel about the cactus garden. If you asked me if I wanted a cactus garden, I would have said no. I even would say that in the middle of the day, when the cactus garden was not around. But then I get home, and there's this beautiful little oasis of plants that are hard to kill that makes me sort of happy.

I feel iffy about my relationship with Nathan, at least when he's not around. It happened too quickly, too easily. I'm suspicious. He's a boyfriend that just sort of fell out of the sky. It was as if I had tripped over a tree root and landed in a relationship. It didn't feel like it should have happened. Or at least, that's how I felt until he showed up, and then I was grateful to have something that was wonderful and easy to keep alive.

It's complicated.

"Dahlia stumbled into another murder," said Daniel.

"You're kidding," said Nathan. "You should have called me."

This was a fair point, but Charice had her own issue to pursue.

"What do you mean Dahlia stumbled into a murder, Daniel?" asked Charice. "You were there too. You stumbled together."

"I suppose," said Daniel. "But Dahlia threw up on the guy. And she was possibly lured to her doom. I'm just the bodyguard."

"Why wasn't I the bodyguard?" asked Nathan.

"You had to teach," I said. "And besides which, I don't need a bodyguard." Which is again, a terrible thing to say, because as this story will bear, I apparently need a bodyguard very badly. Foreshadowing.

But this didn't impress anyone, particularly Charice, who was now onto stage two of her what I can only assume was foreplay with Daniel, which was that she was now feeding the pasta to him. It was like watching *Lady and the Tramp*, but with humans instead of dogs, and filthy.

I got up and sat down in our common-room sofa. Nathan followed along.

"Tell me about your day," he said. Nathan sat down next to me, very next to me, and I sort of fell over onto him. He's a very thin guy, Nathan, with a bony lap (and shoulder blades that can cut glass), but I couldn't think of a better lap to be in at the moment.

"It was horrible," I said. And I gave him all the details. Swan, and Doctor XXX, and the whole terrible business. Nathan, unlike Charice, has a real weakness for interrupting narratives with witty remarks, but this time he took the whole story in without comment.

"You don't have to go back, you know," said Nathan. Which was sensible, really, but the wrong thing to say, because I wanted to go back. It wasn't smart, but it's what I wanted.

"Charice has hired me to figure out who Doctor XXX is," I said. "So I guess I kind of do."

"Plus I want to win!" shouted Daniel.

Nathan, for his part in this, shot a look at Charice that was perhaps the most irritated I've ever seen him. This made me strangely happy. Both because he was being protective of me, which was nice, and because it's rewarding to be reminded that normal people should be irritated by Charice's behavior.

"You know what I think we should do," said Nathan.

"Something with model trains?" Nathan was obsessed with trains, and while I'm willing to geek out over just about anything, model trains are one of the few things that I have no patience for.

"No," said Nathan. "Although," he added, his face transforming, "if you're up for that, I did get the Walthers catalog. We could look at it together."

"That will never happen," I said. "And not just tonight. I mean ever."

"Fine," he said. "Well, it wasn't my suggestion anyway. I say we go out!"

"That sounds exhausting."

"We can go to the Tivoli. We'll see the most foreign movie they have. Super foreign. Something in Khoe or Pitjantjatjara."

Is Nathan a hipster? He generally denied the idea, but then he was given to saying things like "Let's see a movie in Khoe or Pitjantjatjara." You decide.

"As tempting as that sounds," I told Nathan, "I don't think I want to partake of any plan that involves me moving even slightly."

"We could Netflix and chill," said Nathan. "Or even just Netflix."

"Or even just chill," said Daniel, who really ought not to be eavesdropping on our conversations. But I digress.

I enjoy Nathan Willing. I like his clothes. I like his cacti. I can even put up with his shoulder blades, which, seriously, can cut your face. But I didn't want him around just right now.

Mostly because I planned on doing unwise Internet stalking, and I knew that Nathan would disapprove. I didn't feel like telling him that, though, and so I went with:

"I'm thinking I'm just going to pass out," I said.

"You could pass out at the Tivoli. They have alcohol."

"Let's just connect tomorrow instead, okay? Vomiting on corpses will really take it out of you."

Which is a line that's hard to argue with.

CHAPTER TWENTY-ONE

When Nathan left and Charice and Daniel retreated to their room, leaving a trail of noodles behind them, I popped open my laptop and took to the searching. Well, eventually, I did that. I did make myself a gin and tonic, which I know is a little like drinking alone, but my feeling is that you can't drink alone when you're on the Internet. Besides which, I went light on the gin and heavy on the tonic.

Searching was a waste of time, however, because Doctor XXX was not connected to anyone. The name had never been used previously, as far as I could tell, never competed in any other tournaments, never had any connection to anyone I had met.

That sounds like striking out, but it actually was a piece of information in and of itself. Someone had created this identity, just for me. And for Imogen, apparently, which was strange. Why? What was the connection between us?

When you have very little information, the bits that you do have are important. And this was important. If I could figure out what Imogen and I had in common, maybe I could make this whole thing unravel.

I logged back in to Twitch TV and started broadcasting again. This time, I actually was playing a little *Hearthstone*, which I

155

find relaxing and helps me think. The usual gang of knuckle-heads were there watching me, and it was nice to have an audience. I did an Arena run as a Paladin this time, winning the first three games in a row. It seemed like I was having a great evening until chat went crazy.

Doctor XXX was back.

"Hey," typed our mysterious doctor. "Do you have a second?"

Twitch chat was like, Girl, no!, but I did have a second. I told Twitch to keep it together, and opened up a private conversation with the doctor.

"So," I typed. Initially it was going to be a prelude into something else, but after I looked at it, I felt like it was salvo enough. I didn't know who I was addressing here—this guy could be anything from a murderer to the fan that sexed up Swan (unlikely, but still hypothetically possible) to some rando that wasn't even in town. "So" would do.

"Okay," typed Doctor XXX, "I'm really sorry about today. Just so you know, I didn't know anything about Karou. In case you got that idea."

Okay, I thought. *So, not completely a rando.* Someone who knew about Karou. Of course, news of Karou's death had probably made the rounds on social media, so it still didn't mean that he couldn't be messaging me from Stratford-upon-Avon or the Antarctica research station. But it made it less likely. I almost told him that the police were looking for him, but this suddenly struck me as a comment that would likely lead to our doctor vanishing again.

"Why are you telling me this?" I asked.

"Because I feel guilty," said Doctor XXX. "I can't imagine anything crueler than sending you to a room with a violently murdered person. It was an accident. I am so sorry."

It seemed an honest enough answer, but I wanted to plug in the only piece of information I had, even if the transition was a little dickish.

"Why are you following Imogen?" I asked.

There was a very long time before there was a reply. So long that I wondered whether I would have been better off with the police angle. I even alt-tabbed over to my regular Twitch chat channel, where people were taking bets on how I would eventually be killed. Twitch chat is sort of my Statler and Waldorf, now that I think about it.

"I can only be killed by a Highlander," I said into camera, which redirected them into a whole different conversation. Like Statler and Waldorf, they were easy to redirect. *Why do we always come here? / I guess we'll never know.*

Doctor XXX didn't vanish, though. He finally responded.

"What?" he typed.

Three minutes for "What?" Either he was very VERY shocked, or he was just multitasking. I pressed further.

"You're only following two people," I typed. "Me and Imogen. LadyBlazer is her username. I was just wandering why."

"I don't know who that is," typed Doctor XXX.

Sure you don't. I clicked on his profile and discovered that now he was only following one person. Me. I guess that explained what he was doing for those three minutes.

It was my turn to take a moment. I could argue with this clown, but what was the point? I wish I had taken a screenshot, but what would I have done with it? Thrown it in his face? To what end? What I really wanted was more information from him.

"Oh," I typed. "I guess I got confused. Do you want to meet tomorrow at the tournament?"

I sent him a link to the *Major Redding*. Admission aboard the boat—in contrast to the hotel—wasn't free. But it seemed unwise to point that out.

"I'll be there if you want to meet up," I typed. "You can explain this problem of yours to me. Be sure to wear that green cap of yours."

And this time, Doctor XXX was gone for good.

I streamed for a little bit more, although clearly I was elsewhere, because I lost the next three games. But the bizarre strangers of the Internet were not done with me, because I got yet another message. From another doctor.

Doctor XY: "Hey babe!"

It was only a matter of time before my problems became a meme, and I ignored this doctor, who I assumed was just a knucklehead having fun.

"Do you know why they call me Doctor XY?"

I also ignored this question, whose answer I assumed involved a penis.

But Doctor XY kept sending me new messages.

"Can you meet me tomorrow at the *Major Redding*? I have a special surprise for you. Something prickly."

Ugh, I moused over to mute the guy and he added:

"You could wear that T-shirt I like. The black one with the pink unicorn that doesn't fit you."

And that got my attention, because I didn't wear that shirt when I streamed precisely because it didn't fit me. I had left it in the dryer a little too long, and I just hadn't gotten around to throwing it away yet.

"Who is this?" I asked.

"Meet me on the main deck of the *Major Redding*. It'll be a surprise."

CHAPTER TWENTY-TWO

I awoke with a sense of hope. In itself, this is probably a mistake. But what can you do? Part of it was that I had slept, which is almost always helpful—to any problem, up to and including comas. Also, I felt better about Daniel and Charice. Still a little anxious—I'll admit that I wasn't entirely on board with friends of mine growing up without me. But I was coming to terms with it. And if I could accept that, probably solving a murder couldn't be that hard.

Still, a sensible person might have said: you know, there are multiple unknown men who are going to meet me aboard a steamboat. One of them may have lured me to find a corpse. Another wants me to wear tightly fitting T-shirts. Maybe, just possibly, this would be a good opportunity to take a sick day.

Can private eyes do that? Did Sam Spade ever just tell a guy, listen, this Maltese Falcon sounds intriguing, but today I'm just staying in bed and watching the Game Show Network? They should be able to do that. The sensible ones would, at any rate.

However, as we have thoroughly established, I am not a sensible private eye. Technically I'm not even a private investigator, but it's fun to say. I got up extra early—so full was my hope— and found Charice making eggs in our kitchen.

Alone.

She was back in Balrog gear, and sure enough had put enough foundation on her bald cap that she was entirely Charice colored.

"Egg?" she asked me.

"Where's Daniel?" I asked.

"I don't know," said Charice. "He said he had some business to take care of."

It was seven thirty in the morning, and I could not possibly imagine what sort of business that might be. Banks were not open yet. Target wasn't even open yet, and it certainly wasn't the right time of day for drug deals. But the difference between Charice and myself was that I was consternated by this mystery and Charice was dreamily scrambling eggs.

I didn't know what to make of Daniel, with his meeting men in bathrooms and disappearing at dawn. I asked Charice:

"So how serious are you about Daniel anyway?"

Having not answered her question about eggs, Charice apparently decided that I did not want one, and sat down at the table with her own breakfast, which she proceeded to cover with inhuman amounts of pepper and shredded cheese.

"Daniel's a blast," she said. "But you know me, I'm not really much of a planner."

Honestly, superhuman amounts of black pepper. If you ate this egg, you could possibly become a superhero with pepper-based powers.

I both wanted to ask more and not ask more. Charice liked saying that she was not a planner, but it was transparently not true. Last week, she had engineered a pillow-fort party that actually involved multiple floors and a Slip 'N Slide. She planned plenty; she just liked to pretend that it happened by accident.

It seemed like the next question would be "So have you and Daniel thought about getting married?" but I didn't want to give Charice the idea. And hell, it was Charice. Maybe they had already gotten married. Maybe they had eloped in the night.

Whatever discomfort I was feeling was completely ignored by her, however. She just ate her egg.

"I'm glad you spent the day with Daniel. I'm glad you had fun," she said. Charice was just glossing over that I hadn't had fun, really, although this wasn't particularly Daniel's fault, even though he did leave me in a room with a corpse.

"You are my best friend," I told Charice. "So please don't move to California."

"Dahlia," she said, "I love your nonsequiturs."

"Yes," I said.

I did not expand upon my reasoning to Charice, which had many parts. They were:

1. Daniel and Charice fall hopelessly in love.
2. They become married or domestically partnered or enter into some kind of Vulcan wedding ritual.
3. Daniel is lured by the call of the greasepaint to New York or California.
4. Charice follows him.
5. I am left alone, and I suppose devolve into some sort of *Grey Gardens* spinsterhood, which doesn't quite work because I was never a socialite, but I'm painting with broad strokes here.

I did not expand upon this reasoning, because it is mostly a stupid reasoning and largely based on irrational fear. Besides which, who's to say I couldn't move to New York or California myself, aside from the fact that apartments in New York are priced and also sized about the same as Faberge eggs. And that California is basically God's sunbaked rebuke of hippies.

But I digress.

Charice's car was, of all things, being detailed. For reasons that were unclear to me—and by unclear, I mean that I did not want to ask—Charice was having fake-wood detailing put on her Scion. Was this some part of her nesting process with Daniel that she wanted her ride to look like grandma's station wagon? Who knows? But it was a thing that was happening, regardless.

So we took a cab instead. And since Daniel was meeting us there, we'd have a ride home. Assuming nothing terrible happened, hahahahahahahahaaha.

The *Major Redding* was much more of a destination than the Endicott. It was a steamboat docked along St. Louis's riverfront. Even just pulling up to it, you felt like you were in for an experience. I wouldn't exactly call an old-timey steamboat geeky, per se, but there was something geek-like about it, at least in its insistence about what it was. It was like a boat doing cosplay—even from a great distance, it looked kooky and weird, and you could see what it was going for.

Charice paid our cabbie, tipping generously, as was her habit, and we made our way toward the dock. Another observation: it was crowded today. I don't know if it had been press from the murder (there's no such thing as bad publicity, right?) or just the natural interest in the finals of the tournament, but there were folks here. Waiting to get in, even.

The line aboard the *Major Redding* snaked beyond a long red-carpet-covered ramp leading to the harbor, and scads of pale, scowling gamers waited in a line. The scene was a lot more luxe than yesterday. The carpet leading to the *Major Redding* was luxe. The air around the *Major Redding* was luxe.

I, for one, kept staring at the boat, which was sort of hypnotic. It looked like the offspring of a luxury liner and a wedding cake. There were so many white arches. And so many layers. It was a beautiful piece of architecture, and I'm sure someone who was knowledgeable about that sort of thing would say something like "an excellent example of antebellum embellisment huma-dah huma-dah huma-dah," but mostly I was wondering if I could break off parts of the arches and eat them.

I don't know why the line was moving so slowly, however, and Charice and I had been there for a while before Tricia and Kyle came up to us.

"Dahlia," Tricia called. Oh, and also Undine, I suppose, because they were walking around with that child carrier again. "You decided to stick it out to day two!"

At the time, I thought that Kyle and Tricia must have been happy to see me, although now that I think back over it, I think mostly that they wanted to break in the line. That's what they managed, anyway.

"Nice Balrog play," said Kyle.

Charice punched him. Not a hard punch, by any means, but not mime either.

"Wow," said Kyle. "Not in the face."

"You guys seem chipper," I said. And they did. There was almost a rosy glow about the two of them. "Undine let you sleep last night?"

"Undine lets us sleep every night," said Tricia.

"Lucky you," I said.

"Eh," said Tricia. "She not at the no-sleeping stage. We'll suffer in a couple of months."

Two thoughts at once. One, it struck me that I really didn't know anything about babies. Well, perhaps not _nothing_ but it certainly wasn't a topic that I should be making small talk on. I'd put it about at my knowledge of African capitals. Cairo, Cape Town, and...I'm out.

The other thought was a dim surprise that Charice wasn't picking this baby up and, I don't know, running off with it as though she were Rumpelstiltskin. But Charice wasn't doing anything. She had removed her gloves and was checking her phone. Aside from the punch, which was pretty half-meant, Charice seemed completely absorbed in her own world.

Probably texting with Daniel.

"You feeling good about your odds today?" I asked Kyle, although Tricia answered.

"I'm feeling great about it," she said. "It was a tragedy about what happened to Karou, but you know, it's working in our favor."

"He would have wanted us to win this money," said Kyle.

"You still stuck with the fourteen-year-old?" I asked Kyle.

"Yeah." He shrugged. "But it could be worse. The kid's not half-bad."

The line breaking continued when Remy joined our group—not immediately, but after a little small talk that I'm neglecting to include. I couldn't tell you what was taking the front of the line so long, though, because there was no movement whatsoever. Maybe everyone was breaking.

"So my mother knows nothing about the murder," said Remy.

"Oh, good," said Tricia. "We were so worried."

"I stole her phone, just in case," said Remy.

"Really?" I asked, getting involved with this kid despite myself.

"Well, not stole. Took. I took her phone. I figured she was less likely to read about the murder if she didn't have it. Also, if she learns about it later and tries to pick me up earlier, it will be hard for her to find me."

The line started moving all at once, and very quickly. Charice looked a bit sad, although she may have been acting, since Balrog was not really known for a sunny disposition.

"I'm surprised that Daniel's not here yet," she observed, which at least answered the question about why she was down.

I wasn't sad about Daniel not being here, because I really wanted to be eliminated from this damned tournament. As a rule, I try to avoid abject humiliation. It's my least-favorite humiliation. And our next match was going to be streamed and commented on. Literally commented on. There would be sportscasters saying things like: "Frank, it looks like Dahlia has no idea what she's doing. Do you think that's possibly a ruse to lure her opponents into overconfidence? / No, Terry, I don't."

"He'll show up," I told her, and really wasn't very concerned about the matter either way.

CHAPTER TWENTY-THREE

Charice had been glumly hoping that Daniel had gotten here ahead of us, but at the registration table our regular redhead—now dressed in a suit—ooh la la!—confirmed that he was still among the missing. Our match was one of the earlier ones of the morning, and I had a bad feeling that we'd get disqualified. Did I type "bad feeling"? I'm sorry, I meant "exuberant feeling."

Regardless, as much I didn't want to lose a match in front of a crowded group of spectators, I wasn't overly rattled about it until I got to the room in which the match was being shown. This was the opposite of yesterday, with its modest little viewing room. It was a damned theater, with seating for maybe a few hundred folks, and it felt huge. Part of it was the bedecked nature of the *Major Redding*, which was everything you could possibly want from a vintage theater. Cream-colored columns, red carpet, lush seating, and my God was there gold paint in there. There was enough gold paint in that room that a Bond villain might plausibly ask: "Too much?"

The person who was not in there, however, was Daniel. In a few minutes, they'd call our names and we'd lose, I supposed, although this was only fitting given how many times we had won by our opponents doing the same thing.

I was feeling smug about when I felt cold metal claws at the back of my neck.

"Charice?" I asked, because who else would sneak up behind me and gently touch the back of my neck with metal claws?

But first I should explain: Vega. In case you don't know who that is, Vega is a *Street Fighter* character who is sort of a cross between the Phantom of the Opera and Wolverine. He wears a white mask with a cursive "V" on it, has a creepy-ass metal claw, and is also kind of wearing a Spanish bolero. Put all together this way it sounds like he should look ridiculous, but in fact the effect is rather alarming, particularly when those claws are at your neck.

"Why did you change costumes, Charice?" I asked, rather hopefully, given the circumstances.

"I didn't change costumes," said Vega. "This is Daniel."

Of course it was. Charice was the only person I could think of who would do something so creepy and awful without any reflexive regret or concern, and now that I knew it couldn't have been her, I should have guessed. It was Daniel, the Other Charice.

"You realize how awful it is for you to sneak up on me this way, given the whole corpse-lure situation, right?"

I would say that Daniel looked chagrined, but he didn't really, given that I couldn't see his face through that white mask. He sounded chagrined, though.

"You know, you're right," said Daniel. "I didn't even think about it. But I'm trying to be secretive."

"Why?"

"Well, if you must know, I've decided to propose to your

roommate." I turned to look at him, I suppose to hug him, but he said, "Just keep looking forward."

"What do you mean just keep looking forward?"

"I'm in disguise," said Daniel. "I didn't want her to see that I was here."

"You're the worst fucking bodyguard. You sneaked up behind me and put a claw at my neck."

"I couldn't cut bread with these," said Daniel.

"This is not the point," I said. And really it wasn't. "Why are you in disguise? Why not just propose to Charice?"

"Well, I thought I was going to do it today—because you know, scenic beautiful steamboat and everything. That's why I wanted to advance to day two—but then she got that Balrog costume, and I felt it would make the moment look all weird. You know, with her dressed up as a *Street Fighter* villain and me not."

"So you could wait until later," I said.

"Or," said Daniel, "I could also dress up like a *Street Fighter* villain. Then we'd match!"

It was simultaneously hard to argue with and also comprehend this logic. As much as I hated the idea of Charice getting hitched, I had to admit that there was insane logic to the two of them together. Although I could only imagine what that wedding was going to be like.

"Isn't she going to know that the gig is up the moment that you play with me?"

"I've taken care of that," said Daniel. "Someone has sent her a distracting message to go off into a storeroom."

This idea was so repellent and obviously in bad taste that I could instantly see how it would appeal to Charice.

"That someone is you?" I asked.

"I have an accomplice," confessed Daniel.

"So if Charice isn't around, why can't you talk to me, then?"

"I'm hedging my bets. Besides, she might come here first to try to pick you up before she heads off on her little mini-adventure."

I was flattered, frankly, that Daniel would think this. But as a rule, Charice did not include me on all of her adventures. Honestly, I'm not even sure that she told me about all of them, which was fine, because they were often deeply illegal.

"Who are we playing, anyway?" asked Daniel.

"That is so not what I'm concerned with right now," I told Daniel. Why should I be? We were so clearly going to be crushed by whoever had fairly fought their way to day two that I wasn't particularly bothered by the open question.

But the question didn't stay open, because Swan came in and sat down next to me.

"Dahlia," he said. "Well, that's awkward."

"Yes," I said. "We've got to stop meeting like this." The joke didn't land any better this time.

CHAPTER TWENTY-FOUR

We've got to stop meeting like this," I told Swan yet again. This is a habit that I've picked up from my father, which is that when jokes fail, you repeat them. I don't know why I've adopted this particular tic, because it hasn't done much for him, but genetics are destiny, I suppose.

Anyway, I don't even think that Swan processed that I was joking.

"I think the odds of us continuing to meet, under any circumstances, are probably pretty low."

This was undoubtedly true.

"Why are you here now?" I asked, having not yet put together the obvious.

But Daniel had, and he moved his claws from my neck to Swan's. He really couldn't be blind to the effect that the claws were having on people, because the responses were far from subtle, and Daniel was no dummy. Swan actually sprang up in his chair.

"He's our opponent," said Daniel. "We must have gotten paired against Swan and Chul-Moo."

I watched Swan's face as Daniel said this, and he gradually calmed as he realized that this Vega was not a demented

Spanish psychopath plotting to kill him. He relaxed only moderately after putting it together.

"Is that Daniel?" he asked.

"Yup," I said. "A little cosplay Vega for ya nerve," I said.

"Who are you supposed to be?" asked Swan, looking at me uncertainly. "Are you...Dolores Claiborne?"

I was, for the record, wearing a black floral-print blouse that I thought looked very lovely, along with peach H&M pants that, honestly, I didn't think looked that lovely, but were really cheap, and looking lovely is overrated. But Dolores Claiborne? What the actual fuck?

"No," I said. "I'm just me," I said. "What the hell?"

"Oh," said Swan. "I don't know why I said that. Never mind."

"Dolores Claiborne? Kathy Bates is, like, sixty years old."

"She was younger when that movie came out," explained Swan.

"These are some next-level mind games," said Daniel. "He's trying to get in your head."

"I'm not!" said Swan.

I preferred the idea, actually, that Swan was being manipulative to the idea that my regular clothing and stature would lead an independent party to think that I was doing Kathy Bates cosplay. But I didn't have a lot of time to spend on the idea, because an organizer came up to us—thankfully not that damned redhead.

Not much to say about the organizer, but I will note that he had a green cap on, which did put him on my radar. Actually, all of the tournament people did today—green ball caps with the words "Dark Alleys" emblazoned in black on them. Was this a clue, or just the universe making fun of me?

"You guys are up next," said the organizer. "Everyone here?"

"Daniel Simone and Dahlia Moss reporting in," said Daniel, taking the initiative. Which was fine, because if the plane is absolutely going down, it really doesn't matter who's at the helm. Things were more serious today, I could tell, because the organizer actually made us show him our IDs, to make sure we weren't ringers, I suppose. Of course, Daniel had a costume on, and I suppose it could have been anyone there. At an EVO fighting tournament, Jamie Lee Curtis, of all people, attended in disguise, also dressed as Vega. So maybe it wasn't about security. Maybe the organizer was A Fish Called Wanda fan who just wanted to double-check. Daniel even took off his mask, very briefly.

"Are you gonna wear that during the match?" asked the organizer, uncertainly.

"Can I?"

"It's your funeral. Where are your fighting sticks?"

"They're being cleaned," I said, which is a lie that I found more fun each time I said it.

"I see," said the organizer. "I suppose we'll have to fish out the joysticks that came with the machine."

While the organizer was thinking about this, Swan presented his ID, which I really should have looked at to figure out what his name actually was, but I didn't have the idea until later.

"Great," said the organizer. "Where's your partner?"

Swan looked concerned. "He hasn't checked in yet? He told me he was coming here first."

"Your partner is Chul-Moo Yoon? No, I haven't seen him."

"That's very strange," said Swan, and eyed me suspiciously. Like I had kidnapped him.

"What are you looking at me for?" I asked.

"Well," said Swan. "All of your opponents yesterday got disqualified for not appearing."

"Not the kindergarteners," offered Daniel, all too happy to remind everyone that he defeated small children in hand-to-hand combat.

"Okay," said Swan. "But everyone else."

"A man got murdered," I said. "I didn't have anything to do with that."

Again I got a suspicious look from Swan, although, who knows, maybe these were just more mind games.

"Listen," I said. "It's not my fault that your partner is running late."

"You're sure he's just running late," said Swan.

"Cheese and crackers," I told him, with the best over-the-top Maine accent I could manage. "I don't know. I don't go around following your partner."

"What does 'cheese and crackers' mean?" asked Swan.

"It means fuck you, Swan. This is not my fault. Just run out and look for your partner. He's probably in the bathroom shitting himself."

I was getting unduly salty, I admit, but it had been a difficult twenty-four hours.

Swan left, but he did not look overly convinced by my suggestion that Chul-Moo was just waylaid. I wanted nothing more than for Chul-Moo to walk through the door, maybe with toilet paper on his foot, at which point I could crow over everyone. But that didn't happen. Swan was gone, Chul-Moo was missing, and rumors that I was some sort of tournament black widow began making the rounds.

"Someone's cranky this morning," observed Daniel. "He's probably just anxious about his match, you know."

"Yeah, well," I said, finding the Kathy Bates within, "sometimes being a bitch is all a woman has to hang on to."

CHAPTER TWENTY-FIVE

We waited around for a while, and I started to get anxious. It was the crowd behind me that was getting to me. I was sure they were all saying things like: "She's the black widow of the tournament! Everyone who faces her is DOOMED!" Probably paranoia, but you know, gamers do love their memes.

"How much time do we have before the match is officially called?" I asked the organizer.

"Twenty-three minutes."

"I'm going to help look for Chul-Moo."

The organizer looked surprised by this idea. "If he shows up while you're gone, you guys will be eliminated."

"I'll be back with seconds to spare," I said. "No worries."

Persuading Daniel to come along on this trip, however, was more challenging.

"I want to get as far at this thing as we can get," he said. And he sounded so determined that I wondered, just for a moment, if he hadn't somehow messaged Chul-Moo himself. I know he'd turned the trick with Charice. Maybe he'd sent them to the same storeroom.

But I didn't ask that, because it's unseemly to accuse your ostensible friends of wrongdoing, unless the friend is

Charice—who is usually flattered by the idea, or guilty. And often both.

Besides which, Shuler had been right. I was being overly suspicious of Daniel. He didn't kill anyone. He didn't kidnap anyone. He's just this dude, you know.

"I'm going to look for him," I said.

"You should stay here," Daniel said. "Look at the audience we're going to have."

And maybe that's what it was. Actors can't resist a good audience? As far as I was concerned, I would have preferred no audience whatsoever. Ideally I'd be playing alone, in a dark hole, she said, hashtag foreshadowing. But I digress.

"I'm going to look for him."

"You do you," said Daniel.

Of course, the moment I left the theater where the match was being held, it became instantly clear to me that I didn't really have an idea how to go about looking for Chul-Moo. It's easy to say detective-y things—"Follow that car! Let's dust for prints! The game's afoot!"—but significantly harder to actually do them.

That said, I was on a steamboat, which is, as these things go, a very finite place. If you took it as a given that all the individual cabins were off-limits, and I think that you must, how many places could Chul-Moo possibly be?

As I stood there and considered my options, I figured that there were two starting points, right?

1. Chul-Moo was someplace normal. So, on a deck somewhere looking out at the river. In the bar. On a deck chair. Pooping. I could make a quick run-through of all the obvious places, aside from the men's rooms, but

assuming that was the case, he'd probably show up on time anyway.

2. Chul-Moo was someplace terrible.

However, it was Detective Shuler who said to me just yesterday that the answer is not always murder, and he was a homicide detective and ought to know. So I went, for now, with the more positive and probably more likely option. Chul-Moo was yukking it up somewhere, probably. I just needed to figure out where.

And actually, a third option entered my mind, which was odd given that the previous options were sort of (1) alive and (2) dead. But I thought, you know, possibly he's not on the boat at all. Probably that meant he was alive, and thus option one, but really the question was nugatory. If he was dead and not on the boat, it was also not my problem. Maybe he had gotten innocently hit by a car or choked on a peach or something. Or, and this was an even better option, he was alive, but not on the boat. The first question to answer wasn't "Alive or not alive?" but "Boat or no boat?"

And that was a question I could figure out.

CHAPTER TWENTY-SIX

Despite the boat's limited occupancy, and the fact that no one, absolutely no one, at this point was waiting in line, the ticket taker at the dock did not seem overly pleased at my presence. He was a blond kid, fair skinned, and gave off the aura that I was keeping him from something important and urgent. Judging from the closed DS at his table, that important and urgent thing was probably *Animal Crossing.*

"You're sure you can't check your sheet to see if my partner, Chul-Moo, is here?" I changed it to being my partner, because that sounded better than "my opponent's partner, whom I would like to locate so that I don't appear to be a villain." Also it's less syllables.

But the notion didn't move him in the slightest.

"I'm sorry, but I can't tell you that," he said. "It's a violation of privacy. Why don't you call him?"

And that was an interesting idea, too, actually. I didn't have Chul-Moo's number, but Swan did. Why didn't Swan call him? Something to ask later, perhaps.

"I did, but he's not picking up," I said, because the best way to improve an iffy lie is to pile on more lies. "I don't know, maybe his phone is out of power." Bullshit comes to me very naturally, which I *think* is a good skill to have, although not one that you usually list on résumés. "Can you please just help me out?"

"It's a violation of privacy," repeated the blond kid. "I'm sorry."

And he didn't sound sorry in the slightest. He sounded positively irritated that I hadn't taken a hike yet. And yet the information I was looking for was right there—old-school, even. He had a white notebook, the kind that people would sign at a wedding, which was clearly being used to check off the names of all the people on board. A ship's registry, maybe? Who knows?

"This tournament is everything to me," I said, going toward fake sobbing and missing the mark considerably. This is not to say that I was hammy—just the opposite. Apparently I am incapable of expressing genuine emotion. I didn't sound sad in the slightest. Or even honest.

"Yeah, I can't—" started the blond, and hell with it, I just reached over and took the book.

This was clearly not a possibility that the blond had anticipated, because he stared at me openmouthed, even as I ran off. I was a good ten feet away when he yelled:

"Bring that back! I'll get in huge trouble if I lose it."

"I'll bring it back, I promise!" I shouted.

Anyway, all of this is a testament to the power of not being overly tactful.

I skittered down the deck, and came to an open lounge area, which actually was a great place to look for Chul-Moo, if I were going to do that next. Lots of people, sofas, and brass lighting. Also, wallpaper to die for in here.

No Chul-Moo in here, though. Also no Swan. Was Swan

really looking for his teammate? Or maybe Swan had already found him and they were waiting for us at the tournament now. More questions for later.

I opened the book.

But I wasn't able to get very far, because suddenly there was Tricia and Undine.

"Isn't this lounge great?" said Tricia. "I mean, look at this wallpaper."

The wallpaper really had been of note, but I was right at the cusp of figuring something out, and I was on a twenty-minute timer and did not have time for Tricia's decorating tips.

"It's great," I said. "But I'm busy."

"Listen, Dahlia," said Tricia, really sidling up to me. This was a Charician sort of sidle, the kind people use when they want something and are not ashamed of letting you know that right up front. I was prepared to object immediately, but I knew this sort of face. I didn't have to acquiesce to whatever Tricia wanted, but I was certainly going to have to let her ask me.

"What do you want?" I asked. And then, taking a second to observe her, added, "And why are you wearing different clothes?"

"Just a different shirt," said Tricia. Tricia had been wearing a relatively subdued outfit earlier—a green T-shirt that said "Dark Alleys" on it and was maybe early bird swag from the event yesterday, but was now wearing a gauzy zebra-print blouse that was not entirely opaque, and through which I could see her bra strap. Whether she was more dressed up or dressed down now was hard to say.

"Why did you change clothes?" I asked.

"Undine threw up on me," said Tricia. "Beyond throw up,

really. It was next-level vomiting. I had to change. Anyway, I need to go back to the bathroom. And also maybe get a drink."

"Those are different things."

"Well, I need a drink because I got covered in vomit, and I would like to go to the bathroom, because I think maybe there's some throw up in my shoes. Just don't ask."

"You're not going to ask me to watch Undine again, are you?"

"Oh, thank you," said Tricia, not waiting for a yes or no. "You're just the best."

"Wait, wait. Why can't you bring her with you?"

"I could technically, but I feel like it's wrong to order a drink while holding a baby. People are judge-y about that sort of thing."

"You really need a drink that badly?"

"There was vomit in my hair." Tricia gestured to her hair, which was, it had to be noted, wet in places.

"Fine," I said. "But if you see Chul-Moo in the bar, tell him I'm looking for him."

"Why are you looking for him?" asked Tricia again. "What's with you and that guy?"

"Nothing," I said. "Just tell him he has a match. And what do I do if Undine throws up again?"

"Oh," said Tricia, with a dismissive wave. "She's not going do that. She can't possibly have anything left in her."

Undine, for her part, who I observed had also changed clothes, was now sleeping as though she were some sort of blessed cherub. Her tiny little frame bobbed up and down.

"I've got a match in, like, ten minutes," I told her. "If you're not back in time, I'm taking her with me."

"I'll be superfast," said Tricia.

This would not prove to be true, although she did at least mime speed walking at me as she left the lounge. Tricia was, quite clearly, a strange lady, but I didn't have enough experience with mothers to know whether her penchant for pawning her baby off to strangers was part of the weirdness or just the normal reactions of a woman that has been thrown up on.

I was less nervous having Undine this time than last, and I pulled her baby carrier up to the sofa, and said:

"Okay, Undine. Let's go through this registry together."

Undine farted quietly, which I took to mean yes.

The registry was in two parts—people who had prepaid and were being checked off, and everyone who paid the morning of. Chul-Moo surely was in the previous group, and so I scanned the list for his name. I even knew his last name now—Yoon—and so it was quick work to find him.

And also to discover that he was among the very first people here. So: Chul-Moo was on the boat.

Hooray, detecting!

The next question was: Where the hell was he?

I waited exactly five minutes for Tricia to come back, but I really disliked the idea of missing my matchup because I'd wandered off. I guess Daniel was starting to rub off on me, because although we were certain to be crushed, I sort of wanted to see it through. I suppose he sold me on the idea. It was better to fight and get crushed than to never fight at all. Or something like that.

So I picked up Undine's baby carrier and headed back toward the theater, where I hoped that Chul-Moo was waiting for me.

Sort of. I felt a little like I was kidnapping a baby, but I did warn her where I was going, so it wasn't really kidnapping. It was mobile babysitting.

Maybe I'm weak, but Undine's baby carrier was a lot heavier than I expected it to be. Carrying her reminded me of the week and a half in junior high in which I played bari-sax. Which was fun, but caused me to teeter around the halls of the school in a lopsided and scoliosis-forming way. I was doing that now, along the deck, and I felt the process would have gone much better if I had been holding a bari-sax now in my other hand. For balance.

It is a truth universally acknowledged that a woman in possession of a small kidnapped infant who is also late for a fighting-game event is in want for a person to delay her on the side of a steamboat. No, wait. Just the opposite of that actually.

"You're not wearing the unicorn shirt," someone yelled out at me.

I really didn't have time for this discussion, but I was able to deduce two things quite quickly from this outburst.

1. The person yelling this at me was Doctor XY, potential lurker.

And also:

2. This was Nathan's voice. Which meant that I had found my lurker.

"What the fuck, Nathan?" I said, turning.

Nathan, for his own part, seemed mostly surprised by the fact that I was holding a large plastic basket that had Undine in it.

"Where did you get a baby?"

"I'm watching her. Why are you here?"

Nathan ran to catch up to me, and he had this light, airy sort of trot, that was actually a little mesmerizing. He moved like a pony, an enchanted one, that sang songs and galloped but still floated over the ground. When I run, I pound the ground as though my feet yearn for the destruction of the earth. He was also dressed unusually for him, in a black leather jacket I'd never seen before and red corduroy pants that were new, too, although the cords were definitely a go-to look.

When he reached me, he smiled and said, "I wanted to watch you play. And plus there were death threats, which seemed like the sort of thing I should be around for. I can be your bodyguard."

"I have a bodyguard," I said, which was stupid, because it just led to this opening:

"Oh, where is he?"

"I'm not sure," I told him. "Probably at this match that I'm late for."

I should have just started walking, and then Nathan and I could have done a walk-and-talk, like they do on Aaron Sorkin shows. But I didn't, probably because of the baby, which Nathan had knelt down in front of and was cooing at.

"Who is this cute little child?" asked Nathan. "Boy or girl?"

"Her name's Undine. Listen, I gotta get moving. And did you send me a mystery message telling me you would meet me in a storeroom?"

"I didn't think it was that much of a mystery. I assumed you knew it was me all along."

"No," I said. "And that's very creepy."

"I told you I had a prickly surprise," said Nathan. "Who else would it be?"

"Some sort of murderer? Maybe the prickly surprise is a deadly poisonous puffer fish."

"See," said Nathan, "you say you don't want a bodyguard, but then you have theories like that. I'm here to take that puffer fish hit for you."

I started walking, lugging Undine along with me. Jesus, she was heavy. If I ever was going to become a parent—years from now, reader, years and years from now, if that happens at all—I was going to need to start working out. Mommy better get swole.

Nathan tagged after me, not offering to carry this thousand-pound baby.

"The thing is, Nathan, there is no deadly puffer fish. You're the puffer fish."

"Are you angry about it?" asked Nathan.

And it struck me, suddenly, that perhaps I was. My mood wasn't being improved by the fact that I was holding a baby carrier that was apparently made of lead, or yttrium, or some other impossibly heavy metal. But I sort of was, actually.

"It was a little thoughtless of you to jerk me around like that. Why not just say: 'Hey, it's Nathan. See you tomorrow,' like people do."

"Well," said Nathan. "I suppose that's fair." Although he was using the tone of voice of someone who did not think that it was fair. He was using the tone of voice of someone who thought it was not fair at all.

"As long as we don't want to 'jerk each other around,'" said Nathan, "how about not telling me that you're exhausted and aren't up for anything, and then stay up and stream for three hours immediately after I leave."

"You watched my stream?" I asked.

"I got an alert that you started streaming before I even made it out of your building. I was still in the elevator! Which is fine. You could just say, 'Hey, Nathan, I'm planning on streaming some tonight.' You know, like people do."

We had made it to the theater, which was great on the one hand, but also a little awkward, because it meant that my discussion with Nathan was ending on a very unresolved note. But it was definitely ending because Daniel leaped out of his chair—still wearing his scary mask and claws—and grabbed Nathan in a hug.

Yeah, Daniel knew exactly how scary he was looking. This was not Charice's fella by accident.

"What is happening?" asked Nathan.

"It's me, Daniel!"

"This is your bodyguard?"

"Yes," I said. "He has claws for stabbing. And he can double-jump off walls. You know, in case that's relevant."

Why I was wasting *Street Fighter* humor on Nathan, I'll never know.

"Thank God you're back. We're going to win again!" said Daniel.

"I didn't realize you guys played this game," said Nathan.

"Our opponents have gone missing again," I said. "I don't even see Swan anymore."

"We're like the Bermuda Triangle of fighting-game players," said Daniel, who was back to emitting deadly radiation levels of happiness. How long was the half-life on this thing?

But Daniel and Nathan were having a dialogue of their own.

"Do you mean that entirely natural, explainable weather patterns that exist around the two of you have been exaggerated by the media in a sensationalistic way?"

"No, I mean we have hoodoo," said Daniel. "Voodoo, even. Possibly juju."

Nathan's response was classically him—he was definitely the Scully in our relationship, although I'm not actually Fox. Maybe a contestant on *The Bachelor*. One of those fodder girls who inexplicably seem to be on the show despite obviously never having seen it. That's me! But I digress. Nathan had a point. It was an accidental point, but even so, he was right about the media. I could see it on the face of the organizer. Our opponents were dropping like flies. It was suspicious.

"We can compare notes on magic rhyming words later," I told the guys. "Let's get this round settled first."

"Sure," said Daniel. "And why do you have a baby?"

I explained the business with Undine to Daniel, who took her presence with good grace, although he didn't go in for cooing. Nor did Swan, who showed up looking frazzled and tired and completely without his partner.

"Is he here? Did you see him?" asked Swan.

"No," I told him. "But he was on the boat earlier."

Swan's face scrunched up at me suspiciously. "How do you know that?" Any goodwill he had had toward me for busting him out of that utility closet yesterday had completely faded.

"I checked the ship's registry. He's here. Or he was."

"I can't fucking believe this," said Swan. "Am I cursed? Is this a freaking curse?"

"Maybe it's us that's cursed," offered Daniel. I wouldn't have suggested this, given that Swan seemed suspicious of us already, but maybe it was the right thing to say, because he looked relaxed by the idea.

"Do you know how much my plane ticket out here was? It's just all thrown away."

I had a few thoughts on this topic, none of which I shared with Swan, but I'll mention to you now. First of all, if least importantly, a trip to St. Louis is never a waste of time. It's a great town! Have fun here! And besides which, dude, you're on a steamboat. How much more picturesque do you want to be?

"Don't be sad," I told him. "Look, cheer up! Here's a baby!"

Swan looked at the baby skeptically, as though he were regarding a rival. "Hello, Undine," he said, coolly. "We meet again."

This is a ridiculous way to greet a twelve-day-old—I'm sorry, thirteen-day-old person, but Swan was cornering the market on ridiculous behavior. I couldn't help but notice that although he seemed angry, he didn't seem angry at Chul-Moo, which I thought was very curious. He was angry at me, or the situation, or Undine, whom I suppose he had met yesterday sometime, but he wasn't cursing out his partner. I'd probably curse at Daniel plenty if he stood me up, and I didn't even want to win. "So what do you think happened to Chul-Moo?" I asked, venturing for the direct approach.

"What do you think happened to him?" asked Swan, vaguely accusatory. I took this neutrally, perhaps because I still had a baby, which tends to make you not sweat the small things.

"Well," I said carefully, surprised by how much audience I was being given by Daniel and Nathan. They were giving me the sort of looks reserved for the moment when the detective puts everything together. I appreciated the vote of confidence, but I wasn't quite there yet, fellas. "I'm wondering if he isn't naked in a utility closet somewhere."

"That's ridiculous," said Swan. "I wouldn't put him in a broom closet."

And that was a very weird response.

"I wouldn't think you did," I told him. "I would have guessed that it was your lady of the night. Maybe she also works mornings."

Swan seemed to recognize that he had made a gaffe, but he didn't acknowledge it any way other than to talk faster.

"Chul-Moo's just not that kind of guy," said Swan. "He wouldn't go in for that. Anyway, I'm going to go look for him. Maybe I'll take your advice about the closets, though."

And he shot out of there like a rocket. He didn't even speak to the organizer to explain what was going on.

"Have you figured out the case?" asked Nathan after he left. "You're making a really great 'I've solved the case' face."

"I haven't," I told him. "But I'm starting to get some ideas."

CHAPTER TWENTY-SEVEN

Since Swan hightailed it, I took it upon myself to explain to the organizer what was happening, because we couldn't all ignore him. I was glad that yesterday's redhead was not on hand to admonish us for our progress through the tournament, because I was feeling bogus enough about it already. The guy on hand was very formal, displaying not the slightest reaction, favorable or unfavorable, as he entered us as the round winners into the logbook. However, we were in a crowded room this time, and the audience was none too pleased. I could hear the rumblings. For one, they had hoped to watch a match—and this news meant no match—and for another, well, this was the kind of rumor that gamers love to spread. Rookie female fighter wins tournament when all of her opponents mysteriously disappear? One more match of this and I was going to be on the front page of reddit.

Daniel, however, was as buoyed at ever. He'd probably love to be on the front page of reddit, actually. He was definitely someone who knew how to make the most of an opportunity. I had expected him to say something else congratulatory to me, because he had a smug look on his face, but he said quite the opposite:

"You know, this rash of winning is becoming a little inconvenient."

"Yes," I said, glancing out at the sea of frowns in the stadium seating before us. "I know what you mean."

"I was planning to retreat with Charice for the rest of the day," said Daniel, "but now we've got another engagement."

"What do you mean engagement?"

"We're scheduled for another match in forty minutes. I'm actually thinking about blowing this one off. Would you hate me terribly?"

This was a surprising thing for Daniel to want, given my interactions with him so far, which had had an improbable sort of *Blue Dragon* "I will not be defeated!" quality to them.

"I wish you'd been this willing to walk away yesterday," I said. "What's changed?"

"Charice is here today," said Daniel. "Plans are afoot."

"Daniel is going to propose," I told Nathan, who seemed to have a question lodged in his forehead.

"Ah," said Nathan. "Congratulations!"

"No congratulations, not yet," said Daniel. "Not until after she says yes."

"She'll say yes," Nathan said. "She's all over you."

"We'll see," said Daniel. "I've lured her into a broom closet, but I know that she won't stay in one place for long."

And Daniel dashed off. I didn't want to stay in a room of gamers that appeared to be grumbling about me, and so I decided we should follow after him, albeit slowly. Nathan tagged along with me, and I realized that he was basically going to be hanging around me for the rest of the day. Which wasn't bad, just unexpected.

"Why is Charice in a broom closet?" asked Nathan, who

had a talent for asking reasonable questions and not letting the insane pass by without comment.

"She doesn't know that Daniel is cosplaying, and he wants to get the jump on her."

"I see," he said, although I wasn't sure that he entirely did. "So what are we doing now? What's the next step in solving the case?"

I did not know what the next step in solving the case was. I wasn't entirely sure there was a case. Someone murdered Karou, sure, and someone sent me a mysterious message. There wasn't a case; there was an asshole. I surely didn't need to go around unmasking every possible asshole in the world.

"I don't know what the next step in solving the case is," I told Nathan. "But I know what the next step in life is."

"Ooh," said Nathan. "That sounds even more inviting. What's the next step in life?"

"We have to get rid of this baby."

Jeez, when I type it out like that, it looks a little sinister. "We have to get rid of this baby." Like I'm going to drown her in a sink. I just want it to go on record here and now that this is not the plan. This ain't Gillian Flynn, folks. I just mean give Undine back to Tricia or Kyle, or if they are not available, a responsible-looking adult. Like a wandering nanny with a magical umbrella, should that come along.

Anyway, I walked along the deck, which had a lovely view of East St. Louis, which sounds like it should be a joke, but actually wasn't. The view would have been lovelier, undoubtedly, if there were magical nannies filling the sky, but it wasn't half-bad.

"Whose baby is this?" asked Nathan. Ah, Nathan, with the logical questions.

"There's a woman named Tricia who had a bathroom emergency."

"Do you know this woman?"

I did not, in all honesty, know Tricia. I actually wasn't sure what her last name was, which really ought to be a thing one knows about a woman whose baby you are carrying around. I mentioned this to Nathan.

"I think that's very, very odd," said Nathan. "It's practically suspicious."

"I don't know about that," I said. I felt I ought to stand up for Tricia, for some reason, although Nathan was probably right. I probably wouldn't have given my baby to Tricia, had our roles been reversed, and of course I somehow had a baby.

"I would pee with the baby," said Nathan.

"Maybe it's more dire than that."

"How dire can it be? It's a baby. All she does is poop and pee, really. It's not like you're going to offend Undine's delicate sensibilities."

"Maybe Tricia's gone into the bathroom to snort a line of cocaine."

"Eh," said Nathan. "You could still bring the baby for that."

It's comments like this that undoubtedly make Nathan Willing seem like a great candidate for fatherhood. I envisioned him dragging a small infant into a poop-smeared men's room, peeing with one hand, holding a baby with the other, and snorting a line of cocaine off the top of the urinal while ducking his head. It could be worse—at least he could multitask.

Finding Tricia, however, was slightly harder than I had imagined. I checked the bar, and there was no sign of her. I went to the women's restroom, perhaps a bit improbably, and she also was not there, although I did just yell out her name, as opposed to looking under every stall. This disquieted me, not because I thought she had been murdered—although, lately that is becoming my go-to thought for a missing person—but because I was fairly certain that she was on the other side of the ship, looking for me, and probably getting increasingly angry and/or anxious about the disappearance of her child.

"You look troubled," said Nathan, and this was putting a fine face on it. There was something basically thunderous about Tricia, and I'm not just talking about her bulk and size, but something fundamental. She was one of those people who were cheerful and affable up until they weren't.

"We've got to get this woman her baby back," I said, "before she goes Mama Grizzly."

"You told her that you had to go play," said Nathan.

This was both a reasonable and profoundly unhelpful thing to say, although I didn't have time to process it. Probably I was overreacting. But I didn't dwell on that either, much because it became apparent to me that the boat was in motion. The *Major Redding* was on the move.

"Are we taking off? Is that supposed to be happening?"

"Of course it's supposed to be happening. Why do you think the tickets were seventy-five dollars and there was a strict occupancy limit?"

I suppose I was more concerned about the murder and the multiple people threatening to meet with me. "Where are we going?" I asked Nathan.

"Just down a town and back," said Nathan. "Enjoy the ride. It'll be great for Daniel's plan."

"It seems so wasteful," I said. "Gamers aren't going to care about this."

"Some of them might," said Nathan. "Besides, they have to do it. It was a Kickstarter stretch goal when they crowdfunded the game. I bet they never imagined that wealthy benefactors would call their bluff."

It was all very vacation-like, but I found it unnerving that Nathan, who hadn't really been paying very much attention to the case, seemed to have a better idea of what was going on than I did.

"Enjoy the view, Dahlia. Let the calming currents of the Mississippi relax you."

It did relax me, improbably enough. Of course, part of the relaxation was the idea that Tricia would be calmed by the idea that Undine and I had to be on the boat, and so if she couldn't find us in the moment, what's the big deal? And I don't know why I was quite so prepossessed with the idea that Tricia was going to be angry with me—she practically forced this baby on me. I was probably thinking of my own mother, who was the sort of person who might pick up and throw a car to save one of her children. I did not want anyone throwing cars at me.

And then, all of a sudden, there was Charice. And the relaxation, such as it was, was over.

CHAPTER TWENTY-EIGHT

Dahlia," said Charice. "You won't believe what just happened to me!"

"You were lured into a broom closet, and then stood up?"

Charice's jaw dropped, and, man, she could do a good jaw drop. Snakes who can eat their prey whole could take a lesson from her. But it wasn't something you saw much of, because she was tough to surprise.

"How on earth did you come up with that?"

"I have a good idea who sent you that message."

Charice, in contrast to Nathan, Daniel, and any sensible person, did not ask me why I was walking around with a baby; although, she noticed the baby, because she bent down and started cooing at her. She stopped being shocked and focused her efforts on Undine, whom she had entirely failed to notice in line with Kyle and Tricia. Boy, she was making up for it now. Charice and babies. There was a thought I wanted to put out of my head.

"Who is this angel you have with you?" she asked.

I was disappointed by this turn, because I wanted to bask in my powers of detection. But no one was having it.

"It's a baby Dahlia kidnapped," said Nathan.

"I didn't," I said. "She was thrust into my arms."

"It was a Moses situation," continued Nathan. "She came drifting down the river. Dahlia is protecting her from angry pharaohs."

"Nothing Nathan says is true."

"Hyperbole!" shouted Nathan.

He was so over-the-top about it that I nearly missed the phone alert I had set up earlier, which was a nice little chip-tune melody that was challenging to hear over his yelling.

"Wait," I said. "Do you know what that sound means?"

"Commissioner Gordon is calling?" asked Charice.

"Our time is up?" ventured Nathan.

"Doctor XXX is streaming. He's not just watching now. He's actually streaming. We can get a visual."

I whipped out my phone and opened up the Twitch app. Charice and Nathan were super interested now, and it even felt like Undine was in on the action, although I'm probably projecting that because her eyes were closed.

In front of me was a white guy, about my age, with a magnificent beard and great hair. Short on the side and with kind of a pompadour on the top. That sounds a little silly to type out, but he looked amazing. He was wearing a maroon V-neck sweater with a navy dress shirt. He was dapper and did not look especially threatening. Another reason he wasn't threatening: The tables had turned; now he was the one broadcasting, and I was the unseen typist showing up in his chatroom. Which felt great.

"Louise," said Doctor XXX. "I thought if I started streaming, you'd show up. I'm so glad I don't have to just keep droning on while I wait for you."

First thing: accent. Doctor XXX was British. I was pretty sure it was real, because it was very particular and not overdone. He sounded a bit like Stephen Merchant, actually, which is prob-ably some regionalism that I don't quite get the details of. But regardless, it wasn't the accent an American would do if you were going to fake a British accent.

"Glad to see you," I typed. "I wanted to meet with you today, actually. I had a few questions about yesterday."

"Well, that's it, isn't it?" said Doctor XXX. "We can't really meet because I'm on the other side of the world, actually."

I had been fooled recently enough by someone faking an accent, so I was bound and determined to check everything here.

"I see," I typed. "So where are you, actually?"

"You haven't heard of it, probably. The South East Dorset conurbation?"

Again, this was a very particular answer.

"South East Dorset what?"

"Conurbation."

"Is that even a real word?" asked Nathan, watching over my shoulder. "Ask him if that's a real word."

I typed Nathan's question, such as it was.

"Of course it's a real word," responded Doctor XXX. "What kind of a question is that?"

"What time is it there?" I asked.

"Three forty-seven," said Doctor XXX.

"Hmm," I typed. "I'll have to check that later."

"I anticipated that you might be suspicious," said Doctor XXX, whose Britishness seemed to expand and expand, like an invasive plant species. "Anything else you'd like to ask me?"

"Yes," I said. "Take me outside," I said. "I want to see the sun in the sky."

Nathan looked impressed. "Dag, Dahlia."

I shrugged.

"Unfortunately, there's not much sun today, but I'll show you the clouds. How's the weather in St. Louis?"

Cloudless. The weather was completely cloudless here. It was drizzling a bit on Doctor XXX, which was beginning to make it look more and more like he really was a round-the-world rando. Anyway, he shuffled around outside some more, and the camerawork was making me a bit nauseated. I was going to tell him that I believed him and to pack it in when he had another great idea.

"Wait," said Doctor XXX. "I've got it. Take a look at this vehicle registration plate."

And he focused the camera on a license plate that was yellow and had an EU sticker on it, and was obviously not American. It was a nice detail, although it was the fact that I observed traffic behind him traveling in the "wrong" lanes that really sealed the deal for me.

"Yeah, okay," I said. "So you're British. Why were you jerking me around?"

"Yes, I feel a bit sheepish about that, actually," said Doctor XXX. "Fun, really. I was just trolling a bit. Someone told me you were a geek detective, and I thought it would be fun to play around with you a tad. But I didn't know anything about a murder, and I don't want to get involved in that. Very unlucky."

"How did you hear I was a detective?"

"You know," he said. "I don't remember, really."

"Was it Wilbur?" I asked. "Did he tell you?"

"I don't know anyone named Wilbur. But it doesn't matter, really. Anyway, I ought to be going now. There's a television program I'd like to watch."

"Why are you following Imogen?"

"Just someone else to troll? Anyway, must be going now. Good luck with your detectiving."

And he was gone, as quickly as he had arrived.

"Who's Wilbur?" asked Nathan.

Traps like this always look amazing when detectives employ them successfully. But the corollary to this is that you look like a moron when you try one out that doesn't work.

"Just a name I made up," I said. "I was hoping to catch him out. Like he would say, 'Oh yes, it was definitely Wilbur,' and I'd say, 'Aha! That's where I've got you! There is no Wilbur.'"

"And then he'd say, 'Drat! Your fiendish trap has caught me! I'm embroiled in a web of my own lies!' I like it," said Nathan.

Yes, that was exactly what I wanted. More's the pity.

"So," said Charice. "At least we know that Doctor XXX isn't trying to kill you. I wonder who sent that message to me. Maybe it was Doctor XY?"

"No," said Nathan. "That was me. I mean, I'm Doctor XY. I didn't send you a message."

"Oh," said Charice, unconcerned by this confession. "What Doctors do we have left?"

"Two things," I said, and I was beginning to feel more confident now. "One: I know who your Doctor is, but I'm sworn to secrecy."

"Ooh," said Charice. "That gives me a pretty good clue. What's thing number two?"

"That guy who just spoke to me? I buy that he's in the South East Dorset Conservation."

"Conurbation."

"Right. Because who would make that up? But he's not Doctor XXX."

"How do you know that?" asked Nathan.

And I really wished I had a better answer, but I didn't. What I had was a hunch, a feeling in my bones. I felt like there was a clue somewhere that I had missed, but I couldn't put my finger on it just yet.

"I don't quite know it yet," I said, "although I've got some strong clues in that direction."

"He was definitely in England," said Charice. "We can agree on that."

"Yes, but I was streaming at midnight last night. Which meant that he was up at four a.m."

"Maybe he works the night shift," considered Charice.

"Maybe," I said. "And maybe he happened to get up at exactly the right time to catch me in the afternoon. Maybe he's some kind of zombie that doesn't require sleep at all. But I think it's more likely that Doctor XXX is someone else here at this tournament, and maybe this conurbation clown is just some friend he got to throw me off the trail."

"I love it when you say suspicious things," said Nathan. This sounded almost like a joke, but it wasn't. Nathan did love it when I said suspicious things. He enjoyed mysteries, at least as long as they didn't involve anyone shooting at me.

"It's not entirely suspicious. It's logical. Did you notice how he didn't want to talk to me when I started asking him questions that only Doctor XXX would know? When we were talking about proving his location, he had all the time in the world."

"So, what's the plan?" asked Charice.

The plan. What I would really like to do would be to look through all of my correspondence with Doctor XXX. And maybe I would do that later. But there were more pressing plans first.

"Before anything," I said, "I've got to get rid of this baby."

"Gotcha," said Charice. "You want to give me any clues as to who my broom closet captor is?"

"It's a pleasant surprise," I told her.

"Ooh," said Charice. "How about a location?"

"Just make yourself visible, and the surprise will find you," I told her. I really wanted to add, "Congratulations," which I include here to show how generous and magnanimous I am, but I didn't, just because I didn't want to give away Daniel's game. Charice, for all her frivolity, is whip smart when you get down to it.

"Well, I do love making myself visible," said Charice. "Toodles." And she literally backdashed away. Like I was going to jump in at her.

"Hey," said Nathan. "I'm sorry about before. I'm not good at this detective stuff. Sometimes I have a hard time seeing the line between improbable and insane."

"It's fine," I said. "Maybe we should follow Charice," I said. "I kind of want to see her be proposed to. Is that weird?"

"I don't think it's weird," said Nathan. "But I think you ought to let her have her moment. Besides," said Nathan, "I have a present for you."

"It's not a cactus, is it?"

"It is a cactus," said Nathan. "How did you guess?"

"Nathan," I said. "You've got stop with the cacti. Did you buy them in bulk at some point?"

"I just like giving you plants," said Nathan.

"But I don't want plants," I said.

Nathan took this as a natural cue to produce said cactus, which was tiny but somehow looked especially dangerous, with formidable spines and no flowers to speak of.

"The Opuntia glochid," said Nathan. "I thought you might appreciate this one. Be careful. It's very prickly." Nathan coughed. "Like someone I know."

I looked at the cactus in front of me, and at Nathan, the strange boy who was holding it. He was remarkably pleased by this development, so much so that I felt obligated to take it.

"What am I supposed to do with this thing?" I asked. "I can't walk around with a cactus all day."

"It's not that big," said Nathan. "You could put it in your purse. It's not like you don't have weirder things in there."

"What could be weirder than a cactus?"

Nathan had worked out this gambit in advance, obviously, because he had an answer at the ready. "A cassette tape of the best of Belinda Carlisle?"

"Alden gave me that," I said, although my brother actually hadn't given me the cassette in question. I was just making him my fall guy. "And my car still plays cassettes. It's hard to find them anymore."

"I'm just saying a cactus will fit right in," said Nathan. "Besides," he said, "if anyone attacks you, you can hit them with it."

"Fine," I said, shoving it into my purse. Actually, I'm using the verb 'shoving' here because it described my mood, but in fact I handled the cactus very carefully. "I accept your glochid of apology, but no more cacti, Nathan. I mean it."

"Yes," he said idly. "We should transition to something else. Perhaps small fruit trees."

"I'm ninety percent sure you're joking right now," I said, "and I'm just not going to acknowledge the other ten percent."

"You know," said Nathan, "this boat is not that big. I'm surprised this baby's mother hasn't found you yet."

This was a fair point. And yes, of course, my mind went to Tricia getting murdered, because apparently that's just what I do now. If Tricia and Kyle were somehow both to get killed, then I would be responsible for this infant forever, which seemed, however improbable, entirely terrifying.

"Okay," I said. "Here's the plan. We find Tricia. I take a moment to look over my conversations with Doctor XXX, and after that—"

"After that, fruit trees and model trains."

CHAPTER TWENTY-NINE

I made it back to the bar and found that Tricia was having a drink. She was kicked back—in a comfy-looking brown leather chair in the corner, and looking torn between twin desires of wanting to drink and wanting to have a nap. She did not look like she was terribly concerned how her husband was doing in today's tournament. She also decidedly did not look like someone who was concerned about a missing baby.

"Great," she said. "You're back."

I felt like I should chastise her somehow, but I wasn't sure for what, and this is usually a good sign that you don't have the moral high ground.

"You get your whole vomit situation resolved?" I asked her.

Tricia was looking wet and clean. Literally, her hair was wet and slicked back, as if she had washed it in a sink somewhere. This was actually a much better look for her, than frazzled and dry, but that's an observation just between the two of us.

"Clean as a whistle," she told me. "Who's your friend?"

"Undine didn't give me any trouble," I said, feeling that this question ought to have been asked, and as it wasn't, I would answer it anyway. Nathan and Tricia just ignored me, however.

"Nathan Willing," said Nathan. "I'm Dahlia's tentative squeeze."

"Everyone's gotta start somewhere," said Tricia. "Thanks for watching Undine for me. If you see Kyle or Remy, tell them to check in. I don't have the energy to keep up with them today."

And then Tricia rested.

We retreated. The bar would have been a great place to go over my computer conversations with Doctor XXX, but I wanted a little privacy, and I felt that if I did that stuff in front of Tricia, she was going to want to make small talk with me the whole time. So we headed out along the deck and found a nice spot with some white wicker furniture and a glass coffee table that looked like it had been ripped from the pages of *Southern Living*.

It was a pretty scene. And Nathan was right, it wasn't being completely ignored by the gaming crowd. There were people out here, watching the sun set and warding off mosquitos. Not as many as there were inside watching the game, but it was still a scene. There have certainly been worse Kickstarter goals.

I opened my computer and started looking through my conversations with this Doctor. I felt like there had to be some kind of clue in there. I looked through who he was following again, and read the conversations aloud with Nathan, who performed the Doctor's voice in a preposterous British accent.

"I know this is going to sound forward," he said, "but I was wondering if you could come to the Endicott Hotel in St. Louis tomorrow."

"The British voice is not helping me. It makes him seem more British."

"Excuse me there, gov'nah—just wondering if you could come to the Endicott Hotel in St. Louis tomorrow, wot wot."

"Are you listening to me?"

"I am," said Nathan. "I just needed to get it out of my system."

I was irritated with Nathan. Moderately, not significantly so, but I had to give him that his British performance of the Doctor's dialogue had put me in exactly the right frame of mind for detective work.

I'll cut out the irrelevant dialogue—although, Nathan and I went through the whole thing—several times—and cut straight to the clues.

"Why are you telling me this?" I asked Nathan.

"Because I feel guilty," said Doctor Nathan. "I can't imagine anything crueler than sending you to a room with a violently murdered person. It was an accident. I am frightfully sorry."

"He didn't say 'frightfully,'" I said.

"I was editorializing a little bit there," said Nathan. "I'm getting bored. Dreadfully bored. A spot of boredom."

I really wanted to thwack him now, perhaps with a cactus, but all of these Briticisms gave me a thought.

"How did he spell 'crueler'?"

"Correctly."

"Correctly, how?"

"I don't understand the question. He used letters, and the like, not emoji or anything."

"Spell it."

"C-R-U-E-L-E-R?"

"So he used the American spelling?" I asked.

"There's a British spelling for 'crueler'?"

"There is. Wot, wot."

"That's a nice little discovery," said Nathan. "But what does it mean?"

I was actually weirdly excited by my little mini-revelation, even as I accepted its limits. Yes, it was technically possible that the Doctor had taken to using American spellings while messaging me, but why? And to catch such a minor one? It wasn't as if he avoided "meet me at the lift with your flatmate." Nope, the likeliest possibility was that he was an American all along.

"It means," I said, doing this slowly not out of a sense of drama, but because I didn't want to fuck it up, "that Doctor XXX is probably on this boat."

"How do you figure that?" asked Nathan.

"Well," I said, "whoever it is, he doesn't want me investigating him. And he wants that to stop, pronto. If he was some guy who went home to Duluth after losing in the tournament yesterday, why would he care that much?"

"Hmm," said Nathan. "Okay. So, do you know who it is?"

I thought about it. I honestly didn't. I knew that Tricia had watched me streaming, though, so it could possibly have been her? But that was nonsense. To what end? And it just as easily could have been anyone; that's the point of streaming. Your stuff is out there live, for anyone to see.

"I don't know who it is," I said. "But whoever they are, they have a friend in Dorset."

"This seems very hard to work out," Nathan considered. "Maybe we go around talking about visiting Dorset with random people until someone says, 'Oh yes, I know Dorset. It's lovely.'"

"Maybe we use the word 'conurbation' in conversation and we see who knows what we're talking about."

"A clever gambit," Nathan said. "But I think it'd be tricky to naturally bring the topic up."

I was still thinking about the streaming thing, however. Every time I streamed, it seemed, Doctor XXX was watching me. This was not particularly shocking, really, because he obviously just had set up some sort of alert to go off whenever I started streaming, just like I had done for him.

And that, I suddenly realized, was a piece of information worth knowing.

"Nathan," I said. "I think I'm going to need as many hands on deck here as I can get. You didn't, by any chance, come here with Masako, did you?" Masako was Nathan's ex-girlfriend and current apartment-mate, of whom I had grown inexplicably fond. She had the soul of a Goth but the clothes of someone who belonged in a Monet painting.

"She had a study date," Nathan said. "Although honestly, I don't think this sort of thing would have been her scene regardless."

"Is there anyone else on the boat you trust?"

"Nope," said Nathan. "I don't even trust you."

This was undoubtedly a reference to the fact that I had harbored some, perhaps unfounded, suspicions that Nathan had planned to murder me on my last case, a fact which he continued to be amused by and bring up.

"We have to find Charice and Daniel," I said.

"This isn't just some plan to interrupt their wedding proposal?"

"No," I said. "Besides which, what better way to celebrate their new life together than to embark on some stealth and surveillance?"

"I can think of some ways," said Nathan.

"Hush, you," I told him.

Finding Charice and Daniel was remarkably easy, because they were wearing costumes, which meant that everyone knew who they were, at least on a boat filled with fighting-game players.

"Have you seen Balrog?" I'd ask strangers. "How about Vega? Was he with her?"

As it happened, they were on the other end of the ship, almost as far away from us as they could possibly get, at least without hurling themselves into the river. There was a crowd around them, and people were having their pictures taken with them.

"Congratulations," I said, at which point, Daniel—still masked—somehow still managed to give me a death glare. I don't even know how that worked. Acting, I suppose.

"Congratulations for what?" asked Charice.

"Uh," I said. "For attracting this wonderful crowd of onlookers!"

"Oh, onlookers," said Charice, as though onlookers were a nuisance she constantly had to deal with. Actually, considering Charice, this was possibly true.

"Listen," I said. "I need you guys for some skullduggery."

"I'm in," said Daniel. "I'm even masked."

Nathan at this point had already heard the plan, and took to dealing with the scattered group of folks who had been posing with Daniel and Charice. Apparently he intended to do some detective work of his own.

"I'm running a little survey," said Nathan. "What are your three favorite conurbations?" Which really is a sort of question that will drive any group into boredom or silence. Even so, it made me feel better about my skills to watch Nathan fail.

"I love skullduggery," said Charice. "It's my very favorite of the duggeries."

I explained my plan, as softly as I could, to Charice and Daniel, who seemed quietly interested by the idea. But I continued to be distracted by Nathan's interviewing, which could not be said to be going very well.

"Summon Water?" ventured one of the crowd members, a kid in a Trixie Mattel tank top.

"That's a conjuration, not a conurbation," I explained to Nathan, who I figured would never have made the connection otherwise. I also wanted to ask questions of the guy who had named "Summon Water" as his favorite conjuration—because that's a mind-blowingly boring answer. It's so boring as to almost be interesting again. But I resisted this noble impulse and kept my eyes on the prize.

"So we're going to need you guys on the most populated parts of the ship. So, the auditorium, the bar, the main deck."

"I'll take the bar," said Daniel. And I wondered, briefly, why he hadn't popped the question yet. Because clearly that hadn't happened. In the unlikely event Charice turned him down, she wouldn't have been sheepish about it afterward. She would have said something like: "Oh, are you congratulating me on my being engaged? No, I'm sorry. I turned Daniel down—I'm just not ready yet." Which sounds awful, but she would have managed it in a warm and inviting way that would have made it seem natural and human, and just one of those things. It was a real talent of Charice's, actually, making unnatural situations feel as though they were no big whoop. I had the opposite talent, which was to make ordinary and non-stressful events feel like a terrible pressure cooker.

But I digress.

"Charice can take the auditorium—I know you love a crowd. Nathan," I yelled, "you can stay over here."

"And you?" asked Charice. "Where will you go?"

"I think I'm just going to walk around."

CHAPTER THIRTY

People took their places, and I started pacing along the side of the ship. I thought it was better to stay a little out of sight, because if Doctor XXX saw me and realized what I was up to, they might just turn their notification off. I wasn't sure what the best way to manage this was. I could either just start a stream, and then leave it running, with the hopes that Doctor XXX would watch me—and that one of my spies might catch him or her in the act. Or, alternatively, I could start and stop streaming many times in succession, which would make the notification go off a lot but may make our Doctor suspicious. Still, if I absolutely knew he wasn't going to watch me, this was my best option.

I waited five minutes for everyone to get into positions, which was sheer optimism on my part, because for all I knew, Charice had run off to join the gypsies. But I took my chances and started my stream.

"Hi, everyone! Guess where am I now?"

Murdered, said Twitch chat. Is it murdered?

"It's not murdered," I told them.

"Buried alive," someone guessed. "Like in that old Twilight Zone episode."

"That was the Outer Limits," said another Twitch chatter, and then a flame war began, as it obviously would, given that we were on the Internet.

"Guys," I said, "this is not the important thing here."

What's the important thing? asked Twitch chat.

"The important thing is that I think I've figured out who killed Karou." And then I shut the stream down, just like that.

I hadn't planned on being quite so melodramatic. I hadn't planned on saying that at all—I had figured I'd go with something like—uh-oh—the Wi-Fi here is getting a little wobbly—but this worked. My goal was to smoke someone out, after all. Why go small?

I stood around a little, waiting to see if anyone called me. I hoped that I'd get a ring from Daniel or Charice saying, "I saw a guy watching your stream" but that didn't immediately happen. I probably should have started streaming again, but now I needed to say something, because Twitch chat was going to want to know who the killer was. It's not the sort of thing they would easily let drop.

But I noticed a figure running at me, full force. It was a kid, hightailing it as fast as he could. I wondered who was chasing him, when I realized: that's Remy, and he's not running from anyone. He's running toward me.

"Dahlia, are you okay?"

"Yeah," I said. "Sure. Why do you ask?"

"I was watching your stream," said Remy. "You said that you knew who Karou's killer was, and then there was a noise, and the stream went black. It was very scary."

"Oh," I said. "No, I'm okay."

"I nearly called the police," said Remy. "It was literally like one of those notes where someone is writing a confession and their hand gives out before they're able to complete the message."

"Well, I'm glad you didn't call the police," I said, which was true, because I wouldn't want to have to explain this gambit to Detective Maddocks. "But why were you watching my stream?"

"I don't know," said Remy. "I was waiting for my match, and Kyle and Tricia have been really busy. And people don't want to talk to a fourteen-year-old."

"But why my stream?"

"Why not your stream?"

"How did you find me?"

Remy had actually been pretty amenable, all things considered, but fourteen-year-olds are uniquely suited to giving eye-rolling disgusted responses to questions they regard as unnecessary. Such as "How was school?" or "What's this song on the radio?" or "Why does this bottle of white wine taste like it has been largely replaced with water?" Remy, without using any words to get the idea across, made it pretty clear that he thought this line of questioning was incomprehensibly stupid.

"I met you," said Remy. "Yesterday. And Tricia said you had a stream, so I checked it out. I also followed you on Twitter."

"You're not Doctor XXX, are you?"

I didn't get an eyeball for this, but it was at least as dumb a question. If I truly were confronting the Doctor, I wouldn't want to go about it in such a mealymouthed uncertain way. But things don't always go perfectly.

"No," said Remy. "But it's a cool name. What do the Xs stand for?"

"What's your favorite conurbation?" I asked Remy, which is truly the work of the desperate.

"Banana cream," said Remy.

"What's your favorite part of England?"

"Hogwarts?"

"Okay, kid," I said. "I guess you're all right."

"Yeah," said Remy. "Of course I'm all right. You're the person I was worried about. I thought you had been murdered or attacked or something."

"Everyone on Twitch seems to think I'm constantly on the cusp of death," I said. "Where did they get this idea?" I mean, aside from agreeing to meet strangers in hotels and also on vessels of the river. But no matter—I wanted to know why I hadn't gotten a phone call about Remy. "Hey, what room were you in when you got the notification that I was streaming?"

"The auditorium," said Remy, with slowly dawning interest. "Why?"

Charice's territory. I should have guessed. I decided that, for better or ill, I was going to trust Remy completely here. Certainly fourteen-year-olds are capable of serious mischief making, but I didn't think this one was, or at least, this particular fourteen-year-old was not responsible for this particular mischief.

"I'm trying to smoke out this Doctor XXX," I told Remy.

"I don't know who that is," said Remy.

"Doesn't matter. Go back to the auditorium, and watch to see if anyone either watches my stream or gets a notification about it."

"How will I know about a notification? There could just be like a little ding or something. Or it could be silent. My notification was."

It could be silent. I hadn't thought about that at all.

"Okay," I said. "I'm going to start streaming over and over again, for like thirty seconds a pop. Watch the crowd and see if anyone looks at their phone. And if anyone seems to check out my stream, or gets up to leave after checking their phone, follow them and find me."

Remy eyes were the size of saucers.

"Wow," he said. "Okay, I'm in."

I decided that I wasn't going to remain stationery this time, especially since I wasn't really going to stream so much as just start and stop over and over. And I wanted to cover more ground, since apparently my spies weren't doing well enough. Where else could someone go?

There was an entire upper deck to the boat that was off-limits, and I could have taken my chances up there, but this seemed like a bridge too far. I decided to try for the opposite direction—checking out the belowdecks area, both because it was sort of great-looking down there—squint and you could imagine yourself as the heroine in a steampunk novel—and because it's where the bathrooms were. And that was a reasonable place to check, right? I mean, if you wanted to surreptitiously watch a video, a stall in the ladies' or gents' room is probably the best you could hope for, in terms of privacy.

I made my way down the stairs, which were carpeted in this variegated brown swirly thing that managed to be swank and also a little ominous. Coming down the stairs, I was reminded of an old text-based game that my brother Alden used to play.

They really don't make games like that anymore—by which I don't mean text-based, although that's also true, but games where you can make one wrong decision and permanently lose. It was a game called *Ballyhoo*, and if you made an irrevocable choice and were doomed forever, the game wouldn't even tell you. It would just give you a clue—like "You have a terrible sinking feeling, and your mind is struck with the image of a burning bridge."

Anyway, I mention all of that now not to plug games of yore, but because I had a terrible sinking feeling, and my mind was struck with the image of a burning bridge. Admittedly, I'm writing this all down after the fact, so I may be creatively remembering the moment, but I don't think I am. Going down those stairs, I had the sense that I was making a considerable error. Not so considerable that it slowed me down in the slightest, but there was certainly a feeling of unease.

Also, it was dim down here. Not "likely to be eaten by a grue" dark, but dim. To continue with our steampunk metaphor, the airship that we were traveling on was running very low on power.

Despite all this, I was blithely starting up and shutting down the stream, although I did at least take enough care as to not fall down the stairs to my death. When I made it to the bottom of the stairs, and faced a long plain hallway that ran along the middle of the ship, I noticed a snippet of music. By snippet I mean snippet—it was about three bars long, and lasted maybe five seconds, if that.

It was also vaguely familiar.

I stopped moving and listened some more. No music. No sound whatsoever.

I started my stream.

Music again. Very faint music. It was so familiar, but I couldn't quite place it. "Dum, ditty dummm, ditty dum-dum-dum."

I stopped my stream. I'm sure my twelve viewers were getting furious with me. I moved a little farther down the hall and tried it again.

This time it was a little louder. "Dum, ditty dummm, ditty dum-dum-dum." I could place it this time, now that I'd heard it a little louder—it was Dhalsim's theme, from *Street Fighter II*. Of all the mysteries I could have solved, resolving this tiny one was obviously the least-important thing I could have put together, but it gave me a boost of confidence nonetheless. If someone's phone alert sound was Dhalsim's theme song, they were probably a pretty serious player.

I moved farther down the hall and started and stopped my stream again. It was only because it was so completely empty down here than I was able to pinpoint, or even hear the sound. Apparently there were also restrooms in the bar, which was where most of the gamers had taken to going.

There were three restrooms down here—a men's, a women's, and a family restroom, which struck me as a lot of bathrooms for a steamboat, but then they were probably doing gangbusters in the bar and all that liquor's got to go somewhere. I had just assumed, naturally, that the sound would be coming from the men's room, but to my surprise and frustration, I found that it wasn't. I started and stopped my stream and, again, found that the sound was coming from the family room.

This was frustrating, not because I had any particular gender-based ideas about who my stalker should be, but because the family room restroom was locked. In fact, of the three restrooms—I checked—it was the only door in the bunch that could lock at all.

I knocked.

"Hello," I said. "Is anyone in there?"

No response.

I decided to lie. "I've got a small toddler that needs to poo really badly." This was a little strange, sure, but it sounds better than "I'm stalking someone who possibly had a British man pose as themselves on the Internet; by any chance, is that you?"

But no response, regardless.

It was probably a little strange that this person had been getting alerts for my stream over and over again, and was doing nothing about it. Why do nothing? After two alerts I would have shut the thing off, actually, especially with the frequency I'd been sending them. But they hadn't.

A few possibilities, right?

1. No one was in the bathroom. Just an abandoned phone. I really liked this idea, because I could still probably figure out who Doctor XXX was—assuming there wasn't a passcode on the thing—and I could also be a Good Samaritan and return his or her phone.
2. Someone was in the bathroom, passed out, asleep, drunk. This was less likely, but hey, I've been to some wild parties before, and it wouldn't be the first time. At least it wasn't my toilet that the drunk guy had passed out on.
3. Violently murdered corpse, obviously.

Now, now, I know you're leaping to number three, but let's pace ourselves. Or that's what I was saying to myself. I was suddenly getting anxious about being alone down here, and as I had started to stream like twenty times now, I decided to put it on for good now. At least this way I wouldn't be alone.

"Hello there, Twitch. How's everybody?"

What the fuck is wrong with your stream? asked Twitch chat.

That's lending the message a lot more coherence than their version, incidentally, which was pure salt.

"Just having a little technical difficulties," I said, "but it's resolved now."

Are you going to play some *Hearthstone* or what? asked chat. Or is this another almost-get-murdered thing?

"Not right away," I said. "I'm just belowdecks at the *Major Redding.*"

It's dark down there, said Twitch chat.

"It is, actually," I said. "It's a little creepy."

I don't like this place, said chat.

"It's fine. It's fine," I told the crowd. "I just am down here because I think I've tracked down the person who is Doctor XXX."

Who's that? asked Twitch chat. It's important to remember that not everyone was watching me yesterday, so they weren't necessarily filled in on the business. I was going to explain, but the rest of Twitch chat explained the business to themselves.

Well, said Twitch chat. Some crazy person asked Louise to meet them at a hotel.

Oh, don't do that, said the newcomers.

She already did. Except the person was missing. And there was a murder. And Louise is still trying to find the guy.

Why would she do that? asked more of Twitch chat.

She crazy, Twitch chat answered.

"I'm not crazy," I said. "I'm suspicious. Besides which, maybe he's involved in the murder. But that's not the point," I went on. "The point is, he's behind that door."

You should get out of that darkened basement, said chat.

"Guys, it's actually not that dark. The camera's just not picking up the light."

It's like Silence of the Lambs down there, said Twitch chat. Buffalo Bill's gonna be coming after you with night-vision goggles in a minute.

Talking to these clowns made me feel very anxious, and paradoxically, also very safe. They had a lot of suspicions—more than me, even—but I felt certain that nothing bad could happen to me while I was bickering. I don't know where that idea came from—maybe my parents?—but there you have it.

"The thing is," I said, "that door is locked."

I also had another thought—was Doctor XXX watching me now? Perhaps he was observing me from the other side of the door, which was a little creepy, actually. Still not quite Buffalo-Bill-with-night-goggles creepy, but getting there. I scanned the list of viewers and did not see his name, which gave me a surge of comfort that was suddenly followed by an inexplicable wave of disappointment. But I didn't have time to wallow in this, because Twitch was on it.

"Hold the lock up to the camera," typed a Twitch chatter.

I did this. And someone linked to a YouTube video about picking the lock of a push-button-locking door. At the time this seemed very impressive; although, in retrospect I realize that the user just googled "unlock bathroom door." But no matter.

"Okay," I said, clicking on and watching the video. Honestly, YouTube can give a budding criminal a lot of tips.

We should not be enabling her, said Twitch chat.

Yes, we should, said other parts of Twitch chat. I want to see what's on the other side.

Probably some embarrassed dude pooping, continued Twitch chat.

And someone started a betting pool for what would be behind the door. Options available included (going from the least-popular choice to the most):

- Pooping guy
- Sexy-time couple
- Sexy-time singleton
- Sleeping old woman
- Dead old woman, maybe like the mother from *Psycho*
- Pooping guy/Dead old woman combo
- Confetti cannon
- Buffalo Bill with night goggles
- We will never know because Dahlia/Louise will not be able to open the door

Admittedly, that last option looked very plausible. Here was another video where people had lock-picking tools. Was this just some cultural touchstone that I missed out on? Do we all just travel around with lock-picking tools now?

Anyway, I was searching through my purse, cursing all the while, because I didn't have any lock-picking supplies, obviously, and I had also forgotten, momentarily, that there was a glochid in there, which gave me a really close call. It's like a horror movie where you open a door and a cat jumps out at you. You unzip your purse, and there's a large spiny cactus. Admittedly, this is a very poor horror movie with not much of a budget.

Use your bobby pins, said Twitch chat.

"I don't have any goddamned bobby pins," I said. "No one uses bobby pins." (And yes, I realize that this is an exaggeration, but I was stressed. Please don't message me on Twitter telling me that you use bobby pins, because I don't want to hear it.)

Come THRU! said Twitch chat.

I did find, at the bottom of my purse, a paper clip. It was honestly pretty inexplicable what it was doing in there. I'd probably been carrying it around since college, but what the hell. I took out the old collegiate paper clip and fashioned it into a little lock-picking device. Like people do.

I popped open the door—where "popped" here is a word that means "slowly pecked at over a period of ten minutes while using language that made Twitch chat blush"—and voilà.

Now there was a new problem.

CHAPTER THIRTY-ONE

It was Chul-Moo, whom I honestly wasn't expecting at this point. And he was in the corner, by the baby-changing station. He wasn't moving, and his eyes weren't open, but he also wasn't obviously dead.

However, he might be dead, and so I put down my laptop so that my stream was facing the bathroom wall.

"It's Chul-Moo," I said, both because I knew that Twitch chat was typing, WHAT'S IN THERE?!? over and over again in all caps, and because, if by any chance I was killed, it would be good for people to know what I was seeing.

Chul-Moo looked fine—I mean, he wasn't disemboweled or legless or anything—but when I went to touch him, I found that he was cold.

"Okay," I said, for the benefit of the stream. "I think he's dead." For reasons that I cannot possibly fathom, I did not decide to immediately flee from the Family Bathroom of Horror, but instead felt I should figure out what killed him, which I accomplished by touching the back of his head, which had blood on it.

"Oh crap," I said. "I've got blood on my hands."

GET OUT OF THERE GET OUT OF THERE! typed Twitch chat. I leaned over a sink and washed my hands, because if I have learned anything from mysteries, it's that when you innocently get a murdered man's blood on your hands, that's obviously when the police show up and you have to say, as blood drips from your fingers, "It's not what it looks like!"

Plus, also, hepatitis C. You can't be too careful, she typed ironically, because then someone smashed my head into the sink.

Before we go on with the narrative, I just want to take a very brief detour to discuss Twitch chat. I make fun of Twitch chat, because they are idiots, but they are also idiots who may have saved my life, so I am grateful to them. And I always sort of liked them before that, to be honest. (But to be clear: idiots.)

However, I want to point out that after I got online next—much later in the narrative…I'm skipping around here, but hear me out—four people had unsubscribed from my channel. Four people! That means that four gents (or gals) saw this scene—heard my head get smashed into the sink, watched my stream go black—and thought:

"Well, I guess Dahlia's dead now. I might as well unsubscribe."

Fuck you, four members of Twitch chat! I mean, honestly. Fuck you.

I should also mention—because I was told this later—that following my head smashing and fade to black, Twitch immediately decided to play a commercial for a Disney hotel. Advertising synergy at work. Who knows, maybe after watching me get murdered, a viewer might think: "You know, I should get moving on that bucket list. A trip to Epcot would really hit the spot."

I was not dead, although wouldn't that be a turn? It's ghost Dahlia—*whoooo!* We urban fantasy now, as Twitch chat would say.

But alas, no, because if I had been dead, my head would have presumably hurt much less.

I woke up in a room that was pitch-black. Pitch-fucking-black. Surely the afterlife had more lighting than this. I also heard a very alarming grinding noise that was hard for me to immediately process, and it felt like the back of my head had been split open. I can't stress head pain enough. This was not hangover territory—a split-open head that I was accustomed to—this was trauma.

My first thought was: *Okay, I'm in hell.* It made sense. But then I realized that I smelled like blood and vomit and, even for Satan, who I'm sure loves bodily viscera, that felt like an odd combination.

I didn't immediately piece together what had happened—I just lay there in the dark—trying to reconstruct what had led me to this moment. I was in the bathroom, and I had found Chul-Moo, who was dead. Not passed out, not innocently dying while in the bathroom like people do, but actually murdered. And someone had—what?—sneaked up behind me? I felt the back of my head to see if it was bleeding and found that it wasn't, but there was surely a giant knot there.

How had this happened? There was a stall in there, which I hadn't checked. Had my assailant been in the bathroom all along? Or had he or she followed me down to where Chul-Moo was? I suppose these questions weren't important, or weren't immediately important, but my mind was all over the place at that point. That'll happen when you get concussed.

So, a darkened room with a dead body. This had moved into Buffalo Bill territory, after all. Twitch chat was fucking right. Pretty soon I was going to have puppies thrown at me by a transphobically conceived character. That was probably what the girl in the well was thinking. You all thought she was crying from fear or lack of water, but she was really thinking about how she was going to have to explain that movie to her grandkids someday. I digress.

I was not going to die in this room. That's not to say I was going to live, but by God, I was going to at least survive long enough to change rooms. I refuse to expire in a room without carpeting.

Speaking of text games—it was inventory time. What did I have on me?

Well, nothing in my pockets—no iPhone, no ID, no purse, no nothing. I certainly had things before I had been knocked out, such as a cactus and an ancient paper clip, and so this meant that whoever hit me had taken my stuff. Also my laptop, but that one I had expected. I took a moment to panic about this—two or three moments, actually—but then I bucked up and moved on. I wasn't the only person here, after all.

I searched Chul-Moo's body as well, getting nicely covered in what was hopefully hepatitis-free blood. There was something long and rectangular in his pocket—and I was earnestly hoping it was some oddly shaped cell phone. It didn't have to be an iPhone. A Samsung Galaxy would have been great. Hell, I would have even welcomed a Jitterbug.

It wasn't any of these things, but it felt familiar in my hands, and I instinctively opened the rectangle in half. It was a Nintendo DS—God bless handheld gaming.

I had wanted a cell phone, which would have been worlds more useful, but this could have been worse. For one, it meant vision. The DS had power, so once I turned it on, a small

amount of white light entered the room. See? This was progress. I was like one of those characters in Alden's text games.

```
>> SEARCH BODY. OPEN DS. GO WEST.
```

So there was no reason to panic at all. Of course, those
games were hard as fuck, and I was killed as often as not, but no
matter. This was not a magical grotto where I was likely to be
devoured by topiary animals. I had this. I could do this.

Inventory. That's what you do in these games. I had a tool
now, which was good.

What was bad: I didn't know where I was, I didn't know
who had attacked me, when or if they were coming back, and
I didn't know how long I had been out. Which is pretty scary if
you think about it all. Terrifying, actually.

Focus on the tool, Dahlia.

The first thing I thought about was using the DS to contact
someone else. Unfortunately, Nintendo's "Friend Code" system
meant that I could only contact people whom Chul-Moo had
been friends with. One of which was Swan, undoubtedly, and
he was at least an even bet for the person who had knocked me
out in the first place. Even if I felt comfortable contacting Swan,
and I wasn't sure that I did, all I could do was send him a message that he might get hours later.

Whoever did this might be back in minutes. What else,
Dahlia?

I thought briefly of changing my StreetPass outgoing message. There was this minigame that Nintendo had about trying
to "tag" as many people as possible with your DS. Your Mii and
their Mii would electronically connect and exchange greetings.
So like: "I'm Dahlia!" and "I like cats!" In this scenario, some

unsuspecting person aboard the *Major Redding* would randomly tag me, and we'd have a conversation like: "SSsup? ;-)" and "HELP ME I'M TRAPPED IN THE BASEMENT."

Not a great plan either. No immediate results, and I didn't actually know I was in the basement. I had no freaking clue where I was. I scotched the idea of using the DS to call for help just yet, and turned it around so that I could use the DS's light to give me a better idea of where the hell I was.

There was still that grinding noise, and a pulsating moving and enormous metal—I don't know what you would call it—I don't know, penis? Let's say penis, that just sort of kept thrusting back and forth. Honestly, that's what it looked like. Okay, maybe, "cylinder" is a better word—give me a break, I just had a concussion. There was a cylinder pushing back and forth, and the resulting motion shot strange shadows on the wall.

I was in the engine room. (Actually my first thought was clock tower—which would have been way more Gothic, if not immediately logical.) It was cramped and smelled sort of tinny and electric, and there were plain white guard rails everywhere. Also, lots of signs that warned: DANGER, which at this point felt like God just making fun of me.

But I was losing the thread. Focus on the puzzle, Dahlia. What else was there to learn?

The DS had a clock on it. So after a little muddling around, I figured out that it was 7:46, which meant that I'd only been out for twenty minutes or so. Assuming that Chul-Moo hadn't changed time zones recently. But regardless, people were probably still upstairs. All I needed to do was get back upstairs, alive, and then from there it'd be a cakewalk.

I was still on the floor for all of this because—and I don't want to underplay this point—my head hurt like hell. I was trying to accomplish as much as I could from the ground because it was going to be hard going once I got up. I shone light on the two ends of the room, and found that there was only one exit.

Well, it was clear enough.

I tried getting up, and then someone, possibly God again, picked up and threw the *Major Redding* at me. Vertigo, vertigoing, vertigone. There was an entire Poseidon Adventure I went on. If you're going to have a concussion—don't do it on a steamboat. I can't think of a worse place for one. A Ferris wheel would be a better choice.

I was glad, actually, that I wasn't being streamed, because the staggering, drunken, jagged motions I made toward the door must have looked awfully ridiculous. Buffalo Bill would have been like: "Girl—just to be clear, I'm still gonna kill you and wear your skin later—but before all that, are you sure you don't want me to get you some Dramamine? Because you're looking rough." Probably.

I made my way to the door, but doing so gave me pause. Who's to say that whoever had failed to kill me wasn't out there keeping guard? I tried to move quietly in the dark—so easy when you're vomitously dizzy—and then carefully, cautiously tried to turn the door. It was almost a relief that it was locked, but I did not want to wobble through the basement of this steamboat looking for a way up.

Another locked door, and me with no bobby pins in my hair. I swore to God that if I lived through this, I would just start wearing a full-on lock-picking kit in my hair. My whole hairstyle would be engineered so that I would have the right tools for the situation. A beehive, maybe? Maybe a wig?

Problems for later.

New plan? Weaponize. This was the engine room, so that

meant that there was a fire extinguisher in here somewhere, right? Also, if there was a fire, I'd be prepared. I was searching the room, trying to figure out where it would be when I made a discovery. That door wasn't, strictly speaking, the only exit. There was a porthole in the room—just a little out of reach.

This was an interesting possibility. In its favor: the possibility of not getting killed. Against it: I wasn't 100 percent sure I could squeeze through it, and I would probably need a rope or something to avoid getting thrown into the Mississippi. Probably the extinguisher was a better plan. (Also, I could attack with a zingy action-movie line like: "Get Extinguished!" or "Flame Off!"—the latter line working best if I were being attacked by Chris Evans.)

Still, leave no stone unturned. I found a brown plastic wastebasket, which I tipped over and stood on top of. I felt guilty about this, actually, because the wastebasket had a bunch of Kleenex that, as far as I could tell, had shit on it, and I'm sure the engineers of the *Major Redding* were going to be horrified whenever they came back in here. A corpse and now fecal matter on the floor.

I stood on the wastebasket and peeked out through the porthole. I could, just barely, squeeze out of it, and ahead I could see the lights of East St. Louis. I'm just going to go ahead and say this: no one has ever been more excited to see East St. Louis than I was in that moment. Screw the crime and the poverty and the East St. Louisness of it—it was beautiful and looked like a mirage against the water. I wanted to live there, forever, and take Nathan, and maybe also Shuler, and start a wonderful little family in the inner city. It looked alive, and I wanted to be alive.

It was at that point that I heard a noise at the door—a metal creaking that I was sure wasn't the normal creaking of the ship, and I thought: *Well, this is not good. This is probably very bad.*

I looked above me and saw that there was no rope, no ladder, no anything, really. To get to the upper deck from here, I would either need to be Spider-Man or one of those cheap plastic wall-crawling toys you'd get from the bottom of cereal boxes. And those don't even really work very well. I looked below and saw nothing but the inky black water of the Mississippi, which I wasn't sure was safe to swim in, even if I wasn't experiencing Count Vertigo levels of dizziness, which I was.

And then someone had my legs.

I'm going to say that it was Chul-Moo who had my legs, because it's more interesting, and also it's kind of what I had thought, on some level. I was now being attacked by zombies. It had come to this. (Note: I was not being attacked by zombies.)

Have you ever been halfway out the porthole of a steamboat, trying to wrest your lower body out of the grips of a murderer? I'm just going to assume this is a universal experience. ("Girl, we've all done that," I can hear you saying.) Was your porthole hard on your stomach? I still have a mark.

Anyway, I'm not good at a lot of things, but I can kick, and it is my forceful kicking that I credit with getting me out of that situation alive. Also in this skill set of mine: screaming. Jesus God, did I scream. Sam Spade never screamed as I did—but it wasn't all just fear. It wasn't fear at all, honestly—I was just hoping I could get someone else's attention.

I was also trying to fake being completely panicked and

irrational, which wasn't that hard because it certainly wasn't very far from the surface.

"HELP! HELP!" I screamed while trying to worm my way out from whoever had held me. "I CAN'T SWIM! I CAN'T SWIM!"

I slipped out of my attacker's grasp and plummeted toward the dark water below and thought: *Dahlia Moss, you have died as you lived. Bullshitting.*

CHAPTER THIRTY-TWO

I can swim. I'm actually a really excellent swimmer, although I can't do the butterfly. I don't even fully understand how that stroke is supposed to work. But I do get the breaststroke, and I did it then, slipping under the water as best I could in case whoever had me had a gun. Probably they didn't, because you know, they could have just shot my ass. People die from that, right? Ass shot? It probably has a more technical name.

I don't recommend diving from a steamboat and swimming underwater after a concussion. I could just imagine the conversation I was going to have with my physician after this. I'm kidding—I can't afford insurance! What physician!

Anyway, I'm still not so excellent a swimmer as to feel like this wasn't a terrifying nightmare. My first thought, even as I swam under the water, ostensibly to safety, was that this was death for me. I mean, wriggling free from a murderer from a porthole on a steamboat and diving into a darkened river is not the sort of thing they teach you on swim team. If you needed me to turn around very quickly at the end of the swimming pool, I was your gal. This was a step beyond. It was more than a step beyond. It was a tower of steps beyond, maybe even the tower in *Vertigo* where Kim Novak throws herself to the rocks.

I stayed underwater longer than I needed to, because I was still pretty certain someone was going to shoot me. Even when I came up for air, I didn't stay above the water long enough to assess, lest I take a bullet in the head. I just kept ducking back under and swimming away from the boat, which seemed like a great idea at time.

I was grateful for my clothes—Kathy Bates knows how to dress for aquatic adventures (also: Thanks, H&M!)—I was especially grateful I hadn't gone in for the gray fluffy shirt I had been considering that morning, which would have soaked up water like a sponge. Ah, the things you consider while fleeing for your life.

I did this for a bit more, and then observed that the *Major Redding* had gotten quite far away from me, quite quickly. You don't really appreciate the speed of a boat until you are overboard. I guess on some level—some completely unrealistic level in which I fancy myself a superspy—I had the idea that I would catch up to the boat and surreptitiously board its other side, like a Navy Seal. The ways in which I resemble a Navy Seal obviously being too numerous to mention here. I'm probably more like an actual seal, now that I think about it. But either way, nothing was happening.

It began to hit me, now that I was running out of "now you will die" adrenaline, the situation had been upgraded from "certain death" to "quite possible death." The water was cold and I was in the middle of the river—which is two miles wide. I could probably swim to shore, but it wasn't a sure bet because I was incredibly tired and my head hurt. The *Major Redding* was drifting off on the horizon, and I decided that I was safe from this imaginary gunman now, and so I just floated there for a second. Maybe I could do this forever, or at least until New

Orleans. Probably there's a metaphor in there somewhere, but I didn't have time for metaphors, or even a chance to collect myself, because I observed there were police sirens coming toward me.

You don't often see that on the river. Then again, I'm sure my floating there was incredibly illegal, and undoubtedly dangerous. A little zip boat was coming toward me, and sirens were flashing, and I wondered, do they arrest people in the water by telling them to put their hands in the air, because a lot of folks could drown that way.

But there were no instructions, just the boat drifting slowly toward me, and when I got close, I was stunned to see my least favorite police detective ever.

"Jesus Christ, Weber. Fish her out of the water."

Detective Douglas Maddocks had a face like a craggy mountain, like Mordor, or Rushmore, if everyone on Rushmore had been deeply scowling. Like, it was Nixon four times. Detective Maddocks had never been happy to see me, but he looked particularly unhappy to see me now.

Detective Weber extended her arms toward me, and it seemed entirely possible that she could pull me out of the water herself. She was a thick woman, Detective Weber—and yet nothing about her was jovial. She was big, with raven-black hair and an abundant midsection. She looked a bit like Dawn French, and so I expected her to be chumming it up with me, but this was not the case.

"Is this who I think it is?" asked Weber.

Maddocks just looked disappointed. "Dahlia Moss. We've got to stop meeting like this."

Oh, how I laughed.

I felt like Maddocks was hoping for some sort of mental jousting—as if he were my nemesis, which isn't really the case. He's a cop, and I generally wish him well. A little pushy, but what the heck. And besides, I already have a nemesis, who's a bank teller named Clara who gloats whenever I am overdrawn, which is often.

"I'm sure you know that it's illegal to swim in the Mississippi," started Maddocks. "But I'm guessing you've got a story for that."

"Something like that," I said. I wasn't sure if I was glad to be alive at this point exactly. I mean, I got on the boat, but this was not the vessel that I dreamed of rescuing me.

"You wanna tell me this story?"

"I was struck in the head. I think I might have a concussion. Also, someone was trying to kill me earlier and I dove off the *Major Redding* to escape."

"Is she crazy?" asked Weber. "Do you want me tase her?"

Weber was joking, I think, and Maddocks said no, although he contemplated the idea for a few seconds longer than he should. I couldn't blame Weber for wondering if I was crazy. She did find me swimming in the Mississippi in a floral blouse, not the mark of sanity, and my story just seemed like something a crazy person might say.

Maddocks, however, did not regard me as crazy, but as trouble. I was his Rose Walker, like in *Sandman*—a dream vortex—except that I was more of a murder vortex, and I wasn't as cool. I doubt that's exactly the reference he would make.

"Why is it," asked Maddocks, "that you think someone is trying kill you?"

I repeated myself. Maybe the concussion was making me hard to understand? "Someone hit me in the head, smashed my head against a bathroom sink, left me in a darkened locked room with a corpse, and grabbed my legs as I tried to escape."

This was enough to quell skepticism from Maddocks for now, who appeared to be digesting the information I had given him. Concussion or not, I'd been able to think clearly enough that I had a question of my own.

"If you didn't come for me," I said, "why are you guys even here?"

"We got thirty-seven phone calls from all over the world," said Weber. "Telling us that someone named Louise was in grave danger."

Aw, Twitch chat. Let's be BFFs forever.

I did not take this moment to explain to Maddocks that I was Louise Granger, which I will chalk up to the concussion, although this is a lie. It would be more accurate to say that I just didn't want to go over it with him right now, and besides which, a murderer was on the loose, and I could talk about it with him later, and then blame the concussion. That's one of the few upsides of a concussion. You can blame anything you want on it, and it's all vaguely plausible. Play the cards you're dealt is what I say.

We pulled up to the *Major Redding*, which I thought had been going rather fast earlier, but now that I was aboard a speedboat seemed rather leisurely. I'm sure if I had any sense I would be reticent to return to the site where someone had tried—not even an hour ago—to kill me. But as we've established, I think, I can get a little overly focused on one idea, to my detriment. My goal: Find out who tried to kill me and then knock them off the *Major Redding* myself. I didn't want them dead. I didn't particularly even want them arrested. I wanted them to get what I got.

We must have made a ridiculous entrance, with police sirens blaring, lights flashing, and of course, I was soaking wet. Not slightly wet, but full-on dripping death, as though I were some sort of horrible Zombie of the Drowned. How could you not look ridiculous? But I could especially tell so because I saw Charice, still in her Balrog garb, staring out at the boat as we pulled up to the *Major Redding*. She looked impressed, which is rarely a good thing.

As we pulled up to the boat, Maddocks gave his partner an instruction.

"Keep an eye on her, Weber."

"Is she a suspect?" Detective Weber asked, which I appreciated very much, as it was the question I was about to pose myself.

"She's just trouble. Dahlia Moss is a nexus of trouble."

I had never heard myself described that way. I had always thought of Charice as being the nexus of trouble. Maybe she had rubbed off on me. Or maybe it had been me all along.

Maddocks got off the boat and climbed gracefully up a rope ladder to a fullish crowd of gamers. I think there were a lot of cell phone cameras filming this, and we were probably on Periscope somewhere. I waved to the crowd, and Weber gave me a weary look.

Maddocks was surprisingly spry at going up the ladder, which when you got down to it, was sort of a gym school nightmare.

A crowd of people, cameras, a difficult-to-scale ladder, and I'm wet. I could have dreamed this in eighth grade.

"I thought Shuler was Maddocks's partner," I told Weber once Maddocks was out of earshot. "What happened? Was there some sort of dramatic meltdown?"

"No," said Weber, who had the same entirely non-elaborative nature that characterized her coworkers.

"You're not going to tell me what happened?"

"You're the amateur sleuth," said Weber. "You tell me."

The nice thing about being an amateur sleuth, I suppose, as opposed to a professional one, is that I can toss off guesses entirely with abandon, since the expectations of me are so low. Again, this is also the rare upshot of having a head injury.

I took a look at Weber, who was an uneasy tired-looking woman with a ring on her finger, and I made a stab at the dark.

"Back from maternity leave," I told her. "Boy or girl?"

Detective Weber did not volunteer the gender of her spawn to me, but she looked amused by my guesswork. Instead she asked me, "How is it that you came to know Shuler?"

In retrospect, the best answer to this question is the same sort of nonresponse she had been giving me, and if I'd had any sense, I'd have answered with something vague like "It's complicated."

But I didn't have any sense, and I said: "Technically, we first met when a client of mine was murdered." You know, the typical meet-cute.

When this got a shocked and not entirely appreciative look from Weber, I naturally took this as opportunity to overshare.

"I mean, technically not a client because I haven't been licensed as a detective yet, but I'm working toward it. Although don't mention that to Maddocks. He doesn't like the subject."

Weber narrowed her eyes at me. "You don't seem like the detective type." I started to object to this, saying something like "That's something coming from you," but I didn't because—honestly—she did seem like the detective type. I mean, if you asked a four-year-old to draw a picture of a detective, they probably wouldn't draw a forty-year-old recently pregnant woman who had the swaggering manliness of Brienne of Tarth, but when you met Weber, there was no arguing with her apparent detectiveness. She had the face for it. She looked like she was going to breathe up clues. She looked like she was doing it now.

Instead I took a different tack.

"Shuler doesn't look like a detective," I pointed out, which was inarguably true.

And Weber gave me a face that suggested that possibly Shuler wasn't much of a detective. I didn't want to engage on this point, and so I gestured for the rope ladder. Less people were watching now, and it seemed safe to assail it without auguring up pubescent gym class nightmares.

"Maddocks asked you to stay with me," she said, stopping me as I reached to climb my way up.

Ah, Weber, but the amateur sleuth pays attention. "No," I told her, "he told you that you should keep an eye on me. I'm going to get a damn towel."

I could tell that Weber was processing deeply, that or she was stalling, and she had trailed me halfway up the ladder when she asked me:

"So, are you the girl that Shuler has a crush on?"

This is not a question that you want to answer on a rope ladder, and I ignored it, I hoped, with great dignity, although great dignity is hard to achieve when you're dripping wet. Maybe only medium dignity. I got to the top deck with three thoughts:

get clothes, ditch this woman, and avoid Charice. Charice was standing right there, beaming at me. "You fell off a steamboat."

"I didn't fall. I was pushed. Someone tried to kill me. Also, Chul-Moo is dead."

Charice was the type of person that you could make this sort of statement to without worrying that she was going to be paralyzed with grief. Or even shock. The news seemed to buoy her, as if the hijinks of getting knocked off a steamboat were not enough.

"Who is Chul-Moo?"

"Male, Asian, and not completely skulled."

"The same dead guy as yesterday?"

"No," I said. "This is a different guy." Although that was an interesting point that I hadn't considered. These two guys had been killed the same way. And actually, they didn't look completely different. Had someone killed Karou yesterday by mistake? Kind of a dreadful thought.

"It's a small world," said Charice, which is precisely the sort of kindhearted, generous observation that one wants to hear after a double murder.

Eschewing sense and reason, I felt the need to explain the situation to Charice more fully. "This was the guy who told me yesterday that he was worried that someone was trying to kill him." He had even told me who he thought was doing it, and I found myself considering Chul-Moo's grim assessment of Mike and Imogen a lot more plausibly than I did the day before. Was it Mike who had grabbed my legs? Imogen? Earlier I would have said certainly not, but now I wasn't so sure.

"You can avenge his death," said Charice. "By catching the killer."

"Sure," I said. "I'll just knock that right out. Er, uh, any news with you?" I asked. I had presumed that Charice would tell me the moment that she had become engaged, but the whole attempted murder thing could plausibly derail the idea.

"No," said Charice, with a hint of suspicion in her voice. "Why do you keep asking me that? What do you know?"

Who's the amateur detective now? I had to distract Charice with her natural catnip, which is hijinks. But this was easy, because Weber was lumbering her way up the ladder, and this was a natural opportunity to kill two birds with one stone.

"This police lady behind me?" I whispered to Charice.

"The policewoman, you're trying to say?"

Exchanges like this were why I was good at dealing with Twitch chat. My actual friends and relations are as difficult and thorny as strangers on the Internet.

"I'm sorry, Charice. Policewoman. Detective. Can you distract her?"

And Charice gave me a Cheshire-cat smile that was so devious and self-satisfied that I was actually concerned for Detective Weber's well-being.

"Oh, Dahlia," she said. "I'll keep her so busy that you won't find her for days."

CHAPTER THIRTY-THREE

If I didn't know Charice as well as I did, I might be concerned that she planned to murder Weber. It was an ominous-sounding line, to be sure. But presumably she meant that Weber would end up going out clubbing with her, which was precisely the sort of utterly improbable and yet strangely commonplace thing that seemed to happen around my roommate. It was like she was the Scarlet Witch—the old Marvel superhero—but instead of manipulating probability to fight crime, her goals were just to have a really good time. If you think about it that way, the Scarlet Witch is exactly the girl you want to hang out with at the bar. Way more fun than Marrow, anyway, who could take out her bones and throw them. Although I guess it depends on the evening you have planned.

Anyway, I didn't stick around to see what sort of tomfoolery was going down there. I'd ask later, probably when Weber invariably joined Charice's wedding party. I had work to do on the ship.

My goals were primarily of a vengeful nature, but this was tough, because despite it all, I still didn't actually have any idea who had done this, which made vengeance challenging. Unless you just want to go kill everyone, like Rambo or some *Buffy the Vampire Slayer* villain. Which was an idea that had an appeal. I, for one, would love to read a mystery where the detective said: "The killer is one of the twelve people in this room. However, I can't quite work out which one of you it is, so I just said to hell with it, and I've poisoned you all. Let God work it out!"

Probably this is head-wound talk.

Still, almost getting killed was an undoubtedly huge development in the case. Like, there had had to be evidence. Possibly I had kicked the murderer—possibly. So if someone had a footprint on their face, that would be a good clue.

More plausibly, I decided that I should check out the bathroom that I was attacked in. I had informed Maddocks about Chul-Moo being in the engine room, but I didn't really have time to mention the whole bathroom situation. Besides which, I wanted to dry off.

I felt very uncertain going down the stairs again—what's the Einstein quote about doing the same thing repeatedly and expecting a different result? But I wanted to dry off, which was the casting vote. Also: I truly wanted a bodyguard now, but no one was around. Not Nathan, not Daniel, not Shuler. And Charice I'd already tasked with nonsense. I would have gone with the fourteen-year-old, if he'd been around. Even Undine. I actually did try to grab a random person—this blond-haired kid who, I swear to God, was the skinniest boy I'd ever seen.

"Hey, guy," I said. "You wanna go down to the bathroom with me?"

Again, head-wound talk, because I could have delivered this request a little more artfully.

"No," said the blond guy.

Keep in mind that I'm actively oozing river water from my clothes and hair, as though I am some sort of terrible mud elemental.

"It's not like that," I said. "I'm just concerned that someone might attack me."

"You'll be fine," said the guy, backing away from me. I had half a mind to chase after him, because I really didn't want to get hit in the head again, but if strangers were actively alarmed by my presence, maybe this was armor enough. However, it didn't come to that point because God bless him, Daniel Simone showed up.

"You missed your match," he said. Which is really quite a thing to say to someone who is dripping water on a steamboat. He didn't ask why I was wet or what had happened to me. He and Charice were going to make it, I could tell.

"You want to come down to the basement with me? I'm doing some sleuthing, and I don't want to get attacked. Again."

"Boats don't have basements," said Daniel. "But sure. You want a towel or something?"

My shoes were the worst, honestly, which I hadn't taken off yet, because it felt sort of undignified to walk around barefoot, but every step I made oozed water. It was exactly as unpleasant as you are imagining.

"Yes," I said. "But first, bathroom. Besides, they'll probably have paper towels in there."

"I think you're well past paper towel."

We headed back down below the decks of *Major Redding*. It felt remarkably less scary with Daniel in tow, who was arguably intimidating looking, especially in the dim light. I mean, he was wearing a mask that was not unlike Jason's, and he had blades for claws. Who is going to bother someone with blades for claws?

"So what happened to you?" asked Daniel as we approached the bathroom.

"Someone smashed my head into a sink and tried to kill me. I escaped into the river."

Daniel took this very calmly, I thought. Much better than my mother would take it, who would probably start thrashing around the floor, screaming, "My baby! My precious baby!" although maybe I'm overselling her reaction. Daniel just looked at me quizzically.

"Is that why the police came aboard?" he asked.

"Yeah," I said. But I suddenly realized that I didn't really want to discuss this with Daniel. It made me seem crazy, going into the details. Eventually Daniel would ask something like "So we're returning to where you were attacked, seriously?" and I would have to defend this entirely reasonable, completely understandable position, which I did not want to defend.

Because of this, I changed the subject.

"You still haven't proposed to Charice yet. What's keeping you?"

"We keep getting interrupted," said Daniel, who was maybe also happy to get off the topic of my near murder. "I didn't appreciate that people would keep coming up to us and asking to have their pictures taken."

"You haven't lost your nerve?" I asked, because I wasn't sure I completely bought Daniel's narrative. Yeah, they were getting interrupted. But every second? All the time?

"I just want to find the right moment," said Daniel. "I want to make it memorable."

And in retrospect, this was the sort of statement that Daniel shouldn't have made aloud, much in the way I shouldn't have been saying dumb things like "but I don't need a bodyguard." But I'm getting ahead of myself.

"She suspects something," I said. "You're going to have to work fast."

And we entered the bathroom, which was not locked this time. I honestly feel like this should have been creepier, or unnerving, but whatever fear might have been augured by the place was dispelled by the combination of blade-claw Daniel and me being dripping wet. And also—it was just a bathroom. It wasn't covered in blood, or bits of skull, or marked in any way. I didn't know if it had been cleaned or if there hadn't been anything to find in the first place.

"There was a corpse here," I said. "In the corner."

Daniel looked in the corner, which was decidedly corpse-free. "I guess someone moved it."

But I already knew that. What I was hoping, I suppose, was that the killer would have left a telltale clue in here. Like a distinctive lapel pin. Or an ID. An ID would have been ideal. But there was none of that.

I was also vaguely hoping that I'd find my laptop in here, which hadn't made it out to the engine room of death, so it had to be somewhere. I even looked in the trash, which had nothing but old chewed gum in it. I wasn't so much trying to find it for clue value as much that I am not made of money. On that note my iPhone was also missing, which I suppose we could have tracked, but the strongest guess was that it was floating along the bottom of the Mississippi. Probably with my laptop.

"Didn't find what you were looking for?" Daniel asked.

"Not a damn thing," I said. "Detecting things ought to be easier. You don't have a laptop, do you?"

"I'm a desktop luddite," said Daniel. "Why?"

"I should get back online. Twitch chat saw me when I got attacked. Maybe they saw who the killer was."

This is what I told Daniel, but it's not what I thought. If Twitch chat saw who hit me, presumably one of the thirty-seven people who called the police would have passed that info along. What I really wanted was to just let them know I was alive, which seemed like the right thing to do.

"Doesn't Nathan usually carry his MacBook with him?" asked Daniel.

"Sometimes," I said. And sometimes was good enough.

You would think that being a dripping elemental of river water would have somehow made me something of a celebrity aboard the *Major Redding*, but this was not the case. I didn't know what Maddocks was doing elsewhere on the ship, or what Charice and Weber had gotten up to, but there was apparently enough chaos that Nathan did not immediately notice me. No one seemed to notice me. Actually that's not true, mostly people were pretending not to notice me, as though I were a shambling river monster. Like something that had been coughed up by a bad Southern Gothic. Dead River Girl yearns for vengeance!

I liked that line, and I had a head wound, so I said it aloud. Naturally that was when Nathan came up to me.

"Jesus Christ," he said. "You're covered in rainwater."

"Not rainwater," I said—honestly, rainwater? "River water."

And he was taking off his shirt, right off his back. "Put this on," he said, "you're freezing."

At the time this had really impressed me. And it still impresses me. Maybe Nathan isn't perfect, a little jokey sometimes, a little glib, but he was giving me the shirt off his back.

Of course, as I recount the event, I'm now struck by the fact that Nathan was not overly surprised that I was soaking wet. I guess he just assumed I had fallen into the water, as if this were something I just did all the time.

"Do you have your laptop with you?" I asked him.

"That's a weird question to ask while you're dripping wet."

"I need it for research."

"I didn't bring it with me," said Nathan. "And I wouldn't give it to you, anyway. It would be an electrical hazard. Take my shirt."

"I don't need your shirt."

I don't know why I was saying this, because it really ranks among "I don't need a bodyguard" in terms of stupidity. Nathan's shirt looked so very dry. I had never seen an article of clothing as dry and as warm looking. He didn't even respond before I started backtracking, in fact.

"I can't put it on here in front of everyone," I said.

"No one will care," Nathan said, which isn't exactly the most romantic angle he could have taken, but I was willing to forgive the line amid the rest of this chivalry. "Hide behind this golden Italian cypress," he suggested.

I was always slightly taken aback by Nathan's referral to plants by their full names. Yes, he had a degree in plant sciences, but this was a man who referred to his love seat, the remote control, a Ginsu knife, and a small plushy doll of Gammara as "that thing." It was also a slightly silly idea, because the "golden Italian cypress"—to my eyes it looked like the sort of potted pine tree thing you'd find in the garden section of a Home Depot—was not remotely big enough to cover my body. But what the hell. I turned my back toward the wall and put on the shirt.

"Do you want my pants?" asked Nathan.

Now that I was experiencing the life-changing magic of dry clothing, I most certainly did. But concussion or no, I had not lost my mind.

"There is no way that your pants would fit on me, Nathan. To even attempt the idea would be an exercise in humiliation."

And the notion of me trying to effectually pull Nathan's skinny jeans over my wet and bloated body clearly cheered Nathan, whom I could practically see chortling at the idea.

A word about shirtless Nathan. I have a real thing for Nathan—I admit it—but this is not a Janet Evanovich-y romp here where Rick ManSlab takes off his shirt to reveal a six-pack, or an eight-pack, or a seven-pack (which is a six-pack and an abdominal hernia, possibly?), or whatever packs guys have these days. Shirtless Nathan looks like a turtle who has somehow gotten out of its shell. He has no body mass! No fat, which is admittedly appealing, but no anything else. He was a brazen little turtle, though, because he seemed cheered by the turn of events.

"So how did you get wet?"

"Chul-Moo is dead, and whoever killed him tried to kill me."

"Which one is Chul-Moo again?"

"You know," I said, "it doesn't matter." It did matter, but it honestly didn't matter to Nathan, and part of managing a successful relationship is understanding your beau's strengths and weaknesses. Mysteries weren't Nathan's strength.

But as if to rebut me, Nathan had a little revelation of his own.

"Your plan worked, by the way,"

"Which plan?" I asked. Quite genuinely. Plans I hatched seemed like an entire lifetime ago. And if I had been hit in the head a little bit harder, it would have been.

"You don't remember it? You had a plan to unmask

Doctor XXX? Boy, one little murder attempt really derails your thinking."

"I will cut you."

"It's Swan," said Nathan. The moment felt dramatic, but it was undercut by Nathan's adding, "And I'm going to find you some pants."

"Don't get me pants—yet. Tell me about Swan."

"He was horrified that his phone kept going off," said Nathan. "I think he figured out what you were up to. He was frantically trying to turn the thing off, and he kept looking around to see if anyone noticed. But I don't think he was paying much attention to me. I was being slick."

"Well, he's never seen you before," I said. "So you wouldn't have had to do anything to go unnoticed."

"That might have been part of it," said Nathan, "but I think mostly it was my excellent slickness."

"Did he," I started—and I didn't know how to ask this without sounding at least slightly crazy—"start watching my stream and then run downstairs, saying, 'That Dahlia! I will smash her head into the sink!'"

This got a quizzical look from Nathan, as it probably should have.

"No," he said. "Did someone smash your head? It looks the same to me."

"We have got to work on your flattery."

"You love my flattery! But no, he didn't do any of that. He turned off his alerts, and then stood very still. I think he's afraid you're going to come up to him."

"As well he should be," I said.

But if Swan was the guy who had been trolling me along—and

apparently had an alibi, since Nathan had watched him not come downstairs and attack me—who the heck smashed my head?

Nathan embarked upon PantQuest, and I—once again bodyguardless—found Swan peering out over the water. He looked terribly sad, even before he saw me, and it struck me that he was a person who was improbably difficult to remain angry at. But I started pretty well:

"What the hell, dude? I dragged you up a flight of stairs. While you were handcuffed to a chair! Naked! And this is how you jerk me around."

I'm not good at anger, as a rule. Me being angry is like trying to hold on to water. Or mercury. Even when I want to hang on to the emotion, it just doesn't work.

Case in point now: Swan looked saddened and completely defeated. He looked like he was going to throw up. I was already wondering why I was yelling at him, since he seemed to be dejected enough already.

"I'm sorry about that," he said. "It was awful. It was dumb and awful. And dumb. But mostly awful."

It was nice, at least, to have skipped over the denial bits. And I would work out the anger later. But first I just wanted to understand what happened, exactly.

"So," I told him. "Explain this dumb and awful plan to me."

"It wasn't supposed to go down like that at all. I was tricked," said Swan.

"By who?"

"Chul-Moo."

"How was it supposed to go down?" I asked.

"Chul-Moo was angry at Imogen because she stole his teammate."

This was not an answer that involved me, and I told Swan so.

"Imogen stole Mike away from Chul-Moo. And we wanted vengeance."

This plan still did not involve me. In most circumstances, I could be patient about these things, but I was still wet—even in Nathan's shirt—and my patience was at a premium.

"How does being angry at Imogen involve me?" I asked.

"We were going to discredit her," said Swan. "Chul-Moo had me wait in that room, and then we contacted you. You were supposed to find me, and you were going to figure out that it was Imogen that met me in there. We were going to have you discredit her for us."

"But it wasn't Imogen in there," I said.

"No, but we were going to leave you clues that it was."

I remembered the perfume in the air, which at the time seemed ridiculous. And the Monopoly-token charm bracelet.

"You're right," I said. "That is a dumb plan."

"Well," said Swan, suddenly defensive about it, "it would have been better if it had gone off. But we didn't end up doing it. You told me that the police were there, which freaked me out, and then when Chul-Moo found out about Karou, we dropped the whole idea. We wanted it to look like she was bribing her opponents, but everyone dropped out anyway. And Chul-Moo fucking betrayed me."

"How did he betray you?" I asked, thinking that betrayal was a decent motive for murder. Although it would be odd to volunteer.

"He depantsed me! That wasn't part of the plan. He just did that after he cuffed me to the chair because he thought it was funny. Such an asshole."

Maybe not murder then, because depantsing is a real third-tier motive for a killing. "And shoes," I said, suddenly thinking. "He also took your shoes."

"Yes," growled Swan. "Another ad-lib of his. Once I was cuffed to a chair, he had all sorts of hilarious ideas."

I was thinking.

"If Chul-Moo took your shoes, why did you have to go out and buy a new pair?" I asked. "Why not just wear the shoes he took?"

"I did! But then you were going around looking for a shoeless Asian guy, and I realized that I couldn't wear my own damned shoes without you asking how I got them. So I had to pretend to lose them. So I ripped Chul-Moo's shoes off his feet and ran out of there. Anyway, you should be talking to Chul-Moo about this. It was all his plan. I was just his victim."

I wasn't sure if this was the right time to tell Swan that Chul-Moo was dead. But it seemed indecent not to mention it.

"Well, Chul-Moo was murdered," I told him. "So I won't be talking to him any time soon." This came out not nearly as soft as I had expected, which I realized because Swan's brain began hemorrhaging.

"What?" said Swan.

"Someone bashed his head in," I said. "Maybe with a fire extinguisher?" I'm not good at soft.

"When?" asked Swan.

"I don't know when," I told him. "After he came on the boat. Someone tried to kill me too. But they missed."

"What?" asked Swan.

I was using my best detective eyes, but I couldn't detect anything from Swan other than shock and disbelief.

"Is that why you're wet?" asked Swan.

I didn't really understand why people kept asking me this question. No, Swan, my being covered in river was an unrelated matter. I thought it would be a fun thing to do after a near-death experience. Is that what he expected me to say?

Of course, he was probably in shock, so I suppose I should be more forgiving. Although, in practice, what I did was take advantage of the shock to badger him with questions.

"So did you do it?" I asked.

"What?" said Swan again. Nothing but "what"s from this guy.

"Did you kill Chul-Moo?" I asked.

"Chul-Moo is dead?" asked Swan.

"Yes," I said. "And someone tried to kill me." No one reacted to that second part of the statement as well as I wanted.

"Am I a suspect?" asked Swan.

"Hell if I know. I'm not the police," I told him. "But you had some sort of secret plan with Chul-Moo, and you're telling people that you were afraid that he was going to betray you. So maybe you killed him? I'm just putting that out there."

"No," said Swan, suddenly anxious. "Don't put that out there. Reel that back in."

"Well, I find that solving crimes is a lot like Rhonda Byrne's *The Secret*. I just put theories out there for the Universe to take hold of."

"I didn't kill Chul-Moo, and I don't think that's how *The Secret* works."

"Well, by the Universe, I sort of mean 'the Police.'"

"I'm really sorry about everything," said Swan. "I didn't mean to mislead you."

This was a complete lie, obviously, because Swan did mean to mislead me. His entire plan was misleading me. That was the plan, period. But it was a good thing to say, nonetheless. Sometimes bald-faced lies can be almost sort of nice.

"The person you should apologize to is Imogen."

"No," said Swan. "Don't tell her. She'll kill me."

And I was inclined there, for a moment, to think: *What a fucking knucklehead.* But then I remembered how anxious Chul-Moo was about getting killed yesterday, possibly by Imogen, and I began to wonder if perhaps Swan wasn't onto something.

I realize that the last time I saw Mike and Imogen in a bar, it was a different bar—but they somehow managed to be sitting in exactly the same places. They also, and I watched them closely, did not display any signs of being kicked—no wincing, or stitches in the side, or footprints across their faces, which I really feel ought to be a clue in a book, even if not here. But exactly the same places. They were creatures of habit, I was guessing. Maybe this was a fighting-game thing, where players are rewarded more for execution than creativity? Or maybe they're just cold, robotic creatures. I told you earlier that Imogen smelled like a cyborg.

"Dahlia," said Imogen, inexplicably happy to see me, "tell me you aren't here to accuse us of more murders?"

"Why are you wet?" asked Mike.

These were not my favorite questions, because (1) I was here, if not to accuse them of murder, at least to float the idea by them, and (2) I was getting tired of answering the question about being wet.

"Well," I said, not really knowing the best way to do this, "as it happens, those two questions are somewhat related."

"Oh God, is she going to start a story?" asked Imogen to Mike.

"I think she's going to start a story."

It was difficult to imagine that someone who had tried to kill you earlier would then snark their way through your confrontation with them, but who knows? I didn't know if they were guilty or not, but I did know they were snarky.

"The story is that someone tried to kill me, and that I had to dive into the river to escape."

"That's terrible," said Mike, looking genuinely shocked. "But how are those questions related?"

"She doesn't know who tried to kill her, and she really has come here to accuse us of another murder," Imogen said, then sighed.

"Seriously?" said Mike, who was less sad today and more put out. "Why would you think that I would be murdering people? At a tournament with a ten-thousand-dollar prize. It's actually insulting."

"I don't think you're involved, Mike," I told him. "I just have some questions for Imogen."

Mike looked immensely pleased by this, and any minor concerns he might have felt for his fighting-game partner were drastically dwarfed by his surging excitement about being deemed innocent.

"Whoop, whoop!" said Mike. "Who's innocent? I'm innocent!"

"Oh Jesus," said Imogen grimly.

"Chugga-chugga-chugga—Oh, hey Imogen, do you know what that sound is?"

"You saying chugga-chugga-chugga like a jackass?"

"It's the murder train, and it's coming into the station! Watch out! Watch out, Imogen! You're gonna get hit by the murder train."

Fighting-game players, I will observe here, are a bizarrely competitive group of people. These were teammates, I want to point out.

"I am not going to get hit by the murder train," said Imogen.

"Should I step away?" asked Mike. "So you can ask Imogen these murder questions?"

"Don't step away," said Imogen. "I'm happy for you to ride the murder train along with me."

While I'm pointing things out, I'm also just going to put out there how unconcerned these two were about my nearly getting killed. No one was overly alarmed by this development. I didn't even get a hug. But I digress.

"So, Imogen," I said. "The reason that I wanted to talk to you is that the guy who got killed was Doctor XXX—who had been threatening you."

"Karou had been threatening me? He seemed like such a sweetheart," she said, and she looked appropriately shocked.

"No, not Karou: Chul-Moo."

And now it was Mike's turn to look shocked. "Wait, what happened to Chul-Moo?"

"Karou was yesterday's killing, Chul-Moo was today's."

There was a long pause. A very long one. I watched their faces gradually transform to anger.

"That's awful!" said Mike. "Why would you tell us this?"

"We have more matches to fight," said Imogen. "That's terrible. We just don't need this bad news right now."

"Jesus," said Mike. "I feel like I should have a drink."

"No drinking until the tournament is over," said Imogen. "Seriously, though, why would you bring this to us?"

The answer, I felt, was pretty obvious, but I was feeling more and more like a jackass as I developed it aloud.

"Well, Imogen—a man threatens you, tells you you should have never been born, apparently has a plan to discredit you, and then winds up dead. I'm not trying to be the boogeyman, but the police are eventually going to connect those dots themselves."

"Dahlia," Imogen said, "I really don't want to seem glib about this, like I'm perfect or unstoppable or some sort of superheroine, but—if every guy on this ship who had threatened me or said something terrible to me got killed today—it would be like we were on the *Black Pearl*."

"Even I'd be dead," said Mike.

"You wouldn't be dead," said Imogen dismissively.

"I guess not. But my legs might be broken."

Imogen thought for a moment, quietly, and considered. "You know, that might be true."

CHAPTER THIRTY-FOUR

I felt both sort of satisfied from the explanations from Imogen and Mike and yet also supremely bummed. When your alibi is that you get so many threats that none of them actually has any currency—well, it's hard to not find that a little depressing. Keep on, Imogen Morland, at least assuming that you didn't try to kill me, at which point, burn in hell.

Also contributing to my sorrow were my pants. I needed dry pants. I needed them badly. Now that my boyfriend was off on a mission to depants some poor woman—hopefully he would charm the pants off her—the fact that I was still wearing wet pants seemed even more intolerable.

I sat down next to the shrub. It had been a hell of a long day. The question that had occupied my mind was not one of mysteries, but was more medical and practical. Is alcohol good for a concussion? I mean, I'm sure it's not GOOD for a concussion—I doubt doctors are at the ER plying victims of head trauma with shots of tequila—but maybe it wasn't bad. Maybe it wouldn't hurt me. Because I would have loved a drink.

I wanted to look this up on my phone—God knows what the engineers at Google must think of me, but of course, it was still missing. I should have had Nathan call it—although

261

presumably whoever had been savvy enough to take it in the first place had taken care of this issue. Probably my beloved phone was in the briny deep. Or the freshwater deep, I suppose. Or the freshwater shallow, at least relative to the ocean. I'm getting sidetracked.

I didn't notice when the guy came up to me, because I was fiddling with my pants, which were a problem. I was wearing pants that were seemingly made of sponge. I was SpongeBob SquarePants. Even after being dry all this time, I was just leaking water everywhere. And my pants were sagging terribly—I was showing a lot of waistline. More panty than I was comfortable with—which was, generally, to be clear—any panty at all, but I was moving past slightly seductive and straight into drunk crazy woman. With my pants sagging this much, I could have been the sort of youth that Bill Cosby would lecture about, and also roofie.

So that's why I didn't notice him. Not because I'm a lousy detective, okay? The answer is wet pants.

"Hey there, pretty lady," he said, "are you here for the tournament?"

It's a dangerous thing to straight-up call a stranger a beautiful lady, but he had a couple of things going for him. For one, I was soaking wet, still, and felt like some sort of monstrous merwoman. Like a naga, or a sahuagin. So, in that particular moment, I didn't mind hearing that I didn't look sahuaginesque. He was lucky. Another thing he had going for him was that he didn't say: "Hey there, pretty lady—why are you at this tournament?" which I had gotten once already. And not to be discounted, he was a good-looking fellow himself, with a surfer vibe and a tight black T-shirt I approved of. I know that it shouldn't matter, but it kind of did. Wet pants. Concussion.

And he had a laptop.

He even opened it up, very suddenly, and seemed to be filming me.

"Are you streaming?" I asked him.

"Yes, indeed," said the guy. "I'm Reynard, and this is live on Twitch."

"Hi, Twitch," I said. "You might know me as Sunkern, or Louise Granger. Probably Louise."

"Did you watch the last round of the tournament—what a beat down!"

"It has been a really exciting tournament so far—nonstop action," I agreed.

"How far did you get in the tournament?" he asked.

"You know," I said, "I'm not really sure. I sort of forgot to attend some matches somewhere along the way."

This made me sound like an airhead, but that seemed preferable to victim. "I was blacked out for a while" just wasn't a good answer. Or at least, it was something that would require a better segue.

And then Remy came moping up to me. He seemed utterly unconcerned that he was being filmed, or that I was soaking wet. He just sat down next to me and drooped.

"Hey, Dahlia," he said, then added, with even less enthusiasm, "Hey, Reynard. We lost."

Then he whispered to me:

"And your plan didn't work out. Nobody did anything with their phone."

Right, that plan. Ah, the ambitious designs of an undrowned woman.

Reynard didn't catch any of this, though, and just wanted to talk about the match. "I saw that bout," said Reynard. "What an upset! Nice Guy Kyle was not playing his best."

Reynard, if that was his real name, was using a fake news-caster-y voice that would have been irritating in any circumstances, but especially when one has been nearly murdered and completely concussed. But mostly I was thinking: How can I steal this chump's laptop?

Remy was leaning on me, which was not cool, Remy, but remarkable in that he was unconcerned about getting wet.

"I just thought we would win," he said. He wasn't crying, but he was a few doors down. He looked heartbroken, and so I hugged the kid with my soggy arms. Maybe I was trying to make up for my cold demeanor with Swan, who was probably just staring out at the water still, saying "what" over and over again. Or maybe I'm just nice.

Reynard was droning on about what a drubbing Remy had taken, which was not cool—and hug or not—laptop or not—I suddenly did not want to be around these two. I should be at the bar, getting a drink. Or at home. With a towel. Thousands of towels. I should just drive to Target and run up and down the bathroom aisle decadently wiping my body over all their towels.

This fantasy was interrupted because I noticed Kyle and Tricia (and Undine) sneaking down belowdecks, probably for yet another bathroom emergency. I was half expecting Tricia to try to pawn her baby off on me. She was holding Undine in her carrier, one-handed—although I noticed that she had a brightly colored Minnie Mouse bandage on her fingers.

And then I solved the murder.

CHAPTER THIRTY-FIVE

Okay, plan time.

"Remy," I said, hugging him closer so that only he could hear me. Reynard must have assumed I was being nurturing. "I have a plan for catching the person who murdered Chul-Moo."

"Wait, what? You mean Karou?"

"Yeah," I said, suddenly deciding that this was not the time to mention murder number two to a fourteen-year-old. "I misspoke. But I need your help."

"Yes?" said Remy, instinctively whispering in response, even though I didn't strictly tell him so. He was an eighth grader. He knew how secrets worked. "What do you need me to do?"

"Distract this goon. And get him away from his computer, which I plan to steal. Then, a few minutes after I've made my escape, find Nathan and Shuler, and hell, Charice. Detective Weber. Whoever you can get ahold of."

"I don't know any of those people!"

"Just look for a policewoman. Tell them I'm belowdecks. Probably in the engine room," I said, suddenly sounding a lot more like Gandalf than I intended. "Now, GO!"

I finished the hug, and Remy, who was a much better actor than I had given him credit for, wiped away an imaginary tear.

"You know, Reynard," said Remy, busting out Kewpie doll's eyes that would have worked on an animated bunny, "I'm really interested in learning about streaming. I need to do a report about it. For school."

"Just google it, dude," said Reynard.

Remy, having immediately decided that guile was not going to work, changed plans all at once, jumping on Reynard's back and noogying him in a way that would have made Dhalsim proud.

"Steal his computer!" yelled Remy, subtlety now gone out the window.

This was not how I imagined this scene going down, but I take my opportunities wherever they come up. I picked up Reynard's laptop and even filmed a bit of the noogying so that this friendly moment might be shared and remembered forever.

And there were viewers—nearly seven thousand of them, which was WAY out of my league. I was originally planning on switching the laptop to my channel, but hell. All I needed were witnesses, and here were seven fucking thousand of them.

And they were furious. It was like I had picked up a beehive filled with swarming angry insects.

Tag24569: What the fuck is this? Where are the games?

Attica1: KIDNIPPING

CHAr43: Ugly Wet Lady, bring back Reynard.

Gerry26: FINISH HIM!!!!

Mondo13422: Call police now. Crazy lady steals computer.

And they went on like this, for pages. Commenting on Twitch was sort of like live tweeting #Sharknado, except that it's less being arch about #Sharknado. It's just all *Sharknado*, all the way down. Being stupid is part of the experience.

"Bring back my stream," shouted Reynard, who did look rather ridiculous. He was down on his knees, and Remy was on his back and was holding him in a sleeper hold. Or what a fourteen-year-old imagined was a sleeper hold.

"Yoink!" I said. And then I took the stream and went belowdecks.

I walked purposefully down the stairs, and kept the stream going with me. I talked to them all the way. I didn't just have a partner in crime; I had seven thousand of them, and it gave me courage.

"Hi, guys," I said. "So this is I guess a kind of kidnapping. My name is Dahlia Moss," I told them. "You can follow me on my own stream at Sunkern. And I'm dragging you to the basement of the *Major Redding*. Do boats have basements?"

I glanced at the stream.

```
WTF??!!!?!?
What? Is? Happening?
FUCK YOU. THIS B**** stole our stream.
Reynard cry now.
The bilge.
WTF.
It's just belowdecks, dumbass.
BILGE. It's bilge.
Take off your shirt!!!
```

About the responses I expected. I continued on, walking farther into the darkness, and heading purposefully toward the engine room.

"Okay so this is the story. Karou was murdered earlier, and I think I know who did it. I'm going to lay a little bit of a trap here, and I just want you fellas to keep watch in case I get killed. Right?"

```
OMG, you're that woman.
It's not a bilge.
Belowdecks.
Is it a cabin?
Take off your shirt!
How's your head?
Why is she wet?
THIS IS THE DEAD WOMAN. SHE'S BACK.
What the fuck is even happening?
I just got here. Is this EVO, or?
It's not a cabin.
Karou got murdered?
DEAD WOMAN BACK!!!!
Yoga murdered.
A++ Would Watch again.
She hasn't had any complaints.
DEAD WOMAN HAS RETURNED!
```

These guys were going to be incredibly helpful, I could tell. Honestly, they might not be horrible. If I got murdered, presumably one of them would call the police. Probably. They'd snark about it first, sure, but police would eventually be called. I'm 80 percent sure of this.

I was getting close to the engine room now, and I could hear noises coming from inside. It was a baby crying.

Okay, I thought. Now, how was I actually going to do this? I needed to set up the stream somewhere so that I would be visible. Right? There couldn't be an end table or something anywhere? I could put the laptop on the floor, but then the stream would just be people's feet. The laptop camera arched, so I tried to swivel it as far back as I possibly could so that hopefully the stream would be able to see me.

Of course, as soon as I opened the door, the camera would be visible, and the jig would be up.

It was at that moment that I decided to take off my pants.

I've been dreading typing that sentence for a while because I've long known that there isn't a way to write it that doesn't turn out insane, but hear me out. (1) They were wet and horrible, (2) I needed to disguise the laptop, (3) given the oversize nature of Nathan's dress shirt, I wasn't really showing anything, and (4) (although this point I realized later) murderers are very disoriented when being confronted by a pantsless woman.

I glanced at the stream, which was a strange combination of misogyny, gratitude, and a creeping sense that something was very wrong.

```
WHAT?
WHAT IS HAPPENING?
Waifu!
WUT.
!!!!!
What is this I don't even.
My waifu.
Waifu!
```

```
This game has everything.
When is next match?
DEAD WOMAN HAS NO PANTS!
```

And so on. I opened the door, and above me, the last match of the tournament started. Down here, it was a whole different kind of crazy.

"Oh gosh," I said, faking surprise when I saw Tricia in the engine room. "I didn't expect to see you guys here."

It wasn't my best line, but as is probably clear from my pant-lessness and possibly concussion, I had left the realm of good decision making. In my defense, I was shooting more for sarcasm, because I'd intended this to be kind of a big reveal, but they didn't get it. I'm not great at sarcasm, apparently. In fact, Tricia and Kyle didn't even question what I was doing there. They just asked me, almost in unison:

"What happened to your pants?"

That was a real problem with this pants-as-disguise plan of mine because it drew a lot of attention to them. Oh well. I went with the honest approach.

"I took them off—they are wet, because someone tried to drown me earlier. You guys don't know anything about that, do you?"

"No," said Tricia flatly. "We don't."

Tricia was already cold to me, but Nice Guy Kyle was still trying to charm. I'm going to chalk it up to my gams.

"Tried to drown you," he said, sounding genuinely concerned. "What happened?"

"Someone struck me in the head, and then left me in this room. I slipped out by jumping into the water from that porthole."

"This room?" asked Kyle. "Spooky." Although, he didn't sound spooked at all.

Tricia, on the other hand, looked supremely spooked, and also seemed quite perturbed by my presence here. Although, she may have just been digesting that I was wearing no pants. Undine, who was in her carrying case in the corner, was apparently asleep, but I felt that if she had been awake and verbal, she would have mentioned the whole pantless thing as well.

"Yes," I told him, pleased to be off the topic of my partial nudity. "I came in here to look for clues," I told him, which wasn't exactly a lie. "What are you guys doing in here?"

"We were looking for a little solitude," Kyle said, adding, "romantic solitude." He looked pleased with his ad-lib, like he had stumbled into something ingenius. Kyle was so happy-looking; it was disconcerting. Although Tricia's face looked like it could have been carved out of stone.

"What could be more romantic than the engine room?" said Kyle, pointing the enormous thrusting mechanical dildo thing that presumably had some kind of useful purpose vis-à-vis the motion of the boat. It wasn't my idea of romance.

I couldn't help but notice at this point that Tricia was slowly moving toward me, staying along the wall. My plan here was to get Tricia on film saying something implicating, but so far I was having no luck. Only Kyle was talking, and not usefully at that.

"Are you guys usually this frisky?" I asked, inanely, because this was not a useful question.

"Yeah, we're trying to conceive," said Kyle, rattling on like a first-year Groundling. "The doctor has Trish taking this drug, and there are certain times where I'm supposed to strike. It's, like, astrology or something."

"I don't think it's possible to conceive right after a birth, is it?"

I don't know why I was getting into this with Kyle. It's clearly a character flaw. Here I was, in a somewhat dangerous situation, and I was going to get myself killed because I was arguing with someone on the Internet who was wrong. And he was on the Internet—being streamed as we spoke. I imagine that #Twitch had a lot of positive and female-embracing things to say about the post-birth bleeding situation. It pains me that I was not able to look at the screen to see them. Oh, poor, poor Twitch chatters. Yours is a brief and fleeting star.

But I digress.

"Guys, I know that one of or both of you did this. You wanna tell me what's up?"

Kyle looked at Tricia. Tricia looked at Kyle. Undine looked at nothing, because her eyes were closed.

"Why are you here," said Tricia, "asking questions? Are you wearing a wire or something?"

"You do seem to stream an awful lot," observed Kyle.

And this was where being pantless was actually not such a bad thing.

"Don't be silly," I told her. "Where would I find a wire on a steamboat?" I asked, although now that I asked the question aloud, this was exactly the sort of thing that was perfectly up Charice's alley. I wish I had thought of that rather than Operation Twitch, but the die was cast now.

"Also, in the unlikely event that I had been wearing a wire, it certainly would have been destroyed when I fell into the Mississippi River. Finally, as you can see, I don't have any pockets. Or pants."

"What makes you think it was us?" asked Tricia. This sounds like an innocent thing to say, but it was delivered in a sort of a "the better to see you with" way that was thoroughly alarming.

"You have bandages all over your fingers," I said.

"Oh, yes," said Tricia, sounding ever more threatening. "I burned myself earlier. On the stove."

"You weren't wearing them earlier," I said.

"The wound was bothering me anew," said Tricia, calmly and unperturbed.

"You haven't, by any chance, seen my purse anywhere?" I asked.

"No," said Tricia, cold. "I haven't."

"You'd recognize it because it has a quilled cactus inside." And God bless Nathan Willing.

Tricia looked amused by this.

"All right," said Tricia. "It was me." This was a line delivered without a lot of embarrassment. Or emotion. It was the sort of "It was me" that you would use to answer a question like, "Who ate the last of the tomato salad? Yeah, I stuck my hand in your purse."

Well, mystery solved.

CHAPTER THIRTY-SIX

Why did you kill Karou? And Chul-Moo?"

"Do what?" asked Tricia, who was not a natural at admitting things. "I don't know anything about that. I just found your purse in the bathroom and put my hand in it."

"Why do you have a cactus in your purse anyway?" asked Kyle, which double murder or not, was a very reasonable question.

"I know that you did this," I said.

"I haven't heard anything yet that says you do," said Tricia. "You sound like you're fishing. Are you sure you aren't wearing a wire? What kind of person asks questions like these?"

I'd really underestimated how suspicious a person Tricia was, who was not taking anything for granted.

"An angry woman with a concussion," I told her.

"Is this blackmail?" asked Tricia. "Is that what you're playing at? You wanna blackmail us? Because let me tell you, dear, we don't have the money for that."

"Not even close," said Kyle.

Tricia, admirably, still hadn't admitted to anything. I wanted to pin her down into an honest-to-gosh confession, but I could tell she was going to be hard to maneuver.

"I don't have any beef with you guys," I told them. "I was no fan of Karou either."

I had no idea where I was going with this; I was just trying to lay down the track fast enough to keep this train from barreling off the tracks. Although, I had to be careful, lest I falsely confess to a double murder myself. That was exactly the sort of notoriety my stream needed.

Tricia looked skeptical, but not altogether unwilling to entertain my gambit.

"How did you know him?"

"We went to school together. We played spin the bottle at a party one time, and he refused to kiss me."

I actually said this out loud. I don't know where it came from. It was not my best work.

"What?" said Tricia.

"He kept saying the bottle had spun to the left, over by Pamela Davidson, but it hadn't spun to the left; it was pointing at me exactly."

"That's a pretty shabby reason to want someone dead," said Tricia, who, lest we forget, is a double murderer.

On the one hand, yes, it certainly was. I had grabbed this story from my past, although it was junior high and not college, and not Karou but a guy named Leland Banks, who I didn't want to kiss me in the first place. He was built like a shrimp, Leland. Not shrimpy like he needed to work out more, but shrimpy in that he had bad posture and a face like a crustacean. He was no dreamboat, and yet he acted like the bottle landing on me was the equivalent of bankruptcy on *Wheel of Fortune*. He actually said "Wah-wah-wah" when the bottle landed on me. I was so ticked. Although, I didn't want Leland dead. I haven't even unfriended him on Facebook, even though he mostly posts inane political rants about getting America on the gold standard. But I digress.

It was a strange feeling, here, having my murder motivation being judged harshly by actual murderers. I didn't feel like Tricia should somehow get the moral high ground. But I bit back this impulse.

"Why did you kill him?" I asked her.

"Who says we killed him," said Tricia. "You wanted him dead."

"We loved Karou," said Kyle. "He was a great guy. You're the pantless psychopath who carries a cactus in her purse."

"Enough of the games," I told them, "because I'm pretty sure that you murdered him."

"Nope," said Tricia.

I had another bit of evidence that was somewhat iffier and I hadn't planned on wheeling out at all. But it was clear I was going to need more if I wanted to move these guys from their foothold.

"There are baby wipes in the trash can. Those are for Undine."

Kyle looked ashen, but Tricia was as stolid as ever.

"That's nothing to do with us," said Tricia. "We didn't put those there."

"I think you did."

"Lots of people have babies," said Tricia. "Undine's not the only baby in the world."

"In the engine room of a steamboat?"

Tricia had changed tacks, however. She was the antithesis of the woman on *Perry Mason* who broke down, saying, "It was me. It was me." She would have reached across the stand and slapped Raymond Burr in the face. "How about you shut the fuck up, Perry?"

"We put those there just now," said Tricia.

"So if I touch those now, the poop will feel wet," I said. I could not believe how much I was engaging with the crazy here. My plan involved touching poop. But Tricia was unmoving.

"Undine has dry ass. It's a condition."

"Her shit just comes out dry? Honestly, that's your line?"

Tricia changed tack.

"The baby wipes don't prove a thing. They could have come from anywhere. Lots of people have babies."

"On board this steamboat?"

"Or maybe it's just some weird adult," continued Tricia.

"Some kind of freaky sex thing," volunteered Kyle helpfully.

"There are DNA tests that can be done to prove that they belong to her."

"There's no poop DNA test."

"Actually, I'm pretty sure there is."

Tricia was absolutely unmoving. I was in awe of her, in one sense, but she was also being completely exasperating.

"Anyway," said Tricia, "it doesn't prove that we were down here. Maybe Undine came down here on her own."

"Maybe your two-week-old infant came down to the basement by herself? That's your suggestion?"

"Or with some unseen nanny."

"Why don't you tell me why it is that you killed Karou, Tricia?"

"Maybe someone stole some of Undine's used wipes and put them down here."

And Tricia liked this one, because her eyes lit up with possibility. Despite myself, I couldn't help but engage with this woman's ridiculous alibis.

"So wait, you're proposing that—just to make sure I understand this correctly—that someone stole used baby wipes, covered in shit—and left them in the basement."

"Boats don't have basements," said Kyle, and Tricia and I both rightfully ignored him.

"That's exactly what happened," said Tricia. "In fact, I noticed they were missing from the restroom earlier. I thought a porter had emptied the trash."

"That's deeply implausible," I told her. "Why would anyone do that?"

"To frame us," said Tricia, her eyes blinking at me, practically daring me to defy her.

Kyle, after being ignored, had wisely retreated from the conversation, recognizing that this crazy wife-fu act of denial was Tricia's special role in their relationship. But I was keeping an eye on him, because I was half expecting him to pull a gun on me or some such. Yes, I know I didn't get shot in the ass earlier, but once you've taken a bullet, you get wary of guns. I even was keeping tabs on Undine, because these two were quite a piece of work, and who knew what their offspring was capable of?

"I think," I said, considering the stream that was capturing all this behind me, "that you should give this up and tell me why you did it. What did you have against Karou?"

"I think you put these wipes here," said Tricia. "You hated Karou because he spurned you, and you were out for blood. You planted those things here because you wanted to destroy us."

"I just met you," I told Tricia. "I watched your baby for you. Multiple times!"

"We do appreciate that," said Kyle.

And then I was hit with a terrible truth. I realized it all at once.

"You murdered Karou while I was watching Undine! You didn't have a bathroom emergency at all!"

This didn't exactly crack Tricia, but it did seem to make her slightly embarrassed.

"You fucking asshole!" I said. "What kind of person asks a stranger to watch their infant while they commit a murder?"

Tricia was still backpedaling, but she was backpedaling in a different direction now.

"You weren't a stranger," said Tricia. "I'd seen you stream before. And you seemed like you'd be good with Undine."

"Oh my God," I said, still connecting dots. "I watched Undine for forever this morning. Tell me you did not kill again while I was watching your baby a second time!"

"I did not," said Tricia, her denial in a completely different—and markedly honest—tone this time. "I just needed a break."

"You needed a break because you killed Chul-Moo!"

Tricia was, however momentarily, speechless.

CHAPTER THIRTY-SEVEN

What really makes this exchange embarrassing—embarrassing to me, at least—is that there was a corpse on the floor the entire time that I had failed to notice.

If you will go back and look at the stream transcript later—you will see that—had I been watching—there had been, up to this point, hundreds of comments about the dead body. Here I was trying to needle Tricia with fine little points about soiled baby wipes in a trash can, when I should have just said something like: "Hey, is that a corpse behind you?"

But even without the stream, I eventually noticed that there was a trail of blood—and yuck, I don't know, skull bits?—that led from the near porthole to immediately behind Kyle.

"I'm not setting aside the wipes point," I told Tricia. That was how proud I was of that point, actually. I wasn't willing to let it go. "But there's also a trail of blood, and I don't know, brain that leads behind your husband."

Tricia turned to face the blood, which was a thin smeared red-and-brown streak that was nauseating once you saw it.

"What blood?" said Tricia. "I don't see any blood."

"It's on the floor."

"Where?" said Tricia, who also, I observed, had some of it on her feet. "I don't see any."

"It's also on your shoes," I said.

"These aren't my shoes," said Tricia. "I borrowed them. They had this on them already. It's the new style."

"Would you mind moving a little, Kyle, so that I can see what's behind you?"

Kyle moved—I don't know why—and there was more of Chul-Moo's corpse. Tricia must have kicked him in the head? It was terrifying, really. He seemed to look worse every time I saw him.

"Oh my God," said Tricia. "This is terrible! Who knew this was here?"

"Unnnghh," said someone. That's right, "unnghh." Because behind Chul-Moo was another half-murdered person. It was like a murdered-person white sale down here.

The Not Quite Murdered Person was tall, and dark skinned, and I said:

"Oh my God. You did not knock out Detective Maddocks. That is not good." If you shoot at this king, you best don't miss. I'm sure that Detective Maddocks would not like that joke, actually. However, if I saved his life, he was totally going to owe me. Seriously. He'll have like a blood debt.

Anyway, Tricia and Kyle did not answer. (Neither did Undine.) And so I answered their earlier question, "Who knew this was here?"

"Probably Kyle knew he was there," I said, given that his boots have blood on them. Maybe they had been rolling him over, not kicking him. It was probably a little ungenerous to go straight to kicking. There was a giant hole in the engine room that led down to whatever other mechanisms powered the ship, and perhaps they were just trying to roll him in there? I could only guess, because there was no chance I'd get any honest answers from these clowns.

"Well, I had no idea," said Kyle. "I walked over to this part of the room backward."

I admired the even tone that Kyle was able to deliver this line in, which was honestly offhanded and sort of inviting. He looked at me then, a bit searchingly, and shared a look with Undine.

I expected Tricia to say something like "I think she's got us," but then Tricia said, simply: "Check your phone to make sure she's not streaming."

I panicked—seriously panicked—because I was streaming. But then I remembered: I wasn't streaming. Reynard was. I'd kidnapped someone else's stream.

Kyle looked at his phone, and after a moment said: "Nope. She's clean."

"Of course I'm not streaming," I said nervously. "How could I be streaming? You guys stole my computer and phone. That's why I came down here. I want them back."

"I'm sorry I asked you to watch my kid while I *may have* murdered a guy," said Tricia. This was as close to a confession as I would ever get, and so I'm just going to imagine that she didn't say "may have." Actually, I'm just going to imagine that she started weeping and saying, "Yes, yes, Dahlia Moss, your clever deductions have found me out." Why go small?

"Why did you do it?" I asked.

"He cut us," said Tricia. "Right before the tournament. And replaced us with fucking Chul-Moo. We're living hand to mouth here, Dahlia. You can't cut us! We cut you!"

"Okay," I said, accepting this in the limited way I would accept any reason for murder. "I get why you would have been upset with Karou, but what did Chul-Moo do wrong?"

"We maybe got a little carried away with Chul-Moo," said Kyle.

"HE SHOULDN'T HAVE TAKEN THE JOB," said Tricia. "IT WAS OUR JOB."

I did not think it wise to press this point any further. So I asked: "And Detective Maddocks there?"

"I don't know anything about that," said Kyle.

"Oh, come on," I said. "Jesus Christ, guys."

"He's not dead," said Tricia. "He just wandered in here, and we knocked him out. We wanted to just knock you out," said Tricia.

"It's so hard to find good sitters for Undine," said Kyle.

"Okay," I said uncertainly. "Anybody else you guys kill?"

"No," said Tricia, moving toward me. "At least, not yet."

CHAPTER THIRTY-EIGHT

There was a moment, a brief euphoric moment, when I felt invincible. That I could do anything. I had deduced the identity of my attacker, and Karou's murderer—even if the confession was a little wobbly, and I was still decidedly hazy on the details of why exactly Kyle and Tricia had had Karou meet his end—you know, I was doing pretty good work for a beginner. I'd maybe even saved Detective Maddocks from certain death, and he was going to be pissed about that later.

But the moment faded when Tricia started lunging for me. I was taken aback—even given that I had a plan, and I had broadly been suspecting it. It was like a monster movie where the zombies suddenly moved fast. You're: Wait—we've got fast zombies in this lore, do we? You can compensate, but that initial lunge? Scary. Freaky scary.

As an aside, can I mention that I am not a fan of the fast zombie? They're ridiculous. And why are dead people all of a sudden in such great shape? It really cheapens the point of working out if there are just decaying zombies who are more fit than you. I imagine them at the gym, in a huddle, wondering why I am taking so long on the StairMaster.

But I digress.

Tricia was lunging at me, which was good, because it meant she didn't have a firearm. I had kind of assumed that had been the case, given the rash of bludgeonings, but even so: lucky me. I turned, yanked down to grab the computer, and I really wanted to see what the computer said. I imagined it was filled with amazing things about how clever I was, and also, how obstinate Tricia and Kyle were, but I didn't have time. It was probably just as well, because now that I consider it with a little distance, it was probably just a lot of Kappas interspersed with the occasional "show us your tits."

"All right, Twitch chatters—we established that those guys killed Karou, right? The camera caught that?"

I couldn't really read the screen with all the motion, but I was sure that it was filled with "UMmmm, NO," and "Not Really!" and more sarcastic responses to that effect, along with additional Kappas and requests for tits. But I was in the mood for optimism, and I was in no mood to read the comments, even if I had the time and the steady hands.

"I'm glad we agree. So, I'm running for my life right now. I'm hoping some of you called the police while I was down there. Right? Tell me one of you did that."

I had apparently gotten confused in the snaking hallways of the "belowdecks" area—or was it a bilge, did we ever establish that?—because I was fully expecting to arrive at a stairwell, and I did not exactly do that. Instead, I arrived at a dead end, in which there was a nothing but a nice oaken little coffee table— tiny, just large enough for a bowl of fruit, and a largish frowning picture of a white-bearded man in a military outfit. I would later learn that this was Major Redding himself, although I did not take the time to observe that now.

There were two numbered doors here, which presumably led to cabins, but I assumed they were locked. I didn't have time to make a lot of choices here, so I put down the laptop, and I picked up the end table.

When Tricia came around the corner, I hit her in the head with it, which I felt, reasonably, would knock her down. At best it dazed her a tiny amount. Kyle was running down the hall, carrying Undine, which presumably was the reason he had been traveling more slowly. But with Tricia tottering there, there wasn't really anywhere else for me to go. I was boxed in.

"She's got another computer," Tricia said. "She's recording this."

"It's okay, honey," said Kyle agreeably. "We'll just kill her."

Kyle was gingerly putting Undine down—he seemed like a great dad, honestly—aside from him being very weird and also the murders—and unstoppable zombie Tricia just came walking toward me. I saw now that she had a spade in her hand, which is probably what she had hit me with earlier.

And then Nathan, shirtless, ridiculous Nathan, dove on top of her.

Nathan had never looked more ridiculous or perfect or wonderful than he did in that moment. He looked like a Fraggle who was trying to pilot a rhinoceros, which is apparently exactly what was needed.

"Dahlia," he gasped. "I've come to save you."

He was also wearing pink sweatpants that did not stay on his body very well. I later learned, that while I was busy acquiring a confession from Tricia and Kyle—which I totally acquired—he had been on an odyssey of pants. The thing was, Nathan is very thin—almost impossibly thin, and so finding pants that

I, a normal person, could wear—involved multiple trades. Not only had Nathan charmed the pants off a woman for me, he had charmed the pants off two women. And a guy.

If that's not a relationship with a future, I don't know what is.

Of course, I didn't know any of that at the time. I just saw his flailing Muppet hands and his ridiculous oversized sweats, and I observed that if this boy was ready for my jelly, as they said in the aughts, so be it.

Tricia charged forward as if she were some sort of wild animal, like a wildebeest or a kodo, and smashed Nathan's head into the wall. Nathan was holding on to her neck, and it struck me that he was trying to apply some sort of sleeper hold on her, but was doing so very ineffectually. In the meantime, Kyle had carefully unpacked Undine from her carrier—she was sleeping nicely—placed her on the ground in the corner and safely out of the fray, and then thwacked Nathan with the carrier. It would have hit him in the head, had Tricia not twisted, and I wondered if this is what had concussed me, because that spade would have done the job a lot more thoroughly.

I had to do something, and I was being briefly ignored, so I took the picture of Major Redding off the wall, and I hit Kyle in the face with it. This did a lot more damage than I expected it would, in part because it was a really nice wooden frame, and was both nicer and heavier than the coffee table. This suddenly concerned me, because I began to consider that this was probably a very Valuable Painting, but then Tricia started screaming, so I swung the painting at her and hit her—hard—in the back of the knee.

The stream loved this part, and typed the words "FRAME TRAP!!!" hundreds of thousands of times, which is a joke so stupid that I refuse to explain it. They are probably still typing it now.

And then everyone sort of went tumbling. Kyle had fallen to the ground but had picked up a piece of coffee table and hit me in the leg with it. Tricia seemed to go over all at once, almost like she had fallen on the ice. Nathan, of course, went down with her, and someone grabbed at my leg and there I went as well.

We were on the floor, weird and half-naked, and it was now like a terrible murderous game of Twister. We were just wrestling, and it was all sort of awful.

We were dazed—we were all dazed, me from my concussion, Tricia and Kyle from their murder spree, Nathan from his pantsapalooza, Undine from not being able to work her arms or legs, the Twitch chat from having to watch all this plus repeated commercials for Disney hotels.

This stage of the chase, the half-naked dazed portion in which no one was moving particularly, lasted altogether longer than it should. We were tired and getting hit with pieces of wood. No one said so, but in retrospect, I think we all welcomed the break.

It ended suddenly, though, when Tricia managed to pick up my computer, which she probably imagined held incriminating evidence, and ran off, leaving behind her husband, her daughter, and me. This made it the third time she left her child with me.

"Bring back my viewers!" I shouted after her. Or technically,

Reynard's viewers. He was going to make so much money off this. Like, a hundred dollars, maybe two! (This is a dig on Twitch's profit sharing. Hi, Twitch Overlords!)

Anyway, it was perhaps indicative of my mental state that I chased after her. Technically, of course, the computer had no files, no hard-coded anything that could serve as evidence, and Tricia leaving with the stream was doing nothing but incriminating her further. "Let her go; it's her own funeral." That's what a rational person would say. That's what I would say later, with the benefit of a non-concussive state. But what I said then was: "Stop her—she's getting away."

Nathan, who was squaring off against Kyle in what could have been (affectionately) billed as the battle of the wimps, did nothing to accomplish this goal. Nor did Undine, who was resting comfortably, respond to my call.

So I got up and chased her myself.

Tricia was running through the corridors of the *Major Redding* like she was a crazy woman, which I suppose, she was. I still hadn't quite figured out if she had been doing the killing or Kyle, but they both seemed really unruffled by the idea. Say what you will about them, they had a very solid relationship. Anyway, I couldn't tell if she knew where she was going, or if she was just making random decisions at each intersection. I never figured that out, actually.

But we eventually came to a rickety black spiral staircase that she hastily ascended, still holding my laptop. Okay, yes, Reynard's laptop, but I had come to think of it as my own. Besides, seven thousand helpless dude-bros on Twitch chat had been abducted, and it was up to me to save them. So up the stairs I went. Won't someone think of the Kappas?

And hello, non-OSHA compliance, can I just mention these stairs? They were beyond wheelchair inaccessible. They were the antithesis of wheelchairs. It seemed designed to break the spirits of people with disabilities, if not actually their chairs as well. (Or alternatively, this was a very old section of the boat.)

I headed up the stairs and quickly realized why the stairs had been so antiquated. This was a strange portion of the ship that wasn't meant for general use. Probably why it had never been upgraded.

We were backstage, I thought—a wooden area with a white fabric wall. Again, that's really something I noticed more of later. Mostly I was thinking: Destroy Tricia.

"Tricia," I said. "Give it up."

"No," she said. "I can destroy the evidence. I can kill you. I can solve all of this."

"You can't," I told her. "There's nothing to destroy. You're not being recorded, you're being streamed. There are seven thousand witnesses." Probably more now, when you got to it.

I didn't need to explain what that meant to Tricia, who stared at me, bug-eyed. I felt certain that she was not going to go down without a fight, however, and I was not a girl that could put up a fight at this point. What was I thinking? Why did I come up here?

"I will kill you," said Tricia. "It may not solve anything, but I can still kill you."

And then a crowd went, "Awwwww!" just like that. Awwwww! Which is not what you want to hear when someone says, "I will kill you." And yet, it wasn't so bad, because all of a sudden, I knew where we were.

I heroically burst through the screen and was back in the

auditorium, onstage in front of an army of gamers. [Editor's note: This is not what happened.]

Okay, fine, I ran into the screen—which despite being sort of fabric-y, was apparently too thick to just tear through like you're a football team at homecoming. I just crashed into it with sort of a *THWUMP*, which surprised me, but was okay, I guess, because it also surprised Tricia, who felt that this dramatic gesture should have worked. It's the sort of thing that's supposed to work.

Then I was just dazed for a moment, and I lifted the screen and walked under it.

[Editor's note: better.]

There was still the army of gamers, and everyone was looking at me. No game was being projected on the screen, however, which I thought was odd, but then I realized that Charice and Daniel were also on the stage, also looking at me.

Daniel—still in Vega garb—was down on one knee.

My detective brain, concussed as it may have been, was putting it together. Daniel's engagement plan. One-kneed-ness. Crowd going "Aww!"

I looked, and Daniel was holding a ring. He had probably gotten that ring yesterday from Steve Buscemi, because Daniel was a Craigslist's wedding ring sort of guy, I suddenly realized.

"Is this a bad moment?" I asked.

To Charice. To Daniel. To everyone.

Charice, who—despite all of her chaotic little ways, and frankly her chaotic medium-size ways, and okay, yes, her chaotic fucking humongous ways—possesses oceans of patience I lack, simply said: "Yes, Daniel, I will marry you."

And the crowd cheered. I like to imagine that Daniel teared up, but who knows? He was wearing a mask.

It was a perfect little moment, aside from the fleeing a double murderer. Even so, it felt like it existed on its own separate plane. Charice looked so happy, and I felt happy, and it was like I had wandered onto this wonderful magical grotto of love. What was I ever afraid of? Of course I want Charice and Daniel to be together. That's what was supposed to happen all along.

But then I heard Tricia fumbling with the screen, and the spell was broken.

"I'm so sorry, Charice," I said. "I didn't want to step on your moment. But there's just this crazy woman behind this screen with a garden trowel, and she's trying to kill me."

"It's no problem," said Charice, who managed to impart this with a lot of emotion, although I may be projecting.

Then Tricia burst through the screen—okay, fine, lifted the screen and crawled under it—and was stunned to see everyone looking at her. Then Charice—and I may be editorializing a little, but if you don't believe me, you can chalk it up to the concussion—spun around in the classic Balrog turn-punch, complete with the gust of wind sound effect, and punched Tricia in the face.

KO. Perfect Victory.

I mean, that's what someone should have said.

Seriously, though—editorializing aside—Charice punched Tricia in the face. It was sort of awesome. Later, when it was all over, Charice told me:

"See, Dahlia, you don't need a bodyguard. You've got me."

The rest of the day was a blur of chaos, headaches, and sworn statements to the police, who once we hit landfall, started swarming like ants. And I quite literally mean blur, because my head wound was definitely setting in at that point. Nathan completed his circle of pants bartering so that my thighs were at last protected from human view, as God intended. Charice appointed herself my guardian while Nathan was getting grilled by Weber and company.

I had gotten the feeling that folks were regarding me as the slightest bit manic, since it seemed to be everyone's opinion that I should go somewhere dark and quiet and calming. Probably they were concerned about the concussion, in retrospect, but in the moment I thought perhaps I was being lumped in as an unhinged woman. So when I was assigned Charice as a chaperone, I took the opportunity as a chance to accomplish whatever the goddamned hell I wanted.

I was probably getting delirious, because what I really wanted to know was who had won the fucking tournament. Nathan and Charice didn't know, and the police seemed not to even understand the question. So I fought my way above decks until I found Imogen, who judging from her air of resplendence, surely had taken the final round.

"Did you win?" I asked her.

Mike was with her—resplendent in his green cap, which I guess really was ocher, now that I looked at it in this light, and was grinning from tooth to tooth.

"Of course we won," said Imogen.

"Obviously we were going to win," said Mike. "We assumed that's why you dropped out. You realized the inevitability of our victory."

"No," I said. "I dropped out because someone tried to kill me. How can you not remember that?"

"We remembered that," said Mike, who the better I knew

him, I realized was very offended, "we just didn't know that was the reason you dropped."

"Who would have a near-death experience and then keep playing on in the tournament?" I asked Mike.

"I would," said Mike.

"Obviously I would," said Imogen.

"I guess that's why you're champions," I said, and this remark made them both preen, although I didn't actually mean it as a compliment. But no matter.

I ran into Remy, who honestly was the happiest person to see me alive yet, which was surprising, but maybe he was just a happy kid. And yet, as soon as we exchanged greetings he became completely ashen faced.

"My mother is going to be so angry," he said. "I don't know if this much grounded actually exists."

I was quiet then, taking a moment to recount Remy's sins. Let's see, theft, skullduggery, assault, if you count a noogie attack as assault, hiding a murder from your mother, and playing in a tournament with a double murderer, though Dad would probably take some of the heat for that one. I didn't ask, but probably Remy was the guy watching Undine while I was getting assaulted. The first time.

"Yeah," I said. "You're gonna be grounded for a good long while."

Charice showed up, I assumed to try to lure me back down into a small dark calming place, but in fact to give me her phone.

"I really shouldn't," I said. "I keep breaking electronic devices today."

"Oh, I'm not giving you that to keep," said Charice. "You have a caller."

Who would call Charice to reach me?

"Dahlia?"

I had known the answer before I even put the phone to my ear.

"Shuler," I said. "How are you?"

I realized how stupid and inane a question this was. Shuler was fine. I was the person with problems.

"I'm fine," he said. "I'm just glad to hear you're okay."

There was a pause. I was really hoping that Shuler wouldn't say the next thing he said.

"I was watching your stream," said Shuler.

"Oh," I said. "Were you one of the thirty-seven people who called the police?"

"I'm the one person who called the police that they listened to," said Shuler. "Do you have any idea how dangerous all the stuff you were doing was? Incredibly dangerous."

"At the time, no," I said truthfully. "In retrospect, yes."

"I've been sitting here watching your black screen for an hour. Do you know how freaked-out I was getting? A black screen, Dahlia—it's one of the primary metaphors for death."

"Did they make you watch the commercial for the Disney hotel?"

"Hundreds of times. I will never visit that hotel. Epcot means Death to me now. Epcot is Death."

"They have a cool waterslide, though," I said, remembering the commercial.

"That waterslide does look really swank," Shuler admitted.

And we were both silent for a moment. I wanted to say something to Shuler, but I didn't know what. It was an awful feeling—I think it was maybe yearning—but I don't even really know. I did know this: I did not want to be a person in a love triangle. Love triangles were for dummies and people who looked like Kristen Stewart, or both. And "love" wasn't even the right word. This would have been a like triangle, which is too lame to even be a thing.

But I did find myself feeling a very strange emotion—which was the lightest bit of jealousy. Charice knew who she wanted to be with. I couldn't even work that out. Maybe I needed more clues.

It was Shuler who spoke next.

"Do you know what I do when I get nervous?" he said.

"No," I said, feeling that this answer could not be anything positive.

"I buy things on Amazon."

"Oh," I said. "That's not good."

"I bought a skateboard, Dahlia. A skateboard."

"That's very not good. Do you skate?"

"I don't," said Shuler. "But I was thinking maybe I would start."

The notion of Shuler—who had a vaguely wobbly quality to him at the best of times—zipping around Forest Park on a skateboard was innately sort of funny. I expected to say something funny, in fact, but instead I said:

"You wanna maybe go skating sometime? I've got a brand-new pair of roller skates."

"I've got a brand-new key," said Shuler, finishing the phrase. "Also," he said, "I can show you how to pick a damn lock."

By the time I finally got home, it wasn't Nathan who took care of me, whom the police seemed to want to talk to forever. And it wasn't Shuler, who made sure I was okay, but returned to do other work when my health had been assured by paramedics. It wasn't even Charice, who fell asleep so suddenly, it was as though she had been the concussed one. Who knows, maybe she had also gotten concussed. So goes the perils of stage fighting.

It was Daniel, Charice's betrothed, who was inexplicably wandering around our apartment wearing one of Charice's sleep kimonos. He took care of Charice first, obviously, but Charice was easy, because she falls asleep the way all the Chitauri suddenly go limp at the end of the first *Avengers* movie.

He wouldn't be such a bad husband. If you absolutely had to have one.

He made me tea and fluffed my pillow, and he listened to me talk about my day, even though I don't think I was making any sense at all at that point. Also, when my mother called, he told her that I wasn't available because I had gone to a job interview. He did this without even snickering, despite it being ten at night at this point, and not remotely plausible. Acting!

"So you're going to marry Charice," I said.

"So it would seem," said Daniel.

"I'm sorry if I ruined your proposal," I told him.

"Well," said Daniel, "as it happens, I'm the happiest guy in St. Louis today, so I don't think you have much to worry about. Although, it will be hard to top that moment for our wedding."

"I'm terrified of Charice's wedding," I told him, quite honestly. "I don't even want to know what she's going to make her bridesmaids wear."

"She wants you to wear a burlap pantsuit," said Daniel, and I winced.

"Is she angry at me?"

"No," said Daniel, quite surprised. "She's been saying that for ages. Charice loves you, Dahlia. She just wants you in a weird pantsuit."

This made me feel happy, maybe happier than it should, but it had been a long, long day, with many mistakes in it. After a long time, during which I may have briefly fallen asleep, I asked:

"Are you nervous about it?"

"About getting married?" asked Daniel. "Nah. I feel like a flower waiting to open. Maybe that's the kimono talking."

"No," I told him, "you stole that line from Charice. She said the same thing."

"Did I? Well, actors don't steal," Daniel said earnestly. "We reinterpret. So, do you want me to ask you for Charice's hand in marriage?"

"What?" I said, feeling engaged even as I could tell I was drifting back off to sleep. "That would be completely ridiculous."

"But do you want it?"

"Kind of, yes?"

"May I have the hand of your insane but wonderful roommate, Charice, in matrimony?"

"Yes, you may, Daniel," I said, already drifting off to sleep. "And thank you for asking."

We went the next morning for eggs. Me, Charice, Daniel, and Nathan. University City has this great greasy spoon that does breakfast like nobody's business. They serve the eggs in a bowl; that's how greasy we are talking.

We sat at the table and had soupy eggs and waffles. Charice told me that eggs were good for a concussion, which I have since learned is complete nonsense, but it sounded believable at the time.

"What's going to happen to Undine?" Charice was asking.

Where Charice had picked up the name of Tricia's daughter was unclear, but she did have a tendency to pick up unexpected bits of information, like some sort of psychic katamari. Also, like a katamari, she tended to destroy things in her path. I would miss her. Hopefully marriage wouldn't change her too much. Hell, hopefully things would stay exactly as they were.

"Tell me," I said, "that you're not going to try to adopt Undine."

"Maybe just temporarily," said Charice, thoughtfully. "Like respite care until the state figures out what to do with her. You couldn't do it."

"I don't want to do it," I told her.

"You keep falling off balconies."

"I'm pretty sure you have to take classes from the state before they let you do that."

"Hmm," said Charice, in what was a dangerously contemplative sound, given the context.

Daniel, who I had liked very much last night, was irritating the heck out of me now, and was practically necking with Charice. This is broadly unacceptable over dinner, but for breakfast is a high crime. Our waitress, Kellie, kept coming over and glaring at them, and I tried to psychically will her to say something to them, for all the good it would do. She didn't, but I left her a good tip anyway.

"By the way," mentioned Charice, "I invited someone else to our gathering this morning. I hope you don't mind."

I had wondered about that when we had been seated at a table for five, but I hadn't pecked at it. Not everything is a mystery, after all. Sometimes things are dumb coincidences. Most things, actually.

Charice was smiling at whoever was coming along, and I had a few guesses as to who it might be, from least to most horrifying.

- Remy
- Shuler, which would be awkward
- Maddocks, which would be terrifying
- My brother, Alden, which would be inexplicable
- My mother, inexplicable and terrifying
- The broodmother in *Alien* (who just narrowly edges out my own mother)
- A social worker with baby Undine

But I was wrong on all these cases, because it was Emily Swenson. Emily was a dangerously competent lawyer in her thirties, who had been the woman who had gotten me started in on the whole "geek detective" thing in the first place. Emily was the most put-together woman I'd ever seen in real life, and even though she favored pastels that were not at all my style, it was hard not to be in awe of her.

This morning, I'd say she was dressed like a strawberry banana smoothie, all pink and yellow and white. But a really expensive smoothie, with shots of wheatgrass in it.

"Dahlia," she said, and I could almost feel heat coming from a job that would pay actual money, and not merely Twitch notoriety. "I'm sorry I had to call Charice, but your phone doesn't seem to be working."

"I'm very hard on phones," I told her.

"I've got a proposition for you—and don't say yes right away."

And then Emily Swenson handed me a slip of paper that said: "Would you like to become an industrial spy?"

meet the author

Elizabeth Frantz

MAX WIRESTONE lives in Lawrence, Kansas, with his husband, his son, a very old dog, and more books than a reasonable person should own.

introducing

If you enjoyed
THE ASTONISHING MISTAKES OF DAHLIA MOSS,
look out for

THE QUESTIONABLE BEHAVIOR OF DAHLIA MOSS

A Dahlia Moss Mystery

by Max Wirestone

CHAPTER ONE

You don't want Emily Swenson, Lawyer with Money, to confront you at a breakfast bar. Honestly, you don't want her to confront you anywhere, because Emily, despite her peach silk blouses and *Vogue*-layout makeup choices, is an awfully scary lady. But a breakfast bar such as the one I was at, with its all-you-can-eat waffles and syrup packets that you had to individually unwrap, was not the natural habitat of such a person. One doesn't bump into Emily Swenson in a place that sells an omelet called "The Heart Attack." If you encounter her there, it means she was looking for you.

I might have had a head wound, but I could at least put that together. Also, she had slid over a sheet of paper that said: "Would you like to become an industrial spy?"

So, there's that.

We'll get to the paper in a second, but first let's talk about the head wound, because you and I need to get on the same page.

As you may or may not know, I was a bit concussed at the end of my last adventure. It's unseemly for me to be going on about it now, a full story later, because Sam Spade gets concussed three or four times a chapter, and after about three paragraphs he never mentions it again. There is a rule about that sort of thing, which is that detectives aren't supposed to complain about minor injuries from previous books.

Forget that, says I. And who knows, maybe Sam Space couldn't remember the earlier concussions? Maybe he had some real memory-loss issues. Maybe he should have seen a guy.

Anyway, my head smarted, and while I had felt worlds better after getting a nice night of sleep, I'm not going to pretend I wasn't thinking about my vaguely blurry vision for the sake of your narrative smoothness. The head injury was a thing, and it's going to stay a thing for the rest of this story. Mea culpa.

That clear? Now let's talk about the note.

"Would you like to become an industrial spy?"

First, who walks around with notes like that? Emily Swenson, obviously. Maybe she had them for every occasion, and if she had reached in the wrong pocket I would have gotten a note that said: "Up for some arson?" or "I need a man killed."

To be fair to Emily, it wasn't like these were printed on custom-made cards. She had jotted it down on the back on a napkin. Presumably because she didn't want everyone else at the table to hear her probably illegal, certainly unethical offer.

I had been having breakfast with Charice and Daniel, who were being more lovey in public than should be allowed before ten o'clock. I'm not entirely against public forms of affection, but I feel that there should be at least some darkness involved.

Charice pretended not to notice my surprise at the note, as I excused myself from the table.

"Oh, Emily," I said. "You are here to return that library book I loaned you?"

"Sure," said Emily. "That's why I'm here. You want to step out with me for a second."

I say that my roommate Charice pretended not be interested,

but she was doing a pretty good job at it, because she was basically wearing Daniel on her face. From the looks of it, Emily Swenson could have opened a suitcase full of money, dumped it on the table, and said, "I need you to turn this into cocaine," and it wouldn't have fazed her.

We stepped out to Emily's car, which was precisely the sort of luxury car that a super-rich person who doesn't care about cars would purchase. It was simultaneously silver and nondescript and yet paradoxically made of money. It smelled like lemon verbena on the inside, and the leather seats were already warm.

"So," I said, "how have you been?"

Emily just smirked at me, amused by my need to make small talk.

"Let's talk about the job I have in mind for you."

This was probably for the best, because I couldn't tell you the first personal detail about Emily Swenson, which made shooting the breeze somewhat challenging. Sometimes you encounter people in life who are nothing but surface. Beautiful polished people with nothing underneath. Emily Swenson wasn't that exactly—there was plenty going on in there, probably too much—but hell if I had any clue what it was.

"Okay," I said. "You want me to be an industrial spy? Is this what you do, incidentally? Just go around giving people odd requests?"

"Not everyone," said Emily. "Just people with talent and no criminal records."

I preened more at the talent line more than I should have. But like they say, flattery gets you everywhere. And not having a criminal record also helps.

"What are you looking for?" I asked.

"It's not what I'm looking for, Dahlia. It's never about what I'm looking for. It's about what the client is looking for."

"Who's the client?"

"Some general advice, that's rarely a question that you should ask when someone approaches you with a task they've surreptitiously written on a napkin."

Was it, really? It seemed straightforward enough to me. I tried telling this to Emily.

"I generally like to know who I'm working for."

"You're working for me," said Emily, simply.

"And you're working for?"

"Someone who wishes to remain nameless."

"Is it Satan?" I asked. "That's not a deal breaker, by the way. I'd just want to know."

"Please," said Emily, "He already has people."

"Well, what's this about, then?"

"There's a small game development company here in St. Louis called Cahaba Apps. Ever hear of it?"

I hadn't actually, but I didn't pay much attention to local stuff.

"Not in the least," I said.

"You haven't heard of a game called *Ruby's Rails*? I thought you might have played it."

I knew that Emily Swenson wasn't trying to start something, but telling someone that "you thought they might have played *Ruby's Rails*," was effectively just spitting in their face and calling them a filthy casual. *Ruby's Rails* was the sort of game that your grandma would play, assuming she could figure out her phone.

I had played it, actually. Honestly, everyone had. It was the new *Bejeweled*. Not a Match 3 game, but the same kind of idea. It was only halfway a game—it was mostly kind of a zenlike activity.

In the game, you're running a train system, and you're

delivering gems—in games like these it's always either gems or candy—from mines to towns. And you're delivering people to mines. And you build houses and hotels, kind of like Monopoly. Actually describing it makes it seem more complicated than it is—because you need more gems to build more track, that's important—but in practice it's incredibly straightforward and relaxing. It's gaming's equivalent of a lava lamp.

I did not get into this with Emily.

"Yes, Emily," I told her. "I am familiar with *Ruby's Rails*."

"See," said Emily. "I knew you would be perfect for this."

"But what is this?"

"The company that developed the game has been purchased by a larger developer who has a plan for the IP. They're developing a new game together, and there appear to be some holdups."

"Holdups like?"

"The new game is significantly behind schedule, and I've heard that the company is entirely dysfunctional. Possibly there may be some sort of internal saboteur. I'd like you to go in there and let me know what's happening."

This wasn't so undoable. It's not like I would be breaking into a safe and stealing secrets. Although it was still a lot to take before waffles.

"Do you have a cover for me?" I asked. "I don't know what you know about the gaming industry, but under what possible auspices could I be there? I can't code, I'm not an artist, and I can't play a musical instrument, much less compose."

"I've never understood," said Emily, addressing me with those engulfing green eyes of hers, "why you always so strongly point out all the things you cannot do. If you outlined the things you could do with half the enthusiasm of your failings, you wouldn't need my little job."

As insights went, this was both depressingly accurate and yet also slightly off the mark. Accurate because Emily was certainly right—it was easy to get me going on all the things I failed at. As it was, I was working up to a zinger that I'm still a little sad to let go of. But off the mark because I wasn't at all disappointed about Emily job. I was excited.

"I just want to make sure I'll fit in," I said. "What will I be doing?"

"You'll be a secretary," said Emily. "Receptionist, actually. And just as a temp, for a few days."

This answer was both pleasing and disappointing. Pleasing in that I could do it, but disappointing because a little part of me had started imagining how fun it would be to pretend to be a Professional Artist for a few days. I could wear great clothes and have ridiculous hair. I could, I don't know, talk about how great and misunderstood the Flying Lizards were. It would be awesome until I had to work.

"And what am I looking for?"

"On day one? Just the lay of the land."

And Emily Swenson gave me a check. I'm not going to put the amount here, because 1) I'm starting to worry that the IRS might be reading these things, and 2) it was not lay-of-the-land money. From the amount of money, arson was, to my mind, still on the menu.

introducing

If you enjoyed
THE ASTONISHING MISTAKES OF DAHLIA MOSS,
look out for

THE SHAMBLING GUIDE TO NEW YORK CITY

by Mur Lafferty

Because of the disaster that was her last job, Zoë is searching for a fresh start as a travel book editor in the tourist-centric New York City. After stumbling across a seemingly perfect position though, Zoë is blocked at every turn because of the one thing she can't take off her résumé—human.

Not to be put off by anything—especially not her blood-drinking boss or death goddess coworker—Zoë delves deep into the monster world. But her job turns deadly when the careful balance between human and monsters starts to crumble—with Zoë right in the middle.

The bookstore was sandwiched between a dry cleaner's and a shifty-looking accounting office. Mannegishi's Tricks wasn't in the guidebook, but Zoë Norris knew enough about guidebooks to know they often missed the best places.

This clearly was not one of those places.

The store was, to put it bluntly, filthy. It reminded Zoë of an abandoned mechanic's garage, with grime and grease coating the walls and bookshelves. She pulled her arms in to avoid brushing against anything. Long strips of paint dotted with mold peeled away from the walls as if they could no longer stand to adhere to such filth. Zoë couldn't blame them. She felt a bizarre desire to wave to them as they bobbed lazily to herald her passing. Her shoes stuck slightly to the floor, making her trek through the store louder than she would have liked.

She always enjoyed looking at cities—even her hometown—through the eyes of a tourist. She owned guidebooks of every city she had visited and used them extensively. It made her usual urban exploration feel more thorough.

It also allowed her to look at the competition, or it had when she'd worked in travel book publishing.

The store didn't win her over with its stock, either. She'd

never heard of most of the books; they had titles like *How to Make Love, Marry, Devour, and Inherit in Eight Weeks* in the Romance section and *When Your Hound from Hell Outgrows His House—and Yours* in the Pets section.

She picked the one about hounds and opened it to Chapter Four: "The Augean Stables: How to Pooper-Scoop Dung That Could Drown a Terrier." She frowned. *So, they're* really *assuming your dog gets bigger than a house? It's not tongue-in-cheek? If this is humor, it's failing.* Despite the humorous title, the front cover had a frightening drawing of a hulking white beast with red eyes. The cover was growing uncomfortably warm, and the leather had a sticky, alien feeling, not like cow or even snake leather. She switched the book to her left hand and wiped her right on her beige sweater. She immediately regretted it.

"One sweater ruined," she muttered, looking at the grainy black smear. "What *is* this stuff?"

The cashier's desk faced the door from the back of the store, and was staffed by an unsmiling teen girl in a dirty gray sundress. She had olive skin and big round eyes, and her head had the fuzz of the somewhat-recently shaved. Piercings dotted her face at her nose, eyebrow, lip, and cheek, and all the way up her ears. Despite her slouchy body language, she watched Zoë with a bright, sharp gaze that looked almost hungry.

Beside the desk was a bulletin board, blocked by a pudgy man hanging a flyer. He wore a T-shirt and jeans and looked to be in his mid-thirties. He looked completely out of place in this store; that is, he was clean.

"Can I help you?" the girl asked as Zoë approached the counter.

"Uh, you have a very interesting shop here," Zoë said,

smiling. She put the hound book on the counter and tried not to grimace as it stuck to her hand briefly. "How much is this one?"

The clerk didn't return her smile. "We cater to a specific clientele."

"OK...but how much is the book?" Zoë asked again.

"It's not for sale. It's a collectible."

Zoë became aware of the man at the bulletin board turning and watching her. She began to sweat a little bit.

Jesus, calm down. Not everyone is out to get you.

"So it's not for sale, or it's a collectible. Which one?"

The girl reached over and took the book. "It's not for sale to you, only to collectors."

"How do you know I don't collect dog books?" Zoë asked, bristling. "And what does it matter? All I wanted to know was how much it costs. Do you care where it goes as long as it's paid for?"

"Are you a collector of rare books catering to the owners of... exotic pets?" the man interrupted, smiling. His voice was pleasant and mild, and she relaxed a little, despite his patronizing words. "Excuse me for butting in, but I know the owner of this shop and she considers these books her treasure. She is very particular about where they go when they leave her care."

"Why should she..." Zoë trailed off when she got a closer look at the bulletin board to the man's left. Several flyers stood out, many with phone numbers ripped from the bottom. One, advertising an exorcism service specializing in elemental demons, looked burned in a couple of places. The flyer that had caught her eye was pink, and the one the man had just secured with a thumbtack.

Underground Publishing
LOOKING FOR WRITERS

Underground Publishing is a new company writing travel guides for people like you. Since we're writing for people like you, we need people like you to write for us.

Pluses: Experience in writing, publishing, or editing (in this life or any other), and knowledge of New York City.

Minuses: A life span shorter than an editorial cycle (in this case, nine months).

Call 212.555.1666 for more information or e-mail rand@undergroundpub.com for more information.

"Oh, hell yes," said Zoë, and with the weird, dirty hound book forgotten, she pulled a battered notebook from her satchel. She needed a job. She was refusing to adhere to the stereotype of running home to New York, admitting failure at her attempts to leave her hometown. Her goal was a simple office job. She wasn't waiting for her big break on Broadway and looking to wait tables or take on a leaflet-passing, taco-suit-wearing street-nuisance job in the meantime.

Office job. Simple. Uncomplicated.

As she scribbled down the information, the man looked her up and down and said, "Ah, I'm not sure if that's a good idea for you to pursue."

Zoë looked up sharply. "What are you talking about? First I can't buy the book, now I can't apply for a job? I know you guys have some sort of weird vibe going on, 'We're so goth and special, let's freak out the normals.' But for a business that caters to, you know, *customers*, you're certainly not welcoming."

"I just think that particular business may be looking for someone with experience you may not have," he said, his voice level and diplomatic. He held his hands out, placating her.

"But you don't even know me. You don't know my qualifications. I just left Misconceptions Publishing in Raleigh. You heard of them?" She hated name-dropping her old employer— she would have preferred to forget it entirely—but the second-biggest travel book publisher in the USA was her strongest credential in the job hunt.

The man shifted his weight and touched his chin. "Really. What did you do for them?"

Zoë stood a little taller. "Head researcher and writer. I wrote most of *Raleigh Misconceptions*, and was picked to head the project *Tallahassee Misconceptions*."

He smiled a bit. "Impressive. But you do know Tallahassee is south of North Carolina, right? You went in the wrong direction entirely."

Zoë clenched her jaw. "I was laid off. It wasn't due to job performance. I took my severance and came back home to the city."

The man rubbed his smooth, pudgy cheek. "What happened to cause the layoff? I thought Misconceptions was doing well."

Zoë felt her cheeks get hot. Her boss, Godfrey, had happened. Then Godfrey's wife—whom he had failed to mention until Zoë was well and truly in "other woman" territory—had happened. She swallowed. "Economy. You know how it goes."

He stepped back and leaned against the wall, clearly not minding the cracked and peeling paint that broke off and stuck to his shirt. "Those are good credentials. However, you're still probably not what they're looking for."

Zoë looked at her notebook and continued writing. "Luckily it's not your decision, is it?"

"Actually, it is."

She groaned and looked back up at him. "All right. Who are you?"

He extended his hand. "Phillip Rand. Owner, president, and CEO of Underground Publishing."

She looked at his hand for a moment and shook it, her small fingers briefly engulfed in his grip. It was a cool handshake, but strong.

"Zoë Norris. And why, Mr. Phillip Rand, will you not let me even apply?"

"Well, Miss Zoë Norris, I don't think you'd fit in with the staff. And fitting in with the staff is key to this company's success."

A vision of future months dressed as a dancing cell phone on the wintry streets pummeled Zoë's psyche. She leaned forward in desperation. She was short, and used to looking up at people, but he was over six feet, and she was forced to crane her neck to look up at him. "Mr. Rand. How many other people experienced in researching and writing travel guides do you have with you?"

He considered for a moment. "With that specific qualification? I actually have none."

"So if you have a full staff of people who fit into some kind of mystery mold, but don't actually have experience writing travel books, how good do you think your books are going to be? You sound like you're a kid trying to fill a club, not a working publishing company. You need a managing editor with experience to supervise your writers and researchers. I'm smart, hardworking, creative, and a hell of a lot of fun in the times I'm not blatantly begging for a job—obviously you'll have to just take my word on that. I haven't found a work environment I don't fit in with. I don't care if Underground Publishing is catering to eastern Europeans, or transsexuals, or Eskimos, or even Republicans. Just because I don't fit in doesn't mean I can't be accepting as long as they accept me. Just give me a chance."

Phillip Rand was unmoved. "Trust me. You would not fit in. You're not our type."

She finally deflated and sighed. "Isn't this illegal?"

He actually had the audacity to laugh at that. "I'm not discriminating based on your gender or race or religion."

"Then what are you basing it on?"

He licked his lips and looked at her again, studying her. "Call it a gut reaction."

She deflated. "Oh well. It was worth a try. Have a good day."

On her way out, she ran through her options: there were the few publishing companies she hadn't yet applied to, the jobs that she had recently thought beneath her that she'd gladly take at this point. She paused a moment in the Self-Help section to see if anything there could help her better herself. She glanced at the covers for *Reborn and Loving It*, *Second Life: Not Just on the Internet*, and *Get the Salary You Deserve! Negotiating Hell Notes in a Time of Economic Downturn*. Nothing she could relate to, so she trudged out the door, contemplating a long bath when she got back to her apartment. Better than unpacking more boxes.

After the grimy door shut behind her, Zoë decided she had earned a tall caloric caffeine bomb to soothe her ego. She wasn't sure what she'd done to deserve this, but it didn't take much to make her leap for the comfort treats these days—which reminded her, she needed to recycle some wine bottles.

The Shambling Guide to New York City

THEATER DISTRICT:
Shops

Mannegishi's Tricks is the oldest bookstore in the Theater District. Established 1834 by Akilina, nicknamed "The Drakon Lady," after she immigrated from Russia, the store has a stock that is lovingly picked from collections all over the world. Currently managed by Akilina's great-grandaughter, Anastasiya, the store continues to offer some of the best finds for any book collector. Anastasiya upholds the old dragon lady's practice of knowing just which book should go to which customer, and refuses to sell a book to the "wrong" person. Don't try to argue with her; the drakon's teeth remain sharp.

Mannegishi's Tricks is one of the few shops that deliberately maintains a squalid appearance—dingy, smelly, with a strong "leave now" aura—in order to repel unwanted customers. In nearly 180 years, Akilina and her descendants have sold only three books to humans. She refuses to say to whom. ∎